SO-AXQ-917

EAGLE VALLEY LIBRARY DISTRICT
P.O. BOX 240   600 BROADWAY
EAGLE, CO 81631   (970) 328-8800

SEASON OF WONDER

Also available from RaeAnne Thayne

HQN Books

Haven Point

The Cottages on Silver Beach
Sugar Pine Trail
Serenity Harbor
Snowfall on Haven Point
Riverbend Road
Evergreen Springs
Redemption Bay
Snow Angel Cove

Hope's Crossing

Wild Iris Ridge
Christmas in Snowflake Canyon
Willowleaf Lane
Currant Creek Valley
Sweet Laurel Falls
Woodrose Mountain
Blackberry Summer

For a complete list of books by RaeAnne Thayne,
please visit www.raeannethayne.com.

RaeAnne Thayne

SEASON OF WONDER

HQN™

Recycling programs
for this product may
not exist in your area.

ISBN-13: 978-1-335-00591-5

Season of Wonder

Copyright © 2018 by RaeAnne Thayne

All rights reserved. Except for use in any review, the reproduction or utilization of this work in whole or in part in any form by any electronic, mechanical or other means, now known or hereafter invented, including xerography, photocopying and recording, or in any information storage or retrieval system, is forbidden without the written permission of the publisher, HQN Books, 22 Adelaide St. West, 40th Floor, Toronto, Ontario M5H 4E3, Canada.

This is a work of fiction. Names, characters, places and incidents are either the product of the author's imagination or are used fictitiously, and any resemblance to actual persons, living or dead, business establishments, events or locales is entirely coincidental.

This edition published by arrangement with Harlequin Books S.A.

For questions and comments about the quality of this book, please contact us at CustomerService@Harlequin.com.

® and TM are trademarks of Harlequin Enterprises Limited or its corporate affiliates. Trademarks indicated with ® are registered in the United States Patent and Trademark Office, the Canadian Intellectual Property Office and in other countries.

www.HQNBooks.com

Printed in U.S.A.

To Carly, for all the laughs, walks and joy. You are deeply loved!

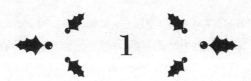

"This is totally lame. Why do we have to stay here and wait for you? We can walk home in, like, ten minutes."

Daniela Capelli drew in a deep breath and prayed for patience, something she seemed to be doing with increasing frequency these days when it came to her thirteen-year-old daughter. "It's starting to snow and already almost dark."

Silver rolled her eyes, something *she* did with increasing frequency these days. "So what? A little snow won't kill us. I would hardly even call that snow. We had way bigger storms than this back in Boston. Remember that big blizzard a few years ago, when school was closed for, like, a week?"

"I remember," her younger daughter, Mia, said, looking up from her coloring book at Dani's desk at the Haven Point Veterinary Clinic. "I stayed home from preschool and I watched Anna and Elsa a thousand times, until you said your eardrums would explode if I played it one more time."

Dani could hear a bark from the front office that likely signaled the arrival of her next client and knew she didn't have time to stand here arguing with an obstinate teenager.

"Mia can't walk as fast as you can. You'll end up frustrated with her and you'll both be freezing before you make it home," she pointed out.

"So she can stay here and wait for you while I walk home. I just told Chelsea we could FaceTime about the new dress she bought for the Christmas dance there and she can only do it for another hour before her dad comes to pick her up for his visitation."

"Why can't you FaceTime here? I only have two more patients to see. I'll be done in less than an hour, then we can all go home together. You can hang out in the waiting room with Mia, where the Wi-Fi signal is better."

Silver gave a huge put-upon sigh but picked up her backpack and stalked out of Dani's office toward the waiting room.

"Can I turn on the TV out there?" Mia asked as she gathered her papers and crayons. "I like the dog shows."

The veterinary clinic showed calming clips of animals on a big flat-screen TV set low to the ground for their clientele.

"After Silver's done with her phone call, okay?"

"She'll take *forever*," Mia predicted with a gloomy look. "She always does when she's talking to Chelsea."

Dani fought to hide a smile. "Thanks for your patience, sweetie, with her and with me. Finish your math worksheet while you're here, then when we get home, you can watch what you want."

Both the Haven Point elementary and middle schools were within walking distance of the clinic and it had become a habit for Silver to walk to the elementary school and then walk with Mia here to the clinic to spend a few hours until they could all go home together.

Of late, Silver had started to complain that she didn't want to pick her sister up at the elementary school every day, that she would rather they both just took their respective school buses home, where Silver could watch her sister without having to hang out at the boring veterinary clinic.

But then, Silver complained about nearly everything these days.

It was probably a good idea, but Dani wasn't quite ready to pull the trigger on having the girls alone every day after school. Maybe they would try it out after Christmas vacation.

This working professional/single mother gig was *hard*, she thought as she ushered Mia to the waiting room. Then again, in most ways it was much easier than the veterinary student/single mother gig had been.

When they entered the comfortable waiting room—with its bright colors, pet-friendly benches and big fish tank—Mia faltered for a moment, then sidestepped behind Dani's back.

She saw instantly what had caused her daughter's nervous reaction. Funny. Dani felt the same way. She wanted to hide behind somebody, too.

The receptionist had given her the files with the dogs' names that were coming in for a checkup but hadn't mentioned their human was Ruben Morales. Her gorgeous next-door neighbor.

Dani's palms instantly itched and her stomach felt as if she'd accidentally swallowed a flock of butterflies.

"Deputy Morales," she said, then paused, hating the slightly breathless note in her voice.

What *was* it about the man that always made her so freaking nervous?

He was big, yes, at least six feet tall, with wide shoulders, tough muscles and a firm, don't-mess-with-me jawline.

It wasn't just that. Even without his uniform, the man exuded authority and power, which instantly raised her hackles and left her uneasy, something she found both frustrating and annoying about herself.

No matter how far she had come, how hard she had worked to make a life for her and her girls, she still sometimes felt like the troublesome foster kid from Queens, always on the defensive.

She had done her best to avoid him in the months they had been in Haven Point, but that was next to impossible when they lived so close to each other—and when she was the intern in his father's veterinary practice, with the hope that she might be able to purchase it at the end of the year.

"Hey, Doc," he said, flashing her an easy smile she

didn't trust for a moment. It never quite reached his dark, long-lashed eyes, at least where she was concerned.

While she might be uncomfortable around Ruben Morales, his dogs were another story.

He held the leashes of both of them, a big, muscular Belgian shepherd and an incongruously paired little Chipoo and she reached down to pet both of them. They sniffed her and wagged happily, the big dog's tail nearly knocking over his small friend.

That was the thing she loved most about dogs. They were uncomplicated and generous with their affection, for the most part. They never looked at people with that subtle hint of suspicion, as if trying to uncover all their secrets.

"I wasn't expecting you," she admitted.

"Oh? I made an appointment. The boys both need checkups. Yukon needs his regular hip and eye check and Ollie is due for his shots."

She gave the dogs one more pat before she straightened and faced him, hoping his sharp cop eyes couldn't notice evidence of her accelerated pulse.

"Your father is still here every Monday and Friday afternoons. Maybe you should reschedule with him," she suggested. It was a faint hope, but a girl had to try.

"Why would I do that?"

"Maybe because he's your father and knows your dogs?"

"Dad is an excellent veterinarian. Agreed. But he's also semiretired and wants to be fully retired this time next year. As long as you plan to stick around in Haven Point, we will have to switch vets and start seeing you eventually. I figured we might as well start now."

He was checking her out. Not *her* her, but her skills as a veterinarian.

The implication was clear. She had been here three months, and it had become obvious during that time in their few interactions that Ruben Morales was extremely protective of his family. He had been polite enough when they had met previously, but always with a certain guardedness, as if he was afraid she planned to take the good name his hardworking father had built up over the years for the Haven Point Veterinary Clinic and drag it through the sludge at the bottom of Lake Haven.

Dani pushed away her instinctive prickly defensiveness, bred out of all those years in foster care when she felt as if she had no one else to count on—compounded by the difficult years after she'd married Tommy and had Silver, when she *really* had no one else in her corner.

She couldn't afford to offend Ruben. She didn't need his protective wariness to turn into full-on suspicion. With a little digging, Ruben could uncover things about her and her past that would ruin everything for her and her girls here.

She forced a professional smile. "It doesn't matter. Let's go back to a room and take a look at these guys. Girls, I'll be done shortly. Silver, keep an eye on your sister."

Her oldest nodded without looking up from her phone and with an inward sigh, Dani led the way to the largest of the exam rooms.

She stood at the door as he entered the room with the

two dogs, then joined him inside and closed the door behind her.

The large room seemed to shrink unnaturally and she paused inside for a moment, flustered and wishing she could escape. Dani gave herself a mental shake. She was a doctor of veterinary medicine, not a teenage girl. She could handle being in the same room with the one man in Haven Point who left her breathless and unsteady.

All she had to do was focus on the reason he was here in the first place. His dogs.

She knelt to their level. "Hey there, guys. Who wants to go first?"

The Malinois—often confused for a German shepherd but smaller and with a shorter coat—wagged his tail again while his smaller counterpoint sniffed around her shoes, probably picking up the scents of all the other dogs she had seen that day.

"Ollie, I guess you're the winner today."

He yipped, his big ears that stuck straight out from his face quivering with excitement.

He was the funniest looking dog, quirky and unique, with wisps of fur in odd places, spindly legs and a narrow Chihuahua face. She found him unbearably cute. With that face, she wouldn't ever be able to say no to him if he were hers.

"Can I give him a treat?" She always tried to ask permission first from her clients' humans.

"Only if you want him to be your best friend for life," Ruben said.

Despite her nerves, his deadpan voice sparked a smile, which widened when she gave the little dog one of the treats she always carried in the pocket of her lab coat and he slurped it up in one bite, then sat with a resigned sort of patience during the examination.

She was aware of Ruben watching her as she carefully examined the dog, but Dani did her best not to let his scrutiny fluster her.

She knew what she was doing, she reminded herself. She had worked so hard to be here, sacrificing all her time, energy and resources of the last decade to nothing else but her girls and her studies.

"Everything looks good," she said after checking out the dog and finding nothing unusual. "He seems like a healthy little guy. It says here he's about six or seven. So you haven't had him from birth?"

"No. Only about two years. He was a stray I picked up off the side of the road between here and Shelter Springs when I was on patrol one day. He was in a bad way, half-starved, fur matted. I think he'd been on his own for a while. As small as he is, it's a wonder he wasn't picked off by a coyote or even one of the bigger hawks. He just needed a little TLC."

"You couldn't find his owner?"

"We ran ads and Dad checked with all his contacts at shelters and veterinary clinics from here to Boise, with no luck. I had been fostering him while we looked, and to be honest, I kind of lost my heart to the little guy and by then Yukon adored him so we decided to keep him."

She was such a sucker for animal lovers, especially those who rescued the vulnerable and lost ones.

And, no. She didn't need counseling to point out the parallels to her own life.

Regardless, she couldn't let herself be drawn to Ruben and risk doing something foolish. She had too much to lose here in Haven Point.

"What about Yukon here?" She knelt down to examine the bigger dog. Though he wasn't huge and Ruben could probably lift him easily to the table, she decided it was easier to kneel to his level. In her experience, sometimes bigger dogs didn't like to be lifted and she wasn't sure if the beautiful Malinois fell into that category.

Ruben shrugged as he scooped Ollie onto his lap to keep the little Chi-poo from swooping in and stealing the treat she held out for the bigger dog. "You could say he was a rescue, too."

"Oh?"

"He was a K-9 officer down in Mountain Home. After his handler was killed in the line of duty, I guess he kind of went into a canine version of depression and wouldn't work with anyone else. I know that probably sounds crazy."

She scratched the dog's ears, touched by the bond that could build between handler and dog. "Not at all," she said briskly. "I've seen many dogs go into decline when their owner dies. It's not uncommon."

"For a year or so, they tried to match him up with other officers, but things never quite gelled, for one reason or another, then his eyes started going. His previous handler who died was a good buddy of mine from the academy and I couldn't let him go just anywhere."

"Retired police dogs don't always do well in civilian life. They can be aggressive with other dogs and sometimes people. Have you had any problems with that?"

"Not with Yukon. He's friendly. Aren't you, buddy? You're a good boy."

Dani could swear the dog grinned at his owner, his tongue lolling out.

Yukon was patient while she looked him over, especially as she maintained a steady supply of treats.

When she finished, she gave the dog a pat and stood. "Can I take a look at Ollie's ears one more time?"

"Sure. Help yourself."

He held the dog out and she reached for Ollie. As she did, the dog wriggled a little and Dani's hands ended up brushing Ruben's chest. She froze at the accidental contact, a shiver rippling down her spine. She pinned her reaction on the undeniable fact that it had been entirely too long since she had touched a man, even accidentally.

She had to cut out this *fascination* or whatever it was immediately. Clean-cut, muscular cops were *not* her type, and the sooner she remembered that the better.

She focused on checking the ears of the little dog, gave him one more scratch and handed him back to Ruben. "That should do it. A clean bill of health. They seem to be two happy, well-adjusted dogs. You obviously take good care of them."

He patted both dogs with an affectionate smile that did nothing to ease her nerves.

"My dad taught me well. I spent most of my youth helping out here at the clinic—cleaning cages, brushing coats, walking the occasional overnight boarder. Whatever grunt work he needed. He made all of us help."

"I can think of worse ways to earn a dime," she said.

The chance to work with animals would have been a

dream opportunity for her, back when she had few bright spots in her world. Besides that, she considered his father one of the sweetest people she had ever met.

"So can I. I always loved animals."

She had to wonder why he didn't follow in his father's footsteps and become a vet. None of his three siblings had made that choice, either. If any of them had, she probably wouldn't be here right now, as Frank Morales probably would have handed down his thriving practice to his own progeny.

Not that it was any of her business. Ruben certainly could follow any career path he wanted—as long as that path took him far away from her.

"Give me a moment to grab those medications and I'll be right back."

"No rush."

Out in the hall, she closed the door behind her and drew in a deep breath.

Get a grip, she chided herself. *He's just a hot-looking dude. Heaven knows, you've had more than enough experience with those to last a lifetime.*

She went to the well-stocked medication dispensary, found what she needed and returned to the exam room.

Outside the door, she paused for only a moment to gather her composure before pushing it open. "Here are the pills for Ollie's nerves and a refill for Yukon's eye drops," she said briskly. "Let me know if you have any questions—though if you do, you can certainly ask your father."

"Thanks." As he took the medication from her, his

hands brushed hers again and sent a little spark of aware-ness shivering through her.

Oh, come on. This was ridiculous.

She was probably imagining the way his gaze sharp-ened, as if he had felt something odd, too.

"I can show you out. We're shorthanded today since the veterinary tech and the receptionist both needed to leave early."

"No problem. That's what I get for scheduling the last appointment of the day—though, again, I spent most of my youth here. I think we can find our way."

"It's fine. I'll show you out." She stood outside the door while he gathered the dogs' leashes, then led the way toward the front office.

After three months, Ruben still couldn't get a bead on Dr. Daniela Capelli.

His next-door neighbor still seemed a complete enigma to him. By all reports from his father, she was a dedicated, earnest new veterinarian with a knack for solving diffi-cult medical mysteries and a willingness to work hard. She seemed like a warm and loving mother, at least from the few times he had seen her interactions with her two girls, the uniquely named teenager Silver—who had, paradoxically, purple hair—and the sweet-as-Christmas-toffee Mia, who was probably about six.

He also couldn't deny she was beautiful, with slender features, striking green eyes, dark, glossy hair and a dusky skin tone that proclaimed her Italian heritage—as if her name didn't do the trick first.

He actually liked the trace of New York accent that

slipped into her speech at times. It fit her somehow, in a way he couldn't explain. Despite that, he couldn't deny that the few times he had interacted with more than a wave in passing, she was brusque, prickly and sometimes downright distant.

He had certainly had easier neighbors.

His father adored her and wouldn't listen to a negative thing about her.

She hasn't had an easy time of things but she's a fighter. Hardworking and eager to learn, Frank had said the other night when Ruben asked how things were working out, now that Dani and her girls had been in town a few months. *You just have to get to know her.*

Frank apparently didn't see how diligently Dani Capelli worked to keep anyone else from doing just that.

She wasn't unfriendly, only distant. She kept herself to herself. It was a phrase his mother might use, though Myra Morales seemed instantly fond of Dani and her girls.

Did Dani have any idea how fascinated the people of Haven Point were with these new arrivals in their midst?

Or maybe that was just him.

As he followed her down the hall in her white lab coat, his dogs behaving themselves for once, Ruben told himself to forget about his stupid attraction to her.

Sure, he might be ready to settle down and would like to have someone in his life, but he wasn't at all sure if he had the time or energy for that someone to be a woman with so many secrets in her eyes, one who seemed to face the world with her chin up and her fists out, ready to take on any threats.

When they walked into the clinic waiting room, they found her two girls there. The older one was texting on her phone while her sister did somersaults around the room.

Dani stopped in the doorway and seemed to swallow an exasperated sound. "Mia, honey, you're going to have dog hair all over you."

"I'm a snowball rolling down the hill," the girl said. "Can't you see me getting bigger and bigger and bigger."

"You're such a dorkupine," her sister said, barely looking up from her phone.

"I'm a dorkupine snowball," Mia retorted.

"You're a snowball who is going to be covered in dog hair," Dani said. "Come on, honey. Get up."

He could tell the moment the little girl spotted him and his dogs coming into the area behind her mother. She went still and then slowly rose to her feet, features shifting from gleeful to nervous.

Why was she so afraid of him?

"You make a very good snowball," he said, pitching his voice low and calm as his father had taught him to do with all skittish creatures. "I haven't seen anybody somersault that well in a long time."

She moved to her mother's side and buried her face in Dani's white coat—though he didn't miss the way she reached down to pet Ollie on her way.

"Hey again, Silver."

He knew the older girl from the middle school, where he served as the resource officer a few hours a week. He made it a point to learn all the students' names and tried to talk to them individually when he had the chance, in hopes that if they had a problem at home or knew of something potentially troublesome for the school, they would feel comfortable coming to him.

He had the impression that Silver was like her mother in many ways. Reserved, wary, slow to trust. It made him wonder just who had hurt them.

"How are things?" he asked her now.

For just an instant, he thought he saw sadness flicker in her gaze before she turned back to her phone with a shrug. "Fine, I guess."

"Are you guys ready for Christmas? It's your first one here in Idaho. A little different from New York, isn't it?"

"How should we know? We haven't lived in the city for, like, four years."

Dani sent her daughter a look at her tone, which seemed to border on disrespectful. "I've been in vet school in Boston the last four years," she explained.

"Boston. Then you're used to snow and cold. We're known for our beautiful winters around here. The lake is simply stunning in wintertime."

Mia tugged on her mother's coat and when Dani bent down, she whispered something to her.

"You can ask him," Dani said calmly, gesturing to Ruben.

Mia shook her head and buried her face again and after a moment, Dani sighed. "She wonders if it's possible to ice-skate on Lake Haven. We watched the most recent Olympics and she became a little obsessed."

"You could say that," Silver said. "She skated around the house in her stocking feet all day long for *weeks*. A dorkupine on ice."

"You can't skate on the lake, I'm afraid," Ruben answered. "Because of the underground hot springs that feed into it at various points, Lake Haven rarely freezes, except sometimes along the edges, when it's really cold. It's not really safe for ice skating. But the city creates a skating rink on the tennis courts at Lake View Park every year. The volunteer fire department sprays it down for a few weeks once temperatures get really cold. I saw them out there the other night so it shouldn't be long before it's open. Maybe a few more weeks."

Mia seemed to lose a little of her shyness at that prospect. She gave him a sideways look from under her mother's arm and aimed a fleeting smile full of such sweetness that he was instantly smitten.

"There's also a great place for sledding up behind the high school. You can't miss that, either. Oh, and in a few weeks we have the Lights on the Lake Festival. You've heard about that, right?"

They all gave him matching blank stares, making him wonder what was wrong with the Haven Point Helping Hands that they hadn't immediately dragged Dani into their circle. He would have to talk to Andie Bailey or his sister Angela about it. They always seemed to know what was going on in town.

"I think some kids at school were talking about that at lunch the other day," Silver said. "They were sitting at the next table so I didn't hear the whole thing, though."

"Haven Point hosts an annual celebration a week or so before Christmas where all the local boat owners deck out their watercraft from here to Shelter Springs to welcome in the holidays and float between the two towns.

There's music, food and crafts for sale. It's kind of a big deal around here. I'm surprised you haven't heard about it."

"I'm very busy, with the practice and the girls, Deputy Morales. I don't have a lot of time for socializing." Though Dani tried for a lofty look, he thought he caught a hint of vulnerability there.

She seemed...lonely. That didn't make a lick of sense. The women in this town could be almost annoying in their efforts to include newcomers in community events. They didn't give people much of an option, dragging them kicking and screaming into the social scene around town, like it or not.

"Well, now you know. You really can't miss the festival. It's great fun for the whole family."

"Thank you for the information. It's next week, you say?"

"That's right. Not this weekend but the one after. The whole thing starts out with the boat parade on Saturday evening, around six."

"We'll put it on our social calendar."

"What's a social calendar?" Mia whispered to her sister, just loud enough for Ruben to hear.

"It's a place where you keep track of all your invitations to parties and sleepovers and stuff."

"Oh. Why do we need one of those?"

"Good question."

Silver looked glum for just a moment but Dani hugged her, then faced Ruben with a polite, distant smile.

"Thank you for bringing in Ollie and Yukon. Have a good evening, Deputy Morales."

It was a clear dismissal, one he couldn't ignore. Ruben gathered his dogs' leashes and headed for the door. "Thank you. See you around. And by around, I mean next door. We kind of can't miss each other."

As he hoped, this made Mia smile a little. Even Silver's dour expression eased into what almost looked like a smile.

As he loaded the dogs into the king cab of his pickup truck, Ruben could see Dani turning off lights and straightening up the clinic.

What was her story? Why had she chosen to come straight from vet school in Boston to set up shop all the way across the country in a small Idaho town?

He loved his hometown, sure, and fully acknowledged it was a beautiful place to live. It still seemed a jarring cultural and geographic shift from living back east to this little town where the biggest news of the month was a rather corny light parade that people froze their asses off to watch.

And why did he get the impression the family wasn't socializing much? One of the reasons most people he knew moved to small towns was a yearning for the kind of connectedness and community a place like Haven Point had in spades. What was the point in moving to a small town if you were going to keep yourself separate from everybody?

He thought he had seen them at a few things when they first came to Haven Point but since then, Dani seemed to be keeping her little family mostly to themselves. That must be by choice. It was the only explanation that made sense. He couldn't imagine McKenzie

Kilpatrick or Andie Bailey or any of the other Helping Hands excluding her on purpose.

What was she so nervous about?

He added another facet to the enigma of his next-door neighbor. He had hoped that he might be able to get a better perspective of her by bringing the dogs in to her for their routine exams. While he had confirmed his father's belief that she appeared to be an excellent veterinarian, he now had more questions about the woman and her daughters to add to his growing list.

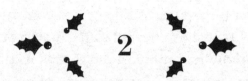

2

After a long, difficult day, following a long, diffi-cult week, all Dani wanted was to pop a batch of popcorn, sit on the sofa and watch something light and cheery with her girls for a few hours. As she stood at the kitchen sink of their three-bedroom cottage drying the last of the dishes Silver had washed after school, she thought that what she would *really* like was a long soak in the tub. By the time her daughters were in bed most nights, she didn't have enough energy left to even run water in the tub.

The kitchen was small enough that cleaning it never took long. The house Frank Morales had provided as part of her internship compensation wasn't big but it was comfortable, with three bedrooms, a living room and a lovely glass-enclosed family room facing the lake, which had become their favorite spot.

Someday she'd like to have a little bigger house, maybe with an actual dining room, but that would have to wait awhile. She had thousands of dollars in student loans to pay back first. Meantime, this house worked well for their needs.

Her life could have been easier. Occasionally, she tormented herself by playing the old what-if game, wondering how things might have been different for her and her daughters if she had been able to ignore her conscience and taken money from Tommy.

If she had accepted the ill-gotten gains her late ex-husband had tried to give for child support, she might have been able to start her professional life as a veterinarian with a clean slate, even with a little nest egg, instead of feeling swallowed by debt. But she would have had to sell her soul in return and she wasn't willing to do that.

Yes, she was tired of the constant scrimping and saving and striving, but at least when she finally made her way to bed each night, she could close her eyes with a clear conscience.

Mostly clear, anyway.

She set the dish towel over the oven handle to dry and made her way to the family room. Silver was, as usual, on her phone while Mia was doing more somersaults, this time on the carpet, while their ancient little mutt Winky watched from her favorite spot on the floor, blocking the heater vent.

"Movie night!" Dani said cheerfully. "Who's ready? I'll make the popcorn. You two just need to pick a show."

"Yay! Movie night. My favorite!" Mia grinned from the floor.

"I think we should watch a Christmas movie. What do you say? *Elf, Grinch, Arthur Christmas* or something off the Hallmark Channel."

The previous Christmas, during Dani's rare moments off from school, they had binge-watched movies on the Hallmark Channel. Dani had felt a little world-weary to truly appreciate the sweet happy endings but Silver had adored them.

It had been several months since Silver had been interested in anything sweet. Right around the time she'd dyed her hair and started begging for the tattoo Dani would not let her get until she was eighteen.

"Elf," Mia declared without hesitation.

"Okay. One vote for *Elf.* What do you think, Sil?"

"I think you're going to have to watch without me." Her daughter rose from the sofa with the long-legged grace she had inherited from her father. "I've got to go. Some friends just texted me and they want to hang out."

Dani felt her temper flare at Silver's matter-of-fact tone but worked to keep it contained. "Are you asking me or telling me?"

Silver's jaw worked. "Asking, I guess. Can I go hang out with my friends?"

At thirteen, she seemed to think she didn't need permission these days for much of anything. Dani had a completely different perspective on the situation.

"Which friends? And what did they want to do?"

"Just friends from school," Silver said, impatience

threading through her voice. "Why do you have to know every single detail about my life?"

"Because I'm your parent and responsible for you. I'm not asking for every detail but I have to know where you're going and who you will be with. Those are the house rules, kid. You know that."

Silver didn't appear to appreciate the reminder. "I thought you might lighten up a little once we moved to the middle of freaking nowhere. Instead, you're worse than ever."

Oh, Dani so did not want to deal with this tonight. Not after the day she'd had. "You're going to want to watch your tone and your attitude, miss, unless you would prefer to spend the night in your room instead of with any friends."

Her daughter glared for a moment and then, with her quicksilver moods lately, her expression shifted to one of resignation. "Fine. I'm going over to Jenny Turner's house. She's in my biology class. She was going to call some other friends so we could watch the latest Marvel movie that just came out. Is that okay with you?"

Dani knew Jenny and her parents. They lived just one street over and her family had two beautiful Irish setters who appeared well mannered and well loved.

"Will her parents be there?"

"Her dad is on a work trip but her mom will be home, she said."

She wanted to say no. Dani had been looking forward to spending a little time together with her daughters. The girls didn't have school the next day because of a teacher training thing and Silver could hang out all day with friends if she wanted while the babysitter was there with Mia.

But Silver had struggled to fit in socially and find good friends since they moved to Haven Point and Dani didn't want to discourage any progress in that area.

"That's fine, then. Do you want me to give you a ride?"

"No. I'll walk. It's just through the block. Can I stay until eleven?"

"Yes, since you don't have school tomorrow. Text me when you're done and I'll pick you up. It doesn't matter how close she lives, I don't want you walking around town so late."

"It's like a block away, Mom. And, again, we're in the middle of freaking nowhere, Idaho. Walking is good for me."

She sighed, choosing to pick her battles. "Watch for cars."

On impulse, Dani hugged her daughter, fighting the urge to wrap her arms around her and not let go. After a moment, Silver hugged her back but quickly pulled away and hurried out the door.

Dani watched after her, trying to ignore the niggle of worry.

How did parents survive these teenage years? She constantly felt like a raw bundle of nerves, always afraid she was going to say the wrong thing and set off an emotional meltdown.

She watched until Silver walked around the corner, then turned back to Mia.

"Guess it's just you and me, pumpkin. I'll make the popcorn. You pick the movie."

"Elf," Mia said without hesitation, which was just fine with Dani.

She was pouring kernels in the air popper when Mia came into the kitchen holding the Blu-ray.

"I found it."

"Good job. Why don't you grab some ice water so you don't have to leave in the middle of the show if you need a drink? Your glass with the elephants on it is still at the table from dinner."

Mia took her water glass and filled it from the refrigerator ice maker.

"Mama," she said, features pensive, after the rattling ice stopped, "why doesn't Silver like us anymore?"

Dani's heart cracked apart a little at the sadness in her six-year-old's voice, mostly because deep inside, she felt as bewildered and abandoned.

"She does, honey. She's just a teenager living in a strange town and trying to make friends. It hasn't been very easy for her."

"I think I liked the old Silver better."

Dani didn't want to tell her daughter that she did, too.

After she finished adding toppings to the bowl of popcorn, she and Mia settled onto the couch. With Mia snuggled against her, Dani felt some of the tension leave her, but she couldn't shake her worry about Silver. She wanted so desperately for her daughter to find good friends who were also decent human beings.

The movie was familiar enough that her mind began to wander. Not for the first time, she wondered if she had made a huge mistake by bringing her daughters to Haven Point.

It had seemed the perfect opportunity. She and Frank Morales had struck up an instant friendship her second year of veterinary school when she'd stayed after a seminar he presented at a conference to ask him some questions.

That initial meeting had developed into a semiregular correspondence. She had a feeling Frank had looked on her as a mentee of sorts. He had been unfailingly patient and kind with her questions about various aspects of veterinary medicine and what went into running a successful practice.

A month before her graduation, Frank had called her with a proposition. He was looking for another doctor to take some of the load at his veterinary clinic. If she liked it here in Haven Point after her year's internship was up, he wanted her to take over the practice.

It was an offer she couldn't refuse, beneficial to her professionally while being perfect for her little family on a personal level.

This was everything she used to dream about, the chance to raise her girls in a safe place surrounded by nice people who cared about each other. Here, people didn't know about Tommy, about his disastrous choices.

Of course, when she'd accepted the internship and moved here, she couldn't have known about the tragic sequence of events to come later, the horror story that unfolded across the country mere weeks after she came to town.

She felt the beginnings of panic again, just thinking

about what would happen if news of Tommy's final moments were to filter through to everyone.

Frank knew, of course. She had to tell him. While he had been kind and understanding, she couldn't imagine the other people in town would accept the truth so easily.

Coming to Haven Point had sounded great in theory but the reality of making a life here was harder than she had imagined. The truth was, she didn't know how to socialize casually, which was a ridiculous thing for a thirty-year-old woman with a doctorate degree to admit.

She had married Tommy when she was seventeen. The years since, she'd been so focused on her girls, on school, on work and on simply *surviving* that she had gotten out of practice when it came to making and keeping friendships.

She didn't know how to relate to these people who were so darn *nice* all the time, and her awkwardness in the beginning had made her leery about accepting new invitations. Then Tommy had become a household name in the worst possible way. Dani knew she couldn't socialize now. She kept finding new excuses not to attend book club meetings or the Haven Point Helping Hands' regular luncheons and after a few months, the invitations had tapered off.

Her girls were struggling, too. Silver had all this attitude all the time, some of that from grief and shame over her father, Dani was certain. Even Mia, who hadn't even known Tommy, had become painfully shy in public, though she was her usual warm, sweet self at home.

Dani had to fix this or they could never make their home here, but she didn't know the first place to start.

"Mama, you're not watching the movie," Mia chided her.

"I'm sorry." She forced a smile and reached for some popcorn. "I'll watch now."

She couldn't do anything at this moment but worry, so she vowed to put it aside for now and focus on something light and silly and fun.

And then maybe take that hour-long soak in the tub after Silver was home and her girls were both safely tucked in bed.

For about the twentieth time in the last fifteen minutes, Yukon went to the back door and peered through the glass toward the backyard and the lake at the edge of it.

Retired police dogs were a lot like retired police officers, in Ruben's experience. They sometimes had a difficult time remembering they weren't on the job anymore.

"Easy, buddy. What's going on?" Ruben scratched the dog's neck in an attempt to calm him but the dog still seemed to want to alert him to something out in the back.

Yukon pulled away and went to the door whining, his attention focused on something near the boathouse, something Ruben couldn't see. He could only hope it wasn't a skunk. He hadn't seen one around here in some time, but one never knew up here. It could also be a black bear or a mountain lion.

Yukon whined again and nudged at the door and Ruben finally rose from the sofa and slipped his feet into the boots he kept by the back door. If the dog needed to go out, Ruben had to let him but he couldn't send him out alone if there might be a potential threat out there.

He pulled on his jacket and grabbed the dog's leash. Ollie trotted over, always ready for some fun, and Ruben had to shake his head at the little dog. "Not you. You've got to stay inside and watch the house while we do a little recon."

Ollie gave what sounded like a resigned sigh and plopped down on the rug to watch as Ruben clipped the leash on Yukon.

"All right, bud. Let's go see what's happening."

The night was cold, mostly clear, with only a few random clouds passing in front of the big moon that hovered just above the mountains. It was the kind of December night meant to be spent by the fire with a special someone.

Too bad he didn't have a special someone.

It had been almost a year since he had dated anyone remotely seriously, and that had been with a teacher in Shelter Springs.

He had met Lindsey while giving a self-defense class organized by Wynona Emmett, sister to his boss and close friend, Marshall Bailey. She had been sweet and warm and kind, but she also had been still in love with her ex-husband, something it had taken both of them six months of dating to fully acknowledge.

Ruben sighed. He missed Lindsey but he *really* missed hanging out with her kids, two cute little boys just a little older than Dani Capelli's youngest girl.

He supposed that spoke volumes about their relationship. His heart hadn't been committed yet, but he had definitely seen things moving in that direction eventually.

At least they hadn't gotten far enough for the situation

to turn ugly, like it did for his brother Mateo, who was in the middle of a nasty court battle for visitation with the stepson he had raised from a baby.

Next time he decided to let his heart get involved, Ruben had vowed it would be with a woman who didn't have children. The only trouble with that philosophy was that he was getting older and so were the women who interested him. He had outgrown his attraction to dewy, fresh-eyed coeds when he was in his twenties. He liked a woman who had been around the block a time or two and had the wisdom and experience to prove it.

Someone like Daniela Capelli, for instance.

He glanced next door, toward her house. The lights were on and he thought he saw someone moving around inside.

He hadn't been able to stop thinking about the woman since he'd left the veterinary clinic earlier in the week. He was no closer to solving the mystery of her, though.

Too bad she had kids—a younger one who seemed afraid of him and an older one who treated him like he had a bad case of head lice every time she saw him.

Yukon whined and pulled in the direction of the boathouse again, which was really just a covered concrete slab where he kept his shiny new cabin cruiser, aptly named *The Wonder.*

Ruben could swear he heard whispers drifting to him on the wind. Was someone there?

Suddenly Yukon's whine turned to a bark and the whispers turned to shouts. Someone yelled, "Run," at the same moment the dog lunged away from Ruben and the leash slipped out of his hand.

He reached for it, but Yukon moved with single-minded speed toward the boathouse, barking away.

Surprised at the unusual behavior from his normally obedient dog, Ruben raced after him. He ordered the dog in Dutch—the language he was trained in—to stay. After only a moment's hesitation, Yukon reluctantly obeyed, too well trained to do otherwise.

"Good boy."

Ruben could hear rustling in the bushes around the boathouse as he drew closer.

"Whoever you are," he called out, "you're going to want to not move. My dog is trained to attack on command. I just have to say the word."

He heard a small sound of distress and aimed his flashlight in the direction of the dog, who had alerted onto a shape crouched close to the ground. The dog wasn't growling. In fact, his tail might even have been wagging, though it was too dark to be sure.

"I should also tell you, I'm a deputy sheriff and I'm armed."

He didn't add that he was armed with only a flashlight and can of bear spray. The intruder didn't need that much information.

"Don't shoot me. Please don't shoot me." The voice was high-pitched and sounded terrified. Either it was only a kid or Ruben and Yukon had scared the cojones off somebody.

"Come on out from there. I won't hurt you. Neither will Yukon, as long as you don't make any sudden movements."

"Can you take his leash? Just in case?"

The voice struck a chord. He'd heard it before, and not that long ago. He tried to place it as he stepped forward to grab Yukon's leash, speaking in Dutch again to order the dog to stay.

"I have the leash but that probably won't help you. I was holding it earlier but he got away from me when he caught your scent."

He sensed the dog wasn't being predatory, he only wanted to play, but the intruder couldn't know that.

"Come on out."

After a long moment, the trespasser slowly rose from the ground, appearing ready to bolt at any moment. Ruben moved into position to block any escape route, and aimed his flashlight at the figure, clothed in a dark coat with the hood up.

Shock rippled through him. "Silver? Silver Capelli? What are you doing here?"

Of all the miscreants in town who might have it out for him—and it was impossible to avoid making a few enemies here and there in his line of work—he never would have pinpointed Dani's older daughter as someone who might trespass on his property.

"Um. Just taking a walk. That's all. I just wanted to, uh, see the water, then your dog scared me and I freaked. I'll, uh, just be going now."

Did she really think he was that stupid? Her house was next to his. If she wanted to see the water, she only had to walk into her own backyard, not scale the fence to come into his.

"Hold on a second."

His flashlight gleamed on something metallic in the

grass. He nudged it with his foot and saw it was a spray can. With a sinking suspicion, he turned the flashlight onto his new boat. Across the hull in glaring red letters he saw "Fascist Pi" written in two-foot-tall letters.

Either she had a thing against math equations or she hadn't had time to finish writing an inflammatory slur against police officers.

"Wow. Nice artwork."

"It was like that when I got here. I didn't see who did it."

He shined the flashlight on her. Again, did he look that stupid? "I can see the spray paint residue on your finger. I believe that's the very definition of red-handed."

She hid her hand behind her back, as if she were five years old and had been caught playing in her mom's makeup.

As he took a step closer, she stepped back, though she lifted her chin. Whether that was instinct or courage, he didn't know. One part of him had to admire her grit, even as he acknowledged that, ridiculously, his feelings were hurt.

What had he done to earn this kind of vitriol? He had tried to be nice to Silver since she and her family moved to Haven Point. He had talked to her a few times when he was making visits to the school and had even cracked a joke or two with her and her friends.

"I have two questions," he said as he flipped on the lights of the boathouse so he could get a better look at her handiwork. "The obvious one is why."

"What's the other question?"

"Answer the first one, then I'll ask the second."

She didn't meet his gaze. She still looked scared but he thought some of her abject terror seemed to be fading. She even reached down to pet Yukon, then faced him with an expression of defiance mingled with a shadow of guilt.

"I don't know," she finally said. "I guess it seemed like a good idea at the time."

It wasn't an uncommon excuse from kids who didn't always think through the consequences of their actions, who considered themselves invincible and were only interested in the thrill of the moment.

He had never personally been able to figure out the thrill of defiling someone else's property. Vandalism as a way to pass the time always annoyed the hell out of him.

"It wasn't. Obviously. It was a very, very bad idea. You see that now, right?"

She shrugged and looked down again without answering. When it became clear she wasn't going to respond, Ruben frowned.

"Second question. Who else did this with you?"

"Nobody," she said quickly. Too quickly.

He had heard other voices, had definitely heard that "run" command ring out across the backyard.

"You're in enough trouble, Silver. Don't compound it by lying to me. We both know that's not true. Who was here with you?"

She lifted her chin again and in the pale light, he saw defiance in her eyes. "Nobody. Only me."

"Why are you standing up for them? They were only too quick to leave you here to face the consequences— and Yukon—by yourself."

"You don't know anything," she snapped.

"I know that was a pretty rotten thing to do, letting you take the rap when you weren't the only one involved. Was this whole vandalism thing even your idea?"

She didn't respond, which he had a feeling was answer enough.

"What's going to happen to me?" she finally asked. "Are you going to arrest me?"

"That depends. Is my boat the only thing you've tagged tonight?"

She looked down at Yukon, as if hoping the dog could help her figure out how to answer.

"Silver?" he pressed.

"No," she finally said, her voice low. "You're going to find out anyway. I might as well tell you. We… I did two other things. A shed down the street where the mean old guy who always yells at kids lives, and Mrs. Grimes's garage door."

Gertrude Grimes taught English at the middle school and had been a cranky old crone back in the day when he went there. The intervening years hadn't improved her demeanor much.

"Are you going to arrest me?" she asked again. Her voice sounded scared and upset and, again, he caught that trace of guilt on her features.

He had the feeling Silver was having a hard time adjusting to life in Haven Point. Was this simply an outward sign of that, or was there more to it?

Technically they were within the town limits, which made this a case for Cade Emmett, the police chief of Haven Point. He could call for an officer and they would take Silver to the police station. She could be charged with criminal mischief and channeled into the juvenile justice system.

Sometimes that was absolutely the best course of action for a wayward teen, a firm and unmistakable wake-up call, but he wasn't sure Silver's actions justified that.

"First you're going to show me everywhere you hit tonight. With luck, we can talk to the owners and persuade them not to press charges as long as you promise to clean up after yourself. Then we need to go talk to your mother."

She opened her mouth as if to argue then closed it again, as if finally realizing just how much trouble she had created for herself.

"I'd rather you just arrest me than take me home," she said glumly. "My mom's going to freak."

"Either way, she's going to find out, Silver. Trust me, you're going to want to pick door number two, the one that doesn't include a trip to juvie."

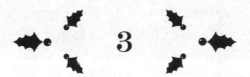

3

As Dani might have predicted, Mia fell asleep about halfway through the movie. Her youngest rarely made it all the way through a show. She would settle in, fully intending to persevere through the whole thing, but every time she curled up and drifted off.

Silver, on the other hand, couldn't bear not seeing things through to the end. If she started a movie, she would do whatever necessary to stay awake until the closing credits rolled past.

The girls had plenty of other differences. Mia loved dressing up, trying on Dani's few nice cocktail dresses and high heels, playing with dolls, drawing her own paper dolls and cutting them out. Silver had never done any of those things. When she was Mia's age, she loved soccer and hockey and watching the Red Sox, though at heart she was a die-hard Mets fan, even at six.

Despite their different personalities, Dani worried about her girls exactly the same.

As she sat in the darkened family room with her sleeping daughter on one side and their aging mutt on the other, Dani's thoughts circled back to her worries that she had made a grave mistake in moving to Haven Point.

All through those long, difficult years working on her undergraduate degree, then the even harder work to her doctorate, she had dreamed of raising the girls in a place just like this, somewhere rural and peaceful, a place of beauty and calm that might offer a tiny chance of protecting her girls from the ugliness of the world.

She wanted better. Better than the hardscrabble, uncertain life she had known growing up, better than the rough-edged world Tommy's family lived in.

With only one goal in mind, she had taken every scholarship that came her way, had worked double shifts, had taken out student loans. All so that she could provide a better life for her daughters doing something she loved.

Nothing was turning out the way she'd planned.

She sighed and nibbled her popcorn. Silver had become a distant stranger and Mia's sudden-onset shyness had become a crutch to her in every social situation. Her teacher said Dani's once bubbly, joy-filled daughter became withdrawn and silent the moment she walked into the school.

Dani wasn't exactly fitting in, either. Not only that, but the natural confidence and sharp intuition she had always felt around animals seemed to abandon her when she was the one making all the hard calls. Frank was so very kind and patient with her, but she still felt as if she was fumbling through everything.

Oh, she hoped this whole move wasn't a huge mistake. But really, what was one more? She'd been making mistake after mistake since she got pregnant with Silver at seventeen.

No. Her girls were her joy. Neither of them was a mistake, though Dani's choice of a man to be their father certainly was.

Mia stirred. "Is the movie over?" she asked sleepily.

"Yes. Come on. Let's get you to bed."

She scooped up her daughter, loving the poignancy of having her small, sweet-smelling shape nestled against her. Sooner than Dani wanted to think about, her baby would be too big for Dani to lift. She was growing so fast.

She carried Mia into her bedroom, decorated in her favorite colors, pink and lavender. After helping the girl under the covers, Dani pulled them up to Mia's chin.

"What about the movie? We didn't finish it," Mia said in a plaintive, sleepy tone, eyes mostly closed.

"Maybe you can watch the rest tomorrow with Silver while the babysitter is here or after I get home from work tomorrow night."

"Okay…" Mia's voice trailed off before she finished the word.

Dani stood beside the bed, Winky at her feet, watching her daughter sleep and feeling the weight of responsibility that had rested completely on her shoulders alone all of Mia's life.

"Come on, Wink," she whispered after a moment.

The little dog led the way outside. In the hallway, the dog suddenly tensed, a small growl in her chest as she hurried to the door.

A moment later, someone gave a firm knock.

Dani glanced at her watch. It was after nine. Who would be coming at this hour? Silver had a key and would have let herself in.

Dani went to the door and peered through the peephole. At first, all she saw was a broad chest clad in a T-shirt and unzipped navy blue down jacket. Her gaze traveled up and she recognized the hard, masculine features of her next-door neighbor.

In the dim glow from her porch light, Ruben appeared dark and dangerous and as gorgeous as ever.

A slight movement caught her attention and Dani shifted her gaze, suddenly realizing he wasn't alone.

Silver stood next to him, eyes wide and nervous and her chin trembling as if it was taking all her energy not to cry.

Dani swore sharply and was glad Mia was in bed and didn't hear it. She had worked for years to clean up her street language but sometimes swear words slipped out in moments of high tension.

Her stomach dropped. *Oh, Sil. What have you done?*

Dani could think of a dozen reasons an officer of the law would be bringing back her child. None of them good.

She wanted to sneak away, to hide in her bedroom and pretend she didn't hear the doorbell, but she was a grown-up. She couldn't pull the covers over her head and ignore her law enforcement officer of a neighbor and whatever dire news he had to impart.

Trouble, like bloodhounds, will always track you down.

With a sigh and a prayer for patience, she opened the door. "Deputy Morales. This is a surprise. What are you doing here? And with my darling daughter, who was supposed to be spending the evening with a friend watching a movie."

"Apparently she found something else to do. May I come in?"

She wanted to say no. She wanted to bar the door against him and her baffling, frustrating child, but, again, adulting carried certain unavoidable responsibilities.

With no choice, she held the door open. Silver didn't meet her eye as she shuffled inside.

"I'm going to bed," she muttered, all prepared to flee toward her room across the hall from Mia's. She looked as if she wanted to be anywhere on earth but here in their living room.

"Guess again," Dani snapped. "What's going on? Why are you not watching a movie with Jenny? Why did Deputy Morales bring you home?"

She slumped into a chair, mumbling something Dani couldn't make out.

"What was that?"

"You're just going to yell."

"Silvia Marie Capelli. What did you do?"

Her daughter folded her arms across her chest and didn't answer. After a moment, Ruben answered for her.

"Instead of hanging out and watching a movie, Silver

apparently decided it would be more fun to take a spray can around town and see what kind of mess she could make with it."

Dani's heart seemed to freeze. She stared at her daughter, shock rocketing through her. "A spray can!"

"She tagged three places in the neighborhood—a garage door at Gertrude Grimes's, an outbuilding at Tom and Mary Miller's, and my new boat."

Nausea churned through her, slick and greasy, and she was unable to think straight through the steady stream of swear words ringing through her head and the effort it was taking not to let them spew out.

Those names he gave were all neighbors and patrons of the veterinary clinic. She had treated one of the Millers' cats and Gertrude Grimes's rather unpleasant schnauzer.

"That's a strong accusation," she said, holding on to a fragile hope that he might be mistaken. "How can you be certain Silver was involved?"

"Show your mom your hand, Silver."

Her daughter gave a heavy sigh and thrust out her left arm, which earned her an amused look from Ruben.

"Nice try. The other one."

After a long moment, her daughter held out her right hand. The forefinger and thumb were covered in unmistakable red paint and Dani's heart sank.

"Silvia. What were you thinking?"

Her daughter remained stubbornly silent, answering only with her habitual nonchalant shrug that drove Dani absolutely crazy.

"In my experience, most of the time the kids involved *aren't* thinking. They get into a herd mentality kind of thing and nobody thinks to question whether what they're doing is a good idea or not."

She could understand that entirely too well. That sort of thinking had landed Tommy in jail when he was an irresponsible teenager and the pattern had continued through his short adulthood.

"Was this Jenny's idea?"

"I didn't go to Jenny's. That was a lie."

"So who was with you?"

"There wasn't anybody else. Just me." Silver said quickly. Too quickly.

"Really? All by yourself, you got it into your head that you would spend a cold December night vandalizing the property of our neighbors? Including a deputy sheriff?"

"Yeah. I guess I did."

"I'm not an idiot," Dani said flatly. "I know you're lying. I need the truth."

Her daughter lifted her chin. "Snitches get stitches. That's what Dad always used to say."

At the reference to her ex-husband, Dani glanced at Ruben, who was watching this interchange impassively.

She could feel heat soak her cheeks. Why did this particular man have to be involved? It was hard enough knowing he was a firsthand witness to her daughter's poor choices. She didn't need him knowing about her own.

"You, of all people, should have learned never to take to heart anything your father might have said," she said quietly.

She could never be quite sure if Silver hated her father or idolized him. The mood shifted constantly.

Since Tommy's violent death three months earlier, Dani was afraid Silver's memories of all those disappointments had begun to fade in the midst of a natural grief over losing her father, even after everything he had done.

"At least he never would have brought me to a stink hole in the middle of nowhere," she snarled back.

No. He would have just broken your heart again and again, until you had nothing left but shattered pieces.

"I happen to like this stink hole," Ruben said mildly.

"You would." Silver's voice dripped sarcasm and Dani stared at her, appalled at her daughter's rudeness to an officer of the law. She had taught both of her girls that nothing good ever came out of being disrespectful to people who were only trying to do their jobs.

"That's enough," she snapped. "Your father has nothing to do with this discussion. This is about you and your own mistakes. I can't believe you would do something like this. How could you?"

"It was easy. You just push the little nozzle on the spray can."

At Silver's flippant tone, Dani's anger spiked.

Sometimes being a parent really sucked.

She dug her nails into her palms to hold on to the fraying edges of her temper, drew in a deep breath and let it out slowly before she trusted herself to speak.

"How much damage did she do?" she asked Ruben.

"Hard to say in the dark. My boat will need some serious cleanup work. It will take the right solvent that won't damage the finish, so I'll need to talk to the marine supply places. We checked out the other places she hit and I'm thinking it would be cheaper in those cases to repaint."

Dani wanted to cry, to just sit right here in the middle of her living room and throw a good, old-fashioned pity party, with a healthy dose of temper tantrum thrown in.

Why couldn't anything be easy? It was hard enough trying to fit into a new place—a new school, a new neighborhood, a new town. Why did Silver have to go and make everything worse, for absolutely no reason Dani could see?

"We'll take care of all costs associated with the cleanup, of course."

Ruben was quiet, watching her out of those big, thick-lashed dark eyes. "Seems to me, Silver should be the one to put in the elbow grease and make it right."

"Me?" Her daughter's eyes widened and she looked appalled.

"Sure. Why not? If you can make the mess, you can clean up the mess. You could always share the burden by letting us know who else was with you tonight, so they can help in the cleanup."

Dani watched Silver's chin jut out with the stubbornness that was as much a part of her makeup as her green eyes and dimples. "No one was with me. How many times do I have to tell you that?"

"You can tell me as many times as you want but I heard voices and saw others running. None of your partners in crime will face the necessary consequences of their actions unless you come clean."

Silver folded her arms across her chest again. "I didn't have any partners in anything. It was only me."

Ruben shrugged. "That's fine. Then you alone can clean up the mess you created. Or I suppose I can go ahead and talk to the property owners and see if they've changed their minds about pressing charges."

Fear flashed across Silver's delicate features. For all her bravado, she didn't like being in trouble. She never had.

"Fine. I'll clean it all up by myself. Can I go to my room now?"

Dani wanted to keep her out there to yell at her some more but she figured some distance between her and her daughter wouldn't hurt right now while she worked a little harder to restrain her temper.

"Go shower and get your pajamas on. I'll be in to you in a minute."

Silver gave one last resentful look to the room in general—as if *she* had anything to be angry about!—and stomped to her room, leaving Dani alone with the deputy sheriff.

She never would have expected it, but she found the man far more intimidating when he was wearing jeans and a T-shirt under his down jacket, instead of his uniform.

The uncomfortable little sizzle of attraction didn't help matters any.

"I don't know what to say to you," she said after Silver's bedroom door closed. "I'm so sorry."

"It's not your fault—unless you were one of the people I saw take off running."

He smiled in response to her narrowed gaze. "Yeah. I didn't think so. In that case, you don't have any reason to apologize. You had nothing to do with it."

"Except I trusted her, when she told me she was going to watch a movie at her friend's house."

"Which friend was she supposed to go to? I can start there. You said Jenny? Which Jenny? I know a few."

She didn't want to answer him. Her tongue felt thick, the words tangled in her throat. Apparently her late ex-husband's disdain for snitches had worn off on her, too.

She sighed. She didn't know how to keep the girl out of it. "Jenny Turner."

"Sean and Christine's daughter."

"That's right. But Silver said she didn't go to her house and it wouldn't surprise me if she just used her name as an excuse, mainly because I know her parents. I can't imagine Jenny would have anything to do with this. I've only met her a few times but she seems very nice."

"She is. But nice doesn't have much to do with it. Even the so-called *good* girls can make mistakes with their friends egging them on."

Was Silver negatively influencing the whole neighborhood? Oh, she hoped not.

"I'm sorry," she said again. To her dismay, she could feel tears burning behind her eyes and blinked as hard as she could to keep them back. "She's never done anything like this before. I can't understand what got into her head."

Ruben's features softened in a way that made him seem far less intimidating. "Don't beat yourself up. She made a mistake and did something stupid. Probably won't be the first time or the last time."

Who would have guessed that she could take such

comfort from the words of a tough deputy sheriff? She wanted to draw them close and hold on tight.

"I did plenty of stupid things when I was her age," he went on. "So did most of my friends. We even got caught a few times. Despite it, we all turned out okay. One's the county sheriff, one is an FBI agent and one is the town police chief. Don't worry. Silver will get through this."

"I suppose you're right. I just wish she had chosen something a little less destructive to the community for her first stupid foray into teenagedom."

"We can't change that now. The only thing she can do is try to make it right and then move forward. The good news is, the other property owners are pretty reasonable people. As long as she makes the effort to fix what she did, things should be okay."

She did *not* want to be in this man's debt but that was exactly where she found herself. He was being extraordinarily kind and she was well aware of just how much she owed him.

"Thank you, Deputy Morales. I appreciate you bringing her home instead of making this a criminal matter."

"After three months of being neighbors, don't you think you could call me Ruben?"

She didn't want anything that would bring them closer together but she didn't know how to avoid it. "Ruben, then. I appreciate the way you have handled things."

"I could have booked her for destruction of property. Technically it is the jurisdiction of the Haven Point PD but I was an officer on scene and could have made that call."

"Why didn't you?" She had to ask.

"I weighed the options, believe me. But when she seemed more frightened about coming home and facing you than she did at the prospect of going to the police station, I figured this was the better choice."

"You must think I'm the meanest mom in the world."

"Your daughter *should* be afraid of the consequences of her actions. She needs to fear disappointing her parents. In my professional life, I see too many cases where kids know their parents will never call them on their bad behavior. Guess what? That only leads to kids who don't know how to function in society."

"I will help her clean up the mess. Please find out the details of what we need to do. We'll make it right."

As if she needed one more thing to worry about in her life right now.

Oh, Silver. What have you done?

"I'll let you know," Ruben said. He was watching her with a strange expression, one of almost approval. Why? She was the bad mother who hadn't even known where her child was that night. She had botched the whole thing, start to finish.

She had *no* business feeling this warmth seeping through her. She couldn't let herself be attracted to Ruben Morales. He was a law enforcement officer who would have absolutely no interest in her, once he knew the truth.

"All right. I'll be in touch tomorrow."

"Thank you."

He studied her for a long moment and she had to wonder what he saw. She had been watching a movie earlier with Mia, though that felt like hours ago. Her hair was probably messy where she had been leaning back against the sofa and she wore casual, comfortable clothes with no shape or style whatsoever.

"Doc? I know you're angry but try not to be too hard on Silver."

"Weren't you just telling me about the parents who never give their children consequences?"

"She definitely needs consequences. That's not what I'm saying. What she did was wrong, no doubt about it. But it might not hurt to remember she's at a tough age, trying to fit in to a new community, which can't be easy for anybody."

Dani was entirely too familiar with what that was like. "I'll be sure to keep that in mind," she said, forcing a polite smile. "Thanks again for your help. Good night, Ruben."

He smiled a little at her use of his first name but also didn't appear to miss the direct hint, especially when she held open the door for him.

"Good night."

He reached down to give Winky another scratch behind her ears, then headed out into the night.

Dani closed the door and stood for a moment in her living room, feeling the heat of her little dog on her slippers. She wanted to sink down onto the floor of her entryway, gather Winky close and cry until she fell asleep, but that was the sort of thing she might have done as a lonely girl in foster care. She was a mother now, with a mother's responsibilities.

Right now, she needed to deal with her daughter.

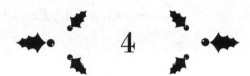

4

She made it as far as Silver's bedroom, then paused outside, still trying to process what had just happened.

How could her child have jeopardized everything like
this? Didn't she understand how precarious things were?
If Dani didn't do well in this internship, if they couldn't
carve a place for themselves here in Haven Point, she
would have to once more pick up her girls and start all
over somewhere else.

They had a nice home here in a nice community.
Where would they go if Haven Point didn't work out?

The worry that always seemed to lurk at the edges of
her subconscious crept ever closer.

She took another deep breath, trying to beat it back
again. She had to do her best to be calm and collected

when she spoke with Silver. Raging at her daughter would accomplish nothing.

Was this some kind of cry for help, tangible proof of everything Silver hadn't said? She wasn't happy here. That truth was becoming unavoidable. She didn't fit in because of her purple hair and her unique fashion sense and, most probably, because of her defensive attitude. She wanted to go back to Boston where she had friends, or even New York to live with Tommy's family.

A parent's job was to discern between a child's wants and her needs. In this case, Dani knew in her gut that her family needed a community like Haven Point.

When she pushed the door open, she found Silver face-down on her bed, the blanket up around her ears. The only light came from Silver's phone, which she was not supposed to have in her bedroom past 10:00 p.m. anyway.

She opened her mouth to yell about that but caught herself. She had other things to worry about right now.

Silver didn't look up when Dani came inside and moved to the bed. She waited her out, standing for a long moment until her daughter finally rolled over and held out her phone.

"Here. I know I'm not supposed to have it. I wasn't texting anyone. I was just looking at pictures of my friends back in Boston."

Dani's heart squeezed with sympathy, but she schooled her features so Silver didn't see.

"Thanks," she said calmly. "I'll put it on the charger in my room."

She said nothing else, just waited for Silver to speak

first and explain herself. "Go ahead. Yell at me. I know you want to."

She did want to yell—to scream and rant and ask Silver what the hell she was thinking. The pain on her daughter's face held her back.

"I'm not going to yell."

"You're not?" Silver's shock was evident in her wide eyes.

"What would that do? It would only make both of us feel worse and wouldn't change what you've done."

"O-okay."

Dani turned on the bedside lamp then sat on the edge of the bed. "A deputy sheriff, though? Seriously? In what alternate reality would you ever think that was okay?"

Her daughter threw her forearm over her eyes, as protection from the light or to avoid her mother's gaze, Dani wasn't sure.

"I don't know," she admitted. "It was a stupid thing to do, okay? I know it was dumb. We... I wasn't thinking."

Dani didn't miss that telltale pronoun. She wanted to pounce on it and make Silver tell her who else had been involved, but somehow she sensed further interrogation would do nothing to move the conversation forward.

"Do you hate it here so much that you want to sabotage everything for all of us?"

A little tear leaked out of Silver's eye and dripped into the hair she had dyed herself. "I miss my friends," she said.

"You know the way to make the sort of friends you want to keep isn't to engage in criminal activity with them, right?"

"I know." She scratched a pattern into her quilt. "Nana says if I really hate it here, I can come live with her back in Queens."

Dani's insides twisted at the mention of her former mother-in-law. "When did you talk to your Grandma DeLuca?"

Silver looked more guilty about this than she had about showing up at the door with a deputy sheriff. "She messaged me and sent me her phone number a few months ago. After, you know. In case I wanted to talk to her about…about Dad and what happened. We've been texting on and off for a while now."

"You know I check your texts. I haven't seen anything like that."

Silver looked away. "I always delete them. I know you don't want me to talk to her. I can stop."

Again, Dani wanted to yell, but did her best to keep control. Silver loved her namesake grandmother, who had been an active part of their lives for her first few years, even babysitting her when Dani had classes.

Dani never would have made it through her undergraduate degree without Silvia DeLuca's help.

Their relationship had become strained after Dani filed for divorce six years ago, but even then she had allowed Silvia DeLuca to see her granddaughters, until the other woman started slyly undermining Dani to them. The final straw had come when Silvia dragged Silver to visit her father in prison without Dani's permission.

Silvia was one of those women who could never see her child as he was. Tommy could do no wrong in her book.

As far as she believed, anytime Tommy found himself in trouble, it was always someone else's fault.

She had been furious about the divorce and even more upset when Dani left for veterinary school in Boston. Their contact had dwindled to Christmas and birthday cards, which was exactly the way Dani preferred things.

"Are you mad that I've been texting Nana?"

"I'm mad that you've been hiding it. We can talk about that later, though. Right now, we need to focus on your actions tonight."

"I made a mistake. It was stupid. It won't happen again."

The words sounded far too well practiced to be sincere.

"No. It won't. You're grounded until further notice. That means extra chores here and at the clinic, no video games, no YouTube and no phone except at school."

Silver huffed but said nothing, obviously knowing she was on extremely thin ice. No doubt she could almost hear it cracking beneath her feet.

"Also, I need you to give me the names of the other girls involved so I can let their parents know and they can help you with the cleanup."

"I told you. It was just me."

They both knew that was a lie but Dani had no idea how to force the truth out of her.

"Fine. You can do the cleanup on your own."

"Fine," Silver said, her voice short. "Is that all?"

"For now."

With a sigh, Dani rose and squeezed Silver's arm. "You know I love you, Silverbell, right?"

Her daughter shrugged, not meeting her gaze.

"I brought you and Mia to Haven Point because we've been offered a chance to make a good life here, a place where you girls would be safe and healthy. A place with low crime, good schools and nice people."

"There were good schools and nice people in Boston. And in Queens before that."

"Agreed. We could have made a good life for ourselves somewhere else. This is the one that felt best. When I got this opportunity, you and Mia and I talked about it and we all agreed we wanted to give Haven Point a chance to become our home. I don't think any of us has really done a good job in that department. I'd like to try harder. What about you?"

"I guess," Silver said.

Dani reached down and hugged her daughter and after a moment, she felt small arms go around her.

Silver rested her head against Dani's chest, just above the thick nest of emotions there. She loved this beautiful, smart, contrary creature beyond words.

"Get some rest. Everything seems better in the morning."

She hoped, anyway. Because right now things seemed pretty bleak for Team Capelli.

"I get to be the candy cane in the school play. You should come see it! I get to sing a solo and everything. Can you come?"

"Wow. That's exciting." Ruben smiled down at Will Montgomery, his boss's stepson and just about the most adorable kid he knew. "When is the play?"

"The Wednesday before Christmas at eleven." Will's

mother, Andie Bailey—married to the sheriff and Ruben's boss, Marshall Bailey—sat in the visitor chair at his desk, waiting for Marsh to get off the phone so the sheriff could take her and their children to lunch on his break.

"Are you sure you don't want to join us for lunch?" she asked.

"Yeah," Will said. "You could sit by me and I could tell you all about my part."

"I hate to miss that kind invitation but I have some paperwork to finish."

The sheriff's department wasn't always a good place for kids, but Andie and the children had brought some shortbread cookies they had made that day to hand out to the other deputies in the office. Ruben had quickly secreted his plate in a desk drawer where everybody else better keep their hands off, if they knew what was good for them.

He loved seeing Will, his sister, Chloe, and their mother, Andie, together with Marshall. The four of them, along with Marshall's son Christopher made a solid, loving unit.

At the same time, his interactions with the family always left him a little…hollow. Not sad, precisely, only more aware than usual of his solitary state.

Ruben never thought he would be thirty-three and alone. He had always wanted a family, always imagined by this point in his life he would have a bunch of kids, a mortgage, a boat in the driveway and a kind, caring wife like Andie.

He had the boat and the mortgage, but not the rest.

"You might like my school program, too." Chloe gave

him her sweetest smile, that one that always stole his heart. She was a few years older than Will but considerably more mature. Some of that had to do with her personality, though some might have been from the tough circumstances of a few summers ago, before her mother married Marshall.

"Are you a candy cane, too?"

"Ruben," she said in an exasperated voice. "We don't have candy canes in the sixth grade program. That's for the little kids. I'm in the choir."

"Let me know when it is and I'll see if I can arrange my schedule."

He had a nephew in her grade at Haven Point Elementary School, so would definitely try to make it.

"It's right after Will's class program."

"Easy enough. I'll add it to my schedule." Maybe that was his destiny, to always be the kindly uncle and friend.

He pushed away that depressing thought as Marshall finished his phone call and came out.

"Did I hear talk that somebody brought cookies?"

Will giggled. "We did! We've got some for you, too, Dad."

That was a new thing, the kids calling Marshall *dad*. Ruben had noticed it the last time he saw them all together. Their own father had been a police officer killed in the line of duty. Marshall had stepped up to take care of all of them and it was obvious the kids loved him.

He could tell Marshall was touched by the word. "Bring them in here before somebody else eats them," he said gruffly.

Will and Chloe grabbed one of their remaining covered plates and charged into their stepfather's office, leaving Ruben with Andie.

"Those two," she said, shaking her head.

"They're wonderful."

"I can't argue with that. I'm enjoying them at this age, but who knows what trouble they'll bring me in about five years or so. Which reminds me, Marshall tells me you had some excitement at your place last night. Some vandalism on your beautiful new boat. How is *The Wonder*?"

He found himself reluctant to discuss Dani and her daughter with Andie, almost protectively so, which he knew was completely ridiculous.

"It was just kids messing around."

"I understand you caught one of them in the act. The new veterinarian's daughter, the one with the cool hair and the unusual name."

"Yes. But please don't spread that around." He really hoped the identity of his vandal wasn't common knowledge. He knew Andie would be discreet. She wasn't going to talk, not even to her friends at the Haven Point Helping Hands, a service and social organization in town.

"I won't," she assured him.

"Silver wasn't the only one involved, but she was the only one I caught. She won't tell me who else was there."

"Snitches get stitches," Andie said.

"Funny. She said the same thing."

"I understand her reticence to implicate others. She's probably worried about retribution. She's, what, thirteen? That's a hard age to start at a new school."

Andie could be a good source of information, he realized. The kids were busy helping Marshall shred some papers in his office so he decided now was as good a time as any to dig a little into his intriguing neighbors.

"What's their story? Dani and her kids? Do you know her at all?"

"She seems very nice and she's a good veterinarian. Right after she came to town, we went to her when Sadie got a bad bee sting in her eye."

"Ouch."

"Right? I would say Dani has a more abrupt bedside manner than your dad, but seemed very kind and caring."

"What about socially? Have you interacted much outside the veterinary clinic?"

Andie shrugged, though she looked intrigued at his line of questioning. Maybe he shouldn't have said anything. He didn't need his friend's wife matchmaking.

"Not really. She seems very...*private* is I guess the word I would use. She came to a few social events when they first moved to town. Again, she seemed nice enough but I'm afraid maybe we overwhelmed her. When McKenzie asked if she wanted to join the Helping Hands, she said no, that she was too busy with her girls and settling into a new town, starting a practice. Same thing when we asked her to join the book club."

"That's fair. Not everybody is a joiner."

"I get it, believe me. The women of this town can be intimidating for even the toughest constitution."

"There are so many of you and you always travel in packs."

"Not always," she protested with a laugh.

"Most of the time, then."

Before she could answer, Marshall came out with the kids and Andie's face completely lit up.

Ruben was aware of a little pinch of discontent again as the two of them kissed. He did his best to ignore it. Marsh had been Ruben's friend long before he became his boss and Ruben was glad the sheriff and Andie seemed so happy together.

He was always aware when he was with them that if the two of them hadn't found each other first, Ruben definitely would have made a move. Andie was the kind of woman he had always thought he wanted—someone soft, warm, compassionate.

Worlds away from a certain prickly, cool, reserved veterinarian.

Somebody should probably tell that to his subconscious, which had filled his dreams with all kinds of inappropriate situations involving the woman the night before.

Friday was a long, difficult day. She would have liked to take the day off since the girls were out of school but her time off was limited as a new veterinarian.

She was lucky enough to have a few good caregivers in her rotation and Gloria, the clinic receptionist and office manager, had a daughter home from college for the holidays who was looking for a little extra cash.

Dani had hoped to be done by two, her usual schedule on Friday, but a bichon frise with an abdominal obstruction came in right as she was wrapping up for the day and the dog required emergency surgery.

The surgery had been much more complicated than she

had expected and she had ended up calling on Frank to help. She found it demoralizing that she had needed his expertise, yet more evidence she wasn't up to the challenge of her new vocation, but Frank wouldn't let her beat herself up.

"Don't ever be embarrassed to ask for help." His eyes—so like his son's—were warm and kind. "I've been in the vet business for more than forty years. Just when I think I've seen everything under the sun, something new walks through the door to prove me wrong. You should never hesitate to call me, even after the practice is officially yours."

She wasn't sure that day would ever come—or ever *should* come. Who was she kidding, to think she had what it took to be a veterinarian? She was a failure. A nothing. Hadn't she heard that enough when she was growing up?

As usual when that negative self-talk intruded, she did her best to focus on how fiercely she had worked to get where she was. All the sleepless nights of studying, the hand cramps from propping a textbook in one hand while rocking a crying baby in the other, the many creative ways she had found to stretch a dollar.

We can do hard things. That was the message she tried to reinforce to her girls. She couldn't help wondering when it would be her turn to do the easy things.

By the time she finally made it home just after five, three hours later than she'd planned, she was exhausted.

"Thank you for staying extra with them," she told Heidi, Gloria's youngest daughter.

"Not a problem. I need the extra cash. I'm saving up to get my belly button pierced."

Since the girl had four rows of pierced earrings and a ring in her lip, what was one more puncture wound? "Glad I could add to the pot, then. Have a good evening."

"Thanks, Dr. C. Silver's been in her room most of the afternoon doing homework and Mia is in the family room."

"Thanks."

After Dani let the babysitter out, she headed to find the easier of her children and found Mia playing quietly with her dolls.

"Hey, sweetie pie. How did your day go?"

Mia shrugged, without looking up at her.

"What's wrong, honey?"

"You said we should never lie but you lied."

Dani scanned over her day, trying to figure out where she had gone wrong this time.

"About what?"

"You said you would be home right after lunch and we could put our Christmas tree up today. Lunch was a long time ago and now it's almost dark and I bet you're going to say you're too tired to put up a Christmas tree."

Going through the hassle of putting up a tree was the absolute last thing she wanted to do right now. After the difficult day, her brain was mush and she wanted to collapse on the sofa and sleep for the rest of the evening.

She had made a promise, though, something she took very seriously.

She sat on the floor beside her daughter. "I'm sorry, Mia. I did tell you I would be home after lunch but then I had a dog emergency. Sometimes that happens when you're a veterinarian. We've talked about it before, remember? This time the emergency was a little bichon frise who had something stuck in her stomach. She was throwing up and couldn't eat or poop."

Her compassionate youngest child looked distressed at that. "Is she okay?"

"She is now. Dr. Morales came in and helped me fix things. It will take a day or two, but Princess Snowbear will be back to herself in a few days."

Apparently saving a dog's life warranted a few points in her book, at least where her youngest was concerned. Mia cuddled up to her. "I like Dr. Morales. He's nice."

"He is, indeed." She would have been in trouble without him during the surgery. What would she do when he finally retired?

She put that worry away for another day. "How's your sister been?"

Mia looked down the hall toward the bedrooms. "I don't know. She stayed in her room almost all day. Earlier, I asked if she wanted to play with my Shopkins and she told me they're stupid and I am, too."

Apparently at least one of her children had no problem being a snitch. "She shouldn't have said either of those things. You're not stupid and neither are your toys, honey."

The two girls were separated by seven years, which sometimes seemed such a vast chasm in their relationship. Sometimes Silver could be the sweetest thing to her sister and sometimes she barely tolerated Mia.

"What did you have for lunch?" Dani asked.

"Grilled cheese sandwiches, only Heidi left the crusts on and I had to cut them off myself."

"That's a hard day all around. Let's see what we can do to make the afternoon and evening better. What do you think about calzones for dinner?"

"I love calzones! Can I help you make them?"

"You got it, kid. Maybe we can talk Silver into helping us, too."

Mia looked doubtful but followed her down the hall. The doorbell rang before they reached Silver's bedroom door.

"Who's that?" Mia asked, looking nervous.

"I don't know. We'll have to answer it to see."

She looked through the peephole and saw a big, solid chest dressed in a brown sheriff's uniform. As she opened the door for Ruben Morales, she told herself it was only her exhaustion that had her feeling a little light-headed.

"Deputy Morales. Hello."

He smiled, looking big and dark and absolutely delicious—something she was furious with herself for noticing.

"Afternoon. I was on my way home but thought I should stop here first to let Silver know about the conversation I had with the graffiti specialist for the county and what it's going to take to clean up her artwork from last night."

Just once, couldn't she see the man when she wasn't exhausted and rumpled and feeling as if she'd been dragged behind his big boat for an hour?

"Come in," she said, holding the door for him. "I've only been home from the clinic for a few moments myself and haven't had a chance to talk to her yet. I'll grab her."

"Thanks. Hi there, Mia."

He smiled at her suddenly shy six-year-old, who somehow managed to give him a nervous smile in return. Dani stood there awkwardly for a long moment, then finally gave herself a mental head-slap and hurried down the hall. She expected Mia to follow her, but instead the girl opted to remain behind with Ruben.

"I told you I'm doing homework, Mia. What do you want?" Silver called out when Dani knocked on her door.

She could feel her shoulders tighten in response. If thirteen was this tough, how on earth was she going to survive the rest of the teenage years? she wondered for the bazillionth time.

"It's not Mia. It's me," Dani said, pushing open the door.

She found Silver on her bed, a notebook propped on pillows in front of her. No doubt she was writing in her journal, detailing how miserable her life was. Silver closed it quickly and while she didn't hide it under her bed, she looked as if she wanted to.

Dani released a breath. "Deputy Morales is here to speak with you."

For just an instant, Silver's mouth trembled with nerves. She looked down at the closed notebook in front of her and fiddled with her pen.

"I'm, um, in the middle of something here. I don't want to lose my train of thought. Can you just find out what he wants?"

"What he *wants* is to speak with you. Come on, honey. Might as well get it over with, right?"

"I guess." Silver sighed and climbed off her bed. She slipped the notebook into the drawer of her bedside table, wiped her hands down her jeans as if they were as sweaty as Dani's, then moved to the doorway.

When they returned to the living room, she found Ruben on the sofa with their dog, Winky, on his lap. Mia was showing him her vast collection of dolls and their wardrobe that Dani could swear was more fashionable than her own.

"What's this one's name?"

"That's Pia. She's my favorite. See, her hair is curly just like mine and her eyes are brown like mine. You have brown eyes, too."

"Yes I do."

"I named her Pia because it rhymes with Mia."

"Perfect. So if I had a doll, maybe I would have to name him Gruben."

Mia giggled, her shyness apparently all but gone, and Dani felt something hard and tight around her heart begin to crack apart a little.

No. She wouldn't let herself be drawn to him. She made disastrous decisions in the men department and right now she couldn't afford another mistake.

"I have three outfits for her but this green dress is my favorite. You can get clothes to match your dolls if you want. I asked Santa for a green dress, too, but I don't know if I'll get it. Silver says it's too expensive and my mom has stupid loans."

"Does she?"

"I did not. I said she has student loans," Silver corrected.

"Though they're certainly stupid, too," Dani admitted.

Ruben looked up and flashed them both a smile that made her feel light-headed again.

"I'm sure they are. It can't be easy."

At the understanding in his voice, Dani was appalled to feel tears well up. She couldn't count the sleepless nights she'd had over the last thirteen years, worrying whether she would be able to provide for her daughters.

"It can be an adventure," she admitted. "It helps that your dad has kindly let us have this place rent-free."

"Dad's good about things like that," he said, then looked around her to where Silver was lurking.

"Hey, Silver. How's it going?"

She shrugged. "Fine. My mom said you wanted to talk to me. I've got a ton of homework, so…"

In other words, get on with it. Silver didn't say the words but she might as well have. Dani tried not to cringe at her rudeness.

"Right. Good for you, doing your homework on a Friday afternoon."

"Like I have a choice. I'm grounded from just about everything else."

"Look on the bright side. With all the studying you'll get, your next report card will be great."

"And if she keeps it up, maybe she'll get a scholarship when she's ready to go to college and won't need those stupid student loans," Dani said.

"Excellent point."

"Did you say you spoke with a graffiti cleanup specialist?"

"Yes." He rose and it seemed to Dani that all the oxygen in the room seemed to seep away. "There's a guy in the road department who takes care of that kind of trouble whenever any Lake Haven County property is vandalized. He's considered our expert. I took the spray can of paint to him and told him what kind of things you'd tagged with it and he's given me a couple of solvents that should work on my boat. For the other places, as I suspected, he says a new coat of paint will be cheaper and easier."

"Okay."

To Dani's relief, Silver seemed to lose a little of her attitude at the sharp reminder of her own actions and mistakes.

"I'm not scheduled for a shift tomorrow, so I figured it would be a good time to get started, especially since we're supposed to have unusually warm weather. Bob, the expert at the county, said we're better off jumping quickly on some of this cleanup. It will be easier now than if you wait a week or so, when the weather is colder."

"I don't know," Silver said. "Like I said, I have a lot of homework."

"She'll be there," Dani said firmly. "What time?"

"Why don't we say ten? We can start at my place and work our way to the neighbors after that. Oh, and bring a sack lunch."

"Seriously? This is going to take all day?"

"Maybe even longer. That's the problem with some poor choices. Cleaning up after yourself takes about ten times longer than the act itself."

Silver looked discouraged, as if she were scouting in her mind for some way out of the hole she had dug for herself.

"She'll be there," Dani repeated.

"Great. We're supposed to have a good day. Dress in layers. It might be chilly in the morning, then warm enough for shirtsleeves by the afternoon. With any luck, you can be done by dinnertime."

Silver's sigh was heavy. "Fine. I'll be there. Can I go now?"

Dani made a shooing motion with her hand and Silver escaped quickly.

"Thank you." Dani had to say it. "You've been much more understanding than I think I would have been in your shoes."

"I was thirteen myself once. I told you, I made plenty of my own stupid choices."

"You said that, but I still have a hard time believing it. You don't strike me as the troublemaker type."

When it came to graffiti, anyway. She could imagine him making all kinds of other trouble for the women of Haven Point.

"You might be surprised."

Mia was tugging on her jacket and it took Dani a moment to register it. "What is it, honey?" she asked.

"I can help Silver clean up," Mia said. Her features were so earnest, Dani felt that suspicious burning behind her eyes again.

"That is a very kind offer." Ruben smiled down at her girl with such sweetness it made Dani's heart ache, for reasons she didn't quite understand.

"Families stick together, no matter what," Mia informed him. "We help each other. That's what Mama says."

He glanced at Dani with that same warmth, which she knew she didn't deserve.

"I couldn't agree more, Miss Mia."

Dani did, too. While she wanted Silver to learn hard lessons about the consequences to her actions, she had thought all along that she would do what she could to help Silver clean up the graffiti, for her neighbors' sakes as much as her daughter's.

"That's a very good idea, sweetie. Yes. Mia and I can help with the cleanup. We'll come with you and Silver tomorrow, as the clinic is closed. We can meet you next door at ten with our work clothes on."

"Great. We'll make a party of it."

"Not *too* much of a party. Silver doesn't need fun, she needs consequences for her actions."

"A subdued party, then. It will be fun for us, but not nearly as fun for her."

He winked at Mia, who giggled with no trace of the shyness she had showed fifteen minutes earlier when he rang the doorbell.

How did he do it, win her over so easily?

Dani supposed it didn't matter. The only important thing, she thought as she let him out of the house, was to constantly be on guard and try her best to make sure he didn't win *her* over.

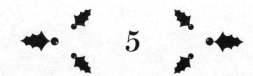

5

Ruben was in deep, deep trouble.

He was fiercely attracted to his neighbor. Something about Dani's complicated mix of vulnerability and chin-up defiance struck a chord deep inside, some place no one else had ever touched.

He didn't want to be attracted to her. She wasn't at all his type. He had always believed he preferred soft, sweet, gentle women—someone like Andie, someone giving and kind, not prickly and defensive.

He might tell himself that all day but it didn't change the fact that he found himself in this unlikely position where he couldn't stop thinking about her, dreaming about her, wondering about her.

What difference did that make? he asked himself as he

finished gathering the supplies they would need to clean up his boat and waited for them to arrive.

Yeah, he was attracted to her, in a way he couldn't remember being to another woman, but that didn't mean he had to do anything about it.

They would be spending most of the day cleaning up graffiti. That's all. He only had to survive several hours in her company without making a fool of himself over her.

Maybe by the end of the day they would emerge as friends. Something told him Dani Capelli needed all the friends she could find.

As usual, his dogs were the first to inform him he had visitors. Ollie went on alert, his ears cocked for just a moment before he rocketed to the front door, Yukon close behind him.

They made it there about fifteen seconds before the doorbell rang.

Friends, he reminded himself. That didn't stop his heartbeat from kicking up a notch as he opened the door.

"Hi, policeman," Mia said, greeting him with her shy smile that stole his heart every time.

"Hi there, Miss Mia. Hi, Silver. Dani."

The other two females at his door didn't look nearly as happy to see him as the little girl was, but Ruben decided not to take it personally.

"You guys ready to do this?"

"Yep," Mia said.

"Yes. The sooner we can get started, the sooner we'll be done," Dani said.

"I know we talked about starting with my boat, but this morning I was thinking we should start with the other places while the weather is good and then make our way back here. Mine can wait, if we have to, plus I have the covered boathouse to protect from the elements a little. Does that work for you guys?"

"Whatever you think. Isn't that right, Silver?"

Her daughter looked like she would rather be anywhere else on earth. "Fine," she mumbled.

"Where do you want to go first?" Dani asked.

"Let's start at the Millers' house. The graffiti seems a little darker there and might take two coats of paint to cover. I talked to Mary this morning and she was able to find matching paint cans from when they had it repainted two years ago, so that should make things easier. I've got some painting supplies from when we redid this place. Rollers and paintbrushes here and a couple of trays."

"And I found a few things at our place, too." Dani gestured to a box at her feet.

"Great. We should be good, then. Silver, why don't you help me with this crate while I grab a few other things."

"That big thing?"

"Yeah. I think you can handle it."

He handed her the heavier of the two boxes, not out of spite but to again reinforce the message that her actions had consequences.

He picked up the other box, gave his usual orders to the dogs to behave, then closed the door behind him.

"You're not taking your dogs?" Mia asked. "They're cute. Maybe they can help us."

"Not today. I'm afraid they would mostly get in the way while we're trying to work. We kind of have to hurry to get two coats of paint on while the sun is shining."

"It is a beautiful day," Dani said. "One of the nicest we've had in weeks."

She was right, the weather was unseasonably warm for December, predicted to get into the high fifties, with no snow in the forecast for at least a few days. The morning sun felt almost warm on his shoulders.

"I'm glad. If it wasn't so nice, we would have to wait until spring to repaint. As it is, we might have to use some industrial space heaters so the paint will dry. We'll see how things go. I've got a couple buddies in construction who might be able to loan us some equipment for a few days."

Dani gave him a look he couldn't read, as if she couldn't quite figure him out. "You're going to a great deal of effort on Silver's behalf. I'm still not sure why."

He glanced at the girl, who walked with her head lowered as they made their way down the street toward the Millers' house.

"I don't know," he admitted, which was absolutely the truth. "I guess maybe this is one little way I can give back to repay all those who've helped me throughout my life. Besides that, around here, neighbors help each other. It's what we do."

She didn't look convinced but he changed the subject before she could press him for answers he couldn't provide.

"Have you met the Millers?" he asked as they approached the house.

"Briefly, when we first moved in. Mary brought us a pie with apples from her tree."

"That was her?" Silver asked, eyes shocked, as if she

hadn't made the connection between a woman who would welcome them to the neighborhood with pie and the people whose property she had vandalized.

"Yes. Mary and Tom Miller," Dani said.

"They're very sweet," Ruben said. "She used to teach math at the high school and Tom worked at the post office for years."

"The man who lives here yelled at us once," Mia said with a frown as they approached the house. "Silver and me weren't even doing anything. Just walking Winky past their house. It scared me."

Is that why Silver had picked this house to tag? Because the man who lived here had scared her little sister?

If it wasn't random vandalism, Ruben had to wonder again what *he* had done to earn her ire.

"He had a stroke a few years ago and sometimes he can be a little grumpy. I'm sorry that happened to you."

Silver met his gaze, shock in her eyes. "Oh. I didn't know."

"Sometimes when people have health problems, they become so focused on that, they aren't always aware of how their words or tone impact others."

"That must be difficult for Mary," Dani said, compassion in her voice.

"Yeah, but she's a trouper. I told her we were coming over. Silver, I thought you might have something you want to say to her."

Silver looked back down at the box in her hands and mumbled something he couldn't hear.

After he knocked on the door, Mary Miller answered wearing a ruffled apron with Christmas trees and candy canes on it. Out of the house wafted the delicious scents of sugar and cinnamon and butter.

"Hello, Ruben, dear."

He leaned in and kissed her wrinkled cheek. "Hi, Mary. I understand you've met Dani Capelli and her daughters, Mia and Silver. We're here to paint over the graffiti."

Her face softened and she reached both hands out and grasped his much bigger one in hers. "You told me on the phone you were coming but I wasn't sure you'd be able to make it. You're so busy! This is so kind of you, Ruben, but I'm not surprised. You've always been such a good boy."

He managed to refrain from rolling his eyes at Dani, who was watching this interchange with interest and, if he was not mistaken, considerable amusement.

"Who's here?" a gruff voice asked from the other room.

"Go back to your show, Tom," she said, her voice patient. "It's Ruben Morales here with that nice veterinarian who moved in down the street with her pretty girls."

Dani's amusement quickly shifted to discomfort when she seemed to remember why they were there. "Silver, don't you have something you want to tell Mrs. Miller?"

The girl mumbled something incoherent, looking down at her sneakers.

"I'm sorry, dear. I don't hear as well as I used to. Could you repeat that?"

Silver looked up. "I'm very sorry I sprayed graffiti on your shed. It was a dumb thing to do. I made a mistake and I'm sorry."

As apologies went, that one was nicely done, Ruben had to admit.

"Well, you're making it right again. That's the important thing. We all make mistakes, choices we wish we hadn't. Why, just this morning, I poured buttermilk in my coffee when I meant to grab half-and-half. Let me tell you, that was quite a nasty surprise."

Ruben had to smile. Grabbing the wrong container out of the refrigerator didn't quite equate to vandalizing others' properties, but he appreciated her trying to make Silver feel better.

"It shouldn't take us long to paint over it, then we'll get out of your way."

"Thank you. The cans are right inside the shed. I don't know when I would have had the chance to clean it up myself, and you know Tom likes the place to look tidy."

Silver winced a little, looking even more guilty. Good.

"Wait a minute. Before you go there to start work, you'd better try these snickerdoodles that just came out of the oven. I tried a new recipe this time and you would really help me out if you would taste them for me and give me your opinion."

"Oooh. I love snickerdoodles," Mia declared. "They're my favorite."

The elderly woman smiled down at the little girl. "Then you'll be the perfect one to try them out and tell me how you like the recipe."

She shuffled out of the hallway, shoulders bent from age and arthritis. A moment later, she returned with a plate piled high with cinnamon-and-sugar-dusted cookies.

"They're a little more flat than my snickerdoodles usually turn out. I might need to add a tad more flour. Try them and tell me what you think."

Ruben took a bite, which was fluffy and sweet and delicious, as far as he could discern.

"Perfection," he said.

"Very tasty," Dani concurred.

"Yumalicious," Mia declared.

Silver nibbled hers, still with an odd expression on her features. "It's, um, really good. Thank you."

The woman beamed at them. "Oh, I'm so relieved. Here. You take these with you, to keep your strength up while you're painting."

She pulled plastic wrap over them and handed the plate to Mia, the only one of them who didn't have her hands full of painting supplies.

"That was nice of her, wasn't it?" Dani said to her daughter when they walked outside.

"I guess," Silver mumbled, her eyes still filled with confusion as they made their way to the shed.

Here, the vandals—he would never believe she acted alone—had covered the side of the shed with multiple huge spray-painted smiley faces and the words *Be Nice*.

"Oh, Silver," Dani exclaimed.

"I was dumb. I know. I don't need you to keep harping on it. Can we just move on now?"

"Good idea," Ruben said, taking pity on her discomfort. "We have a lot of work ahead of us. I brought some wire brushes. I think they're in the box you brought along. Our first step should probably be seeing if we can scrape some of it off before we try painting over it. Why don't you grab them, Silver?"

She didn't look thrilled at the assignment but nodded and started digging around in her crate until she pulled out the brushes.

"Is this what you wanted?"

"Exactly. Just start scraping away at the graffiti. I'm not sure if any will come off, but we can try."

They all went to work, Dani on one side, Silver in the middle and Ruben on the end.

He didn't mind painting and considered himself something of a pro. He'd spent many hours of his childhood earning spending money by helping his dad paint the concrete walls of the veterinary clinic. Those had been great times, where he'd been able to talk to his dad about girls, about life, about where he wanted to be in the future.

There was actually a Zen-like calm in the process, painting over the old and bringing in the new.

"Mommy, can I have another cookie?" Mia asked after a few moments. She was sitting on a garden bench, keeping watch over the cookies as if she expected Mary's garden gnomes to come to life and snatch them away.

"Just one. Let's save the rest for later."

Silver frowned as she continued working the wire brush against the wooden shed.

"What's wrong?" Ruben asked. "You seemed upset earlier about the cookies. Didn't you like them?"

"No. It's not that. They were great. It's just…" She looked down at the plate of cookies in her sister's hand then back at the tidy little house. "Why did she give us cookies?"

"She said she needed testers," Mia reminded her sister.

"But… I did a stupid thing and vandalized her property. Why is she so nice about it? I thought she would yell at me."

She gestured to the mess she had created on the shed. "I mean, if this were my place and some stupid kids, um, a stupid kid messed it up, I'd be seriously pissed."

"I suppose she sees that you're trying to make amends," Dani said. "That's what today is all about, to show our neighbors you're sorry for what you did, right?"

"I guess. I still don't get it."

"I don't care why," Mia said. "I just like the cookies. I'll eat them all if you don't want them."

"I never said I didn't want them," Silver protested, which made Ruben smile.

"She's a nice lady," he said. "Just like Mrs. Grimes, once you get past her gruff shell. After you've been in Haven Point awhile, I think you'll find most people here are kind."

"If you say so," she muttered, looking not at all convinced.

"I do. In fact, in my experience, most people *everywhere* are kind. Sure, there are the selfish jerks out there. People who don't care about anyone but themselves and who are willing to do whatever it takes to get ahead, but they're usually far outnumbered by those willing to step up when they see a need."

"Wow. Do you need me to clean those rose-colored glasses for you?" Dani asked, looking at him as if he had just arrived from another planet filled with do-gooders.

He smiled. "I already polished them this morning, thanks. You can borrow them anytime you want, though."

"No thanks. I prefer to see the world as it is, not as some pretty picture with all the harsh edges blurred out."

Who had hurt her and left her so cynical? The girls' father? He wanted to ask but didn't dare with her daughters looking on.

"Mommy, if Silver doesn't want another cookie, can I have hers?"

"I said one more. Put them away for now. Maybe after lunch you can have another one."

She pouted but was easily distracted when Ruben told her he needed help holding the tray while he poured paint into it.

The little girl was adorable and he was thrilled she seemed to have lost her shyness with him so quickly.

With her curly dark hair and light olive-toned skin, she looked like something out of a Renaissance painting. Her mother and sister did as well. Throw their pictures up in a Venetian chapel and they would fit right in.

Okay, maybe they wouldn't fit in so well right *now* when they were wearing clothes suitable for paint and cleanup work. And Silver might need to lose the purple hair first.

"Do you have a ladder?" Dani asked a few moments later. "I can't quite reach the top."

"Over at my place. I'll grab it if necessary, but let me see if I can reach first."

"Use my brush. It has a longer handle."

She handed it over and their hands briefly connected. He attributed the little burst of heat that flared between them to the wire bristles of the brush conducting electricity. It was a nice theory but didn't quite explain the rosy blush climbing her high cheekbones.

Was it possible Dani was attracted to him, too? It was a fascinating idea, one he desperately wanted to explore, if not for her daughters looking on.

"Watch out," he said gruffly. "I don't want to shower down paint flakes on you."

She moved out of the way while he finished scraping the high spot and brushed off the flakes. When he finished, Ruben stepped back to look at the wall again.

"Good work. We might be able to get by with only one coat, which is good since it has to dry completely before the temperature drops tonight. Winter isn't a great time to clean up graffiti."

He didn't miss the guilt that flashed across Silver's expression. Good. Maybe if she felt guilty enough, she would come clean about who else had been involved with her in the vandalism.

"What now?" Silver asked, a new urgency in her voice.

"Brush off any remaining paint flakes, then you can start rolling on one side and I'll do the other. We'll meet in the middle. This shouldn't take us long."

"What can I do?" Dani asked.

"I've only brought the two rollers. You and Mia can be our cheerleaders."

She rolled her eyes, which led him to the not surprising conclusion that she probably wasn't the sort of girl who went in for short skirts and pom-poms.

"When we knocked earlier, I saw the woodpile close to the house is running a little low. Maybe you and Mia could grab the wheelbarrow and move some of the split logs closer to the house so she doesn't have to," he suggested.

Dani brightened at the suggestion. "That's a great job for us. Come on, Mia."

"Can I ride in the wheelbarrow?"

"Maybe on the way back from the house," Dani said.

For a few moments, he and Silver worked in silence.

"I don't get why we have to paint over the whole thing when the graffiti is only on part of it. Couldn't we just paint that?"

"If we only paint over the markings on the wall, we'll end up with a splotch of new paint that will look almost as bad as the graffiti. Painting the whole wall will hide it better."

She seemed to accept that, though it was obvious she didn't necessarily like it.

"Tell me about where you came from," he said after a few moments. "Boston, wasn't it? Did you like it there?"

"I guess. It was okay. My friends are cool."

"How long did you live there?"

"Since I was nine. That's when we moved from Queens so my mom could go to vet school."

Dani had loaded the wheelbarrow full of wood and was heading toward the house with Mia in the lead. He wanted to ask directly about Silver's father but didn't want to come across as too obvious.

"Just the three of you?" he asked, as unobtrusively as possible.

"And Winky. Her full name is Winky Stinksalot. The Winky part is from Harry Potter."

"Oh, right. The little house elf. You've had her a long time, then."

"We got her when I was a little girl. I found her in a park near our apartment in Queens. She was starving and dirty and didn't have a leash or anything. We put a sign up in the park but nobody ever came forward to claim her so Mom said we could keep her."

That was the most she had ever talked to him, the longest string of sentences he'd heard out of her mouth. He asked a few more questions about the things she liked to do in Boston and New York. Once Silver started, it was as if he had uncorked the bottle. She chattered as much as Mia had earlier, though mostly about her friends and the movies she liked and some of the places they liked to hang out in Boston.

In no time, they were finished with the wall and he had a much clearer picture of their family. They seemed to love each other very much, a message that came through in Silver's conversation.

He had also noticed the girl went to a great deal of effort not to mention her father, in what was an obviously deliberate effort to leave him out of the conversation.

Why? What was the big secret about the man?

"That looks great," Dani said, rejoining them. "I can't see any trace of graffiti. Do you think you'll need a second coat?"

"We may have to see what happens when it dries, but so far it looks like we've got good coverage. How did you two do?"

"We carried about a hundred logs over to the house."

Mia slumped to the ground, apparently completely exhausted.

"Good work. Now Mrs. Miller won't have to walk all the way over here to refill her wood box for a week or two."

Mia looked happy about that, anyway.

"That should do it here. We'll check back later in a couple of hours to see if this will need a second coat. Meanwhile, let's head over to Mrs. Grimes's place and get started on her garage door. I'm warning you, it might be a little harder."

"We can do hard things," Mia said. "That's what our mama always says."

"Exactly right. Good thing we have snickerdoodles to help us keep up our strength."

Dani faced the garage door decorated with more of her daughter's handiwork, her heart sinking at the magnitude of the task ahead of them.

Gertrude Grimes hadn't been as sweet as the Millers. She had been terse and tight-lipped when Silver apologized for her actions. Dani had a feeling her daughter's English grade would *not* be very good this term.

Again, she had to wonder what Silver had been thinking. She couldn't understand her daughter. On what planet would she ever think destroying someone else's property would make her more liked, more popular, more *accepted* in their new community?

Dani sighed. How could she blame Silver, really? She had once been her, defiant and angry, trying to lash out at the world however she could.

Wasn't that the whole reason she had hooked up with Tommy DeLuca?

Tommy had seemed wild and reckless and dangerous, yes, but that had been a big part of his appeal when she was a needy, lonely sixteen-year-old girl.

He had been four years older, a twenty-year-old man who had no business hitting on a teenager, she could see that now. At the time, she hadn't thought anything was wrong with it, she had only been enthralled by his attention.

Like a thirsty, forgotten plant shriveling up in a corner, she had lapped up all of it desperately and had been pregnant with Silver when she graduated from high school.

Ruben Morales, on the other hand, was the complete opposite of her late ex-husband. Okay, except for the dangerous part. Something told her that for all his good-natured amiability, he would be fierce and protective if anything threatened those he loved.

What would it be like to have the love of a man like him?

That was a question she didn't have the courage to even consider.

"Do we need to use the wire brushes again here?" she asked him.

He stood beside her, studying Silver's handiwork.

"I'm afraid that would damage the garage door. I think our best bet here is to try the cleaning agent the county specialist suggested to see if we can get the paint to fade at all, then we'll repaint."

She watched as he reached into one of the crates of supplies for rags.

What was his story? The man was a complete mystery to her. She still didn't understand why he would want to spend an entire Saturday helping them clean up graffiti. So far, they had only worked at other people's houses, too. They hadn't even made it as far as his house to clean up his boat.

He was a fascinating enigma.

"Mia, there are some rags in that box there. Can you hand me a few?"

Her youngest rushed to help him, eager to please her new best friend. It worried her, this instant bond her youngest daughter seemed to have formed with the gorgeous deputy sheriff. Dani wasn't quite sure why Mia had glommed on to him, when she had been so shy around virtually everyone else since coming to Haven Point.

Funny, but Mia had the same reaction to Ruben's father. Usually around men, she was nervous, preferring to talk to them through Dani or Silver, or—more likely—not speak to them at all. Apparently, something about Frank Morales and his son set her at ease.

Dani wanted to think that was a good thing, but she wasn't quite sure.

After they wiped down the door with the cleaner, Ruben stood back to look. "I think some of it has faded, but it still might need two coats."

He grabbed a can of paint and the tray, and he and Silver went to work with the rollers.

"Good work," he said a few moments later. "You're really getting the hang of that paint roller. Maybe this summer, your mom can put you to work rolling a fresh coat of paint on the outside of the vet clinic. The last time it was painted was probably when I did it at your age."

"Did they even have paint in those days?" Silver asked with a sideways grin.

"Yes, but we had to make our own out of natural dyes from the plants we gathered around our covered wagons," Ruben said drily, which earned him an even wider grin from Silver.

"I'm not that old," he said. "Probably not much older than your mom."

"She'll be thirty-one in April," Silver offered, entirely too free with Dani's information.

"Thirty and already a doctor of veterinary medicine? That's impressive."

"Not that impressive. It took me five years to get my undergrad degree, since I was working full-time and had a child, and then another two years of working as a vet tech before I was able to get into veterinary school."

"I still think it's impressive," he said.

She told herself not to be warmed by his admiration but she couldn't seem to help it. Apparently some part of her was still that shriveled houseplant in the corner.

"That should do it," Ruben said a short time later.

"Are we done?" Silver asked.

"I think so. Depending on how this dries, we might not need a second coat here, either, but we'll have to check it for sure in a few hours."

"We still have to clean up your boat," Dani pointed out.

He made a face. "Believe me, I won't forget. *The Won-*

der is only two months old. I've only had her in the water twice."

"I'm really sorry, Ruben," Silver said.

Apparently she was just as susceptible to the man's charm as her younger sister. Okay, and her mother.

"Good. You should be," he said, not unkindly. "Now let's go check the Millers' house and see if it's ready for another coat."

They packed all the supplies back into the crates and headed down the street. When they returned to the Millers', they found the paint on the shed had dried with good coverage.

"You lucked out," Ruben said. "Looks like we don't have to do another coat here. Since that's the case, why don't we break for lunch, then meet back at my place in an hour or so to work on *The Wonder*?"

"Sounds good," Dani said.

"We're having chicken noodle soup," Mia informed him. "I helped put the carrots and the celery in the pot before we left."

"That sounds delicious."

"I bet you could have some," Mia said.

Dani didn't miss the sidelong look Ruben sent her. "That's very kind of you, but I don't want to take all your soup."

"Mom always make tons," Silver said. "You might as well eat with us."

Ruben didn't bother to hide his shock at her seconding her sister's invitation. His gaze met Dani's, a question in them, as if gauging her opinion about her daughters inviting him over. She shrugged.

"We do have plenty and you're welcome. It's the least we can do after all your help today, but don't feel obligated. You could probably use a break from having your ear talked off by one or more of us."

"I was going to grab a quick PB and J sandwich, but chicken noodle soup sounds way better. Listen, I've got a loaf of homemade bread at my place. Why don't I run home and check on the dogs, grab the bread and meet you at your house in fifteen minutes or so?"

In Boston, she might have found it unusual if a man had told her he had a loaf of homemade bread sitting around his house. Haven Point was another story. People did that here, just dropped off a loaf of warm, fragrant, scrumptious bread simply because they had baked extra and thought you might like it.

"That sounds delicious. We'll see you in a few moments. Come on, girls. We need to add the noodles to the soup."

She could have used a little distance from the man, a chance to rebuild all her defenses before spending the rest of the afternoon with him, but apparently she wouldn't be getting that right now.

While one coat of paint seemed to have covered over Silver's graffiti, Dani wasn't being nearly as effective when it came to resisting Ruben Morales.

6

Twenty minutes later, Ruben rang the bell at Dani's house, the loaf of fresh bread under his arm.

The very adorable Mia opened the door for him immediately, almost as if she had been watching for him out the window.

"Hi." She beamed, showing off the gap in her front teeth. "The buzzer just went off, which means the soup is ready."

"Don't I have perfect timing, then?"

"You certainly do," Dani said from the doorway.

Twenty minutes. That's all the time they had been apart, but still, his heart seemed to kick in his chest at the sight of her, fresh and sweet and pretty.

In those twenty minutes, she had redone her hair, pulling back the loose strands that had slipped out of her ponytail throughout the morning as they worked. She looked lovely either way but he wondered how she would react if she knew he was suddenly battling a strong urge to start pulling those strands back out. He kind of preferred the tousled, sexy look of earlier, though he knew full well she hadn't been going for that on purpose.

Her little dog, Winky, greeted him with a friendly yip and Ruben diverted himself from that inappropriate hairstyle temptation by reaching down to scratch the dog's head.

"How were Ollie and Yukon?" Dani asked as she led the way to the kitchen, where plates and bowls had been set around the table.

"They're always happy to see me. Isn't that one of the best things about dogs? Ollie made it clear he didn't want me to leave again. Apparently he doesn't want me to do anything on the weekends but sit around and watch sports."

"I'm sorry we've messed up your routine."

"I'm not," he said truthfully. He said the words with a little more intensity than warranted, which might have been the reason he thought her color rose a little.

"Silver," she called down the hall. "Deputy Morales is here and lunch is ready."

"You and your girls don't have to call me Deputy Morales all the time, you know, like I told you the other day. I would prefer if you all call me Ruben, especially after we've already spent the entire day together."

"Right. Sorry. Habit." She gestured to the loaf of bread in his hand. "Would you like me to slice that?"

"That would be great. Thanks."

Silver came in and finished setting the table while Dani took his loaf of bread to a cutting board near the sink.

"Can I help do anything?"

"No. You're a guest. I'm afraid we only have water to drink. I should have warned you. I don't even have beer."

"Water's fine with me."

"Sit down," she ordered. "Anywhere is fine."

The moment he picked a seat, Mia joined him at the table, moving her chair closer to his. How could any guy not lose his heart to this one?

"You guys getting ready for Christmas yet? I didn't notice a Christmas tree."

"We took our old crappy tree to Goodwill when we moved," Silver said, pulling headphones off to drape around her neck.

"We took *all* our stuff to Goodwill," Mia added.

"Not everything," Dani protested. "Just the stuff we didn't want to move across country."

Silver rolled her eyes. "Everything that wouldn't fit in a little rented trailer the size of a bathtub. The Christmas tree didn't make the cut. Mom said we would pick up another one here but we haven't yet."

"I've been a little busy the last few weeks," Dani said tartly. "It doesn't help that I had to spend my one free day this week cleaning up graffiti, did it?"

"I didn't ask you to help. You offered. I could have done it by myself."

Dani's mouth tightened but she was busy dishing bowls of chicken noodle soup into chunky blue stoneware bowls and carrying them over to the table.

"Mama says we can get a real tree this year, as soon as we find one. I can't *wait*."

"There's a nice lot on the outskirts of Shelter Springs where they sell real trees. A friend of mine runs it, Carlos Urribe. He's a good guy."

"If we mention your name, will we get a discount?" Silver asked.

"Better not. He's still miffed at me over a bet he lost a few months back during the World Series."

"What about you?" Dani asked. "Do you decorate much for the holidays? I don't think I've noticed a tree at your place, either, when I've passed by."

"I love Christmas, don't get me wrong, but I live alone and it doesn't really seem like it's worth all the trouble just for me. I have a little tree in the front room. It's one of those prelit ones and I hang a dozen or so ornaments on it. If I didn't do *something*, I think my sister would probably come and decorate my whole house when I'm not looking."

"Would she really?" Dani looked as if she couldn't comprehend that sort of relationship.

"I've learned not to put anything past my family."

She sat down at the table finally, across from him. "Your family seems very close."

"Sometimes *too* close," he admitted.

She took a piece of bread and buttered it for Mia. "But you settled in Haven Point anyway."

"I lived in Boise when I was in college and when I went through the police academy, but when the job opened at the Lake Haven Sheriff's Department, I was glad to move back. I like it here."

"I do, too," Mia said.

He smiled at her, grateful he had at least one ally among the Capelli women.

"What about you?" he asked. "Do you come from a big family?"

"No," she said, her voice wooden. "Mia, don't slurp your noodles."

So family was a touchy subject. He filed that away for future reference, even as he was astonished at his urge to hold her close and kiss away the pain in her eyes.

"Small families are good, too," he said.

"They are. This is my family," she said, gesturing to her daughters.

"Except Nana," Silver said.

"Your mother?"

"My ex's mother. Late ex," she added quietly.

"I'm sorry."

She opened her mouth as if to say something, then apparently changed her mind. "Thanks," she mumbled.

So she was divorced and then the girls' father died. How sad for all of them. He wanted to ask about the man and what happened to him but decided this wasn't the appropriate time.

Dani changed the subject, asking him more about going through the police academy and why he wanted to go into law enforcement in the first place. He, in turn, talked to the girls about school and their favorite subjects. It turned into one of his most enjoyable meals in recent memory and gave him a much better picture of the family dynamics.

"Girls, hurry and finish your soup," Dani finally said. "We still have to help Ruben clean up his boat."

He thought about telling her he really didn't need her help. After speaking with the graffiti specialist for the county, he had found exactly the right solvent that would easily clean the paint off *The Wonder*. He had tested it the day before to be sure and it had worked like magic.

He *could* clean it himself. At the same time, he believed strongly that Silver needed to be involved in all aspects of the cleanup effort, including something he easily could handle on his own.

"It won't take us long," he assured her. "I can help you clear the table first. The soup was delicious, by the way. Thank you."

"You're welcome. And it's Silver's turn to load the dishwasher. You can help her."

Silver groaned but didn't push her luck.

Smart girl, he thought as he rose and picked up his soup bowl. He was beginning to like her, despite her attitude.

He liked *all* of them. Entirely too much. It was becoming too easy to forget his resolve about not dating women with children.

Not that he and Dani were dating, or anything close to it. She was still brisk with him and somewhat distant, which made his undeniable fascination with her even more puzzling.

Dani refused to let herself be charmed by the man as she watched him tease Silver while the two of them cleaned up the few dishes in the kitchen.

What was his game? Why was he being so nice to them all?

He was an officer of the law and she had an inherent mistrust of him because of it. Growing up in the city, she saw too much corruption, too much inequality and bias and misuse of authority.

He appeared nothing like that. He seemed to be one of the good guys, a caring, dedicated sheriff's deputy who gave up an entire Saturday to help her daughter.

Still, Dani couldn't completely trust his motives.

She and the girls had secrets she would rather he not discover, secrets that might threaten her future here. The more time she spent around him, the likelier the chance that she might let some of those secrets slip to a trained investigator like Ruben.

If she wanted to make a better life for her girls here, she had to be wary about letting down her guard around him.

"Can I play with my dolls?" Mia asked.

"For a few minutes, then we need to head over and help Ruben and Silver clean up his boat. If we get done in time, we'll go pick out our Christmas tree."

"Yay!" Mia did a little circle in the air, which Winky promptly copied.

"Whoopee," Silver said, with no trace of excitement in her voice.

"You don't like Christmas?" Ruben asked.

"I like not having to go to school for two weeks," Silver said, "but the rest of it seems like a lot of work for limited payoff."

Silver's words stuck a little sharp-tipped thorn into

Dani's heart. Had she failed her daughter when it came to instilling Christmas spirit in her?

She hadn't always loved the holiday, either. It was tough being in foster care at Christmas. If her foster family had other "real" children, there were always inherent inequities in the way she had been treated, especially among extended family members.

Most of the time, they probably weren't even aware of it. She had noticed, though, even as she understood. Why should grandparents extend the same effort and energy into finding the right gift for someone who could be gone from their lives the next day?

She had gotten used to it. What other choice had she been given? Eventually, Dani had come to treat Christmas as just another day to get through, this one with a little more chaos than most.

After she had Silver, though, Dani had gained an entirely new perspective.

She had this small, wonderful creature to think about now and Christmas became far more magical when her focus shifted to providing memories for her child.

Dani had always tried to make up for the dearth of material things by giving her girls experiences they wouldn't forget: walking through a light display in a city park, going to the mall to see Santa, visiting nursing home residents who would otherwise be alone—both because it was kind and also to remind her girls that while they didn't have much, they had each other.

The last few years, she had been so insanely busy trying to survive the rigors of veterinary school, she was afraid she had failed in that arena, too.

This year had to be different.

While money was still tight thanks to all those loans she had taken out, gambling toward her future, she was more comfortable financially than she had been in years. That was in large part thanks to Ruben's father and his generosity both in the compensation he was providing her during her internship and his offer to let them live in this small but comfortable house on the lake.

She had been afraid this would be a hard Christmas. The stress and trauma of Tommy's death and the highly charged circumstances around it had taken their toll on her and on Silver. Mia was mostly oblivious, since her father had been a stranger to her, but Silver still grieved.

Despite everything, Dani had grieved as well. She had mourned the pipe dreams she'd cherished as a lonely, foolish teenage girl, swept off her feet by a fast-talking young man who had promised safety and security and the happily-ever-after she had always yearned after.

Those dream castles had turned to sawdust too quickly. His promises had all been an illusion, but at least her girls had come out of her marriage, the two most important things in her life.

In a way, she supposed Tommy had given her the thing she most needed, someone to love. Two amazing some-ones. She could regret many things about her marriage to a man who ultimately chose a life of crime over his family, but she would never regret her daughters.

She wanted to give them the best possible Christmas here in Haven Point.

Whatever game Ruben Morales might be playing, whether he was befriending them to dig deeper into her life in an effort to protect his father, or whether he genuinely wanted to know them better, she would be cautious around him. She had to be. Her girls had no one else to stand for them.

An hour later, she had to acknowledge that keeping her distance from Ruben Morales was easier said than done, especially when he was so very sweet to her daughters.

"Look at that," he said, standing back and admiring the work he and Silver had put in to clean away the graffiti. "It came off perfectly, just like the label on the cleanser said it would."

"You can't even tell it was ever there," Dani said, admiring the sleek, glossy gleam of his boat in the afternoon sunlight with the words *The Wonder* in small script near the stern.

"I'll admit, I was a little worried about damaging the finish, but this stuff is magic. I'm glad it worked so well."

"I do like your boat," Mia said. "It's pretty."

Ruben smiled down at her and Dani tried to ignore the little flutter of nerves inside her.

"Thanks. I think so, too. I never considered myself a boat guy but it kind of seemed a natural fit, since I own a house right on the water. I will say, next time I buy a boat, I'm going to do it at the beginning of the season, not at the end. I'm anxious to get out on her."

Silver rolled her eyes. "Why do guys always consider their boats girls?"

"Because we love them," he answered promptly. "And maybe because they're unpredictable and take more work than any guy ever expects."

This time Dani was the one who rolled her eyes. "And

because men like to think they're the captains of them, but it's really the boat that makes all the rules," she told her daughter, then decided she would be wise to change the subject.

"You guys worked hard today. I'm impressed," Dani said. "I didn't think we would get everything cleaned up in one Saturday."

"Agreed," Ruben said. "I was worried the weather wouldn't hold, but we did it. Lucky for us, the shed at Mrs. Grimes's place didn't need a second coat, either."

"Yay us!" Mia said, beaming her gap-toothed grin.

"You didn't have much to do with it," Silver said.

"Not true," Ruben said. "She was the best cheerleader ever, plus she helped move firewood for the Millers and petted Mrs. Grimes's schnauzer."

Mia beamed at him, clearly smitten. Oh, Dani hoped her little girl didn't get her heart broken.

"Thank you for all your help," she said. "We never would have been able to make things right without it. You really went above and beyond."

"I can't believe I'm saying this, but it really was my pleasure. Despite the work involved, it was a fun day."

Dani was afraid to admit how very much she agreed with him. "Silver. Don't you have something you want to say to Deputy Morales?"

"Ruben," he insisted.

"Thanks again for helping us, Ruben," Silver mumbled. "And I'm sorry I tagged your girlfriend here."

Ruben grinned and patted the side of his sexy boat. "She forgives you. And so do I."

Dani could swear her daughter grinned back for just a moment but she concealed it quickly.

"The good news is, now she should be all ready for the Lights on the Lake Festival next week."

"I want to see that!" Mia said.

"You can watch the parade from your house, but it's more fun to go to Lake View Park downtown, where there are craft and food booths, live music and games for the kids. It's a big party. The biggest one of the season. You don't want to miss it."

Her first instinct was to tell him they would likely do better to watch from their house, but that seemed to play into her antisocial tendencies. She was trying to make a home here, which meant she needed to get out and mingle more.

"Thanks for the reminder. Can we help you clean up?"

"Not much to do. I should be fine."

Mia tugged on her sweatshirt. "Mama, can we go get our Christmas tree now?"

"Yes. Let's go home and clean up, then we'll drive to Shelter Springs and check out the lot Ruben was talking about."

"Do you have a tree stand and Christmas lights for your tree?" he asked.

She hadn't thought that far ahead. "No. I suppose I'll have to pick those up while we're in town."

"I might be able to help you out there, actually. My parents bought an artificial tree a few years ago and they've been storing their old things in my garage. There are a couple of tree stands and at least a half-dozen strings of lights. I can't guarantee they'll all work, but you're welcome to use what you can find."

His offer surprised and touched her, especially as she suddenly realized that purchasing multiple strings of lights and a new tree stand for a real tree might end up costing her more money than if she went ahead and bought a whole artificial tree.

"That's very nice of you. Thank you."

"Silver, come help me dig around in the garage for a minute, will you?"

"Ooh. That sounds fun," she said, her voice dripping with sarcasm. Still, she went with him toward the house and the attached garage, and Dani and Mia followed behind.

His garage was neatly kept and well organized, though not to the point where he seemed like a neat freak. He went to the back of the garage and pulled down a ladder from the ceiling, which made Mia's eyes go wide.

"That's cool! I want one of those in my room!"

"That would be great, except you don't have an attic above your room," Silver said. "Where would you go?"

"I don't care. I want one anyway. Can I have a pull-down ladder in my room, Mama?"

"Let's focus on the Christmas tree for now," she said.

"Can I go up?" Mia asked.

"Better let me handle this for now," Ruben said. "I haven't been up here for a bit and I'm not sure how stable some of the boxes are. But maybe another time."

She made a face but plopped onto the concrete floor to watch as he climbed the ladder then emerged a moment later with a green tree stand atop a box labeled Christmas

Lights, which he held in one hand as he used the other to help in his descent.

"I saw one more box up there that might have some of my mom's old decorations. If you're interested in using them, I'm sure she won't mind."

"Oh, I couldn't."

"Let me grab the box anyway and you can decide after you take a look at what's inside."

He climbed the ladder again and she did her best not to gawk through the fabric of the T-shirt he wore at the play of muscles in his shoulders and his back.

Just as he disappeared into the bonus room, she heard a polite woof and a moment later a yellow Lab wandered into the garage. He was on a leash and at the other end stood Ruben's father.

"Hi, Dr. Morales," Mia chirped. She immediately went to him for a hug, which seemed to thrill him.

"Hello. I wasn't expecting to find you in my son's garage," he told her. "What's all this about?"

"We're raiding your Christmas decorations," Silver told him. "Ruben said it was okay. We're getting a real tree this year and he said nobody is using your old tree stand."

"True enough. What a good idea! I'm sorry I didn't think of it first."

Ruben climbed down the ladder a moment later with another box under one arm.

"Hey, Dad." He set the box down and gave his father an affectionate hug, which made Dr. Morales smile and sent those blasted butterflies fluttering through Dani's insides.

She found it absolutely charming that he loved his parents and wasn't afraid to show it.

"What a kind thing, helping your lovely neighbors with their holiday decorations."

"I didn't think you and Mom would mind."

"Not at all. Not at all."

Frank smiled at them and Dani's heart warmed with gratitude for this man who had completely changed her life. She only hoped she could be worthy of his faith in her.

"I'll help you carry these things next door," he said. "Mia *corazón*, you don't mind holding Baxter's leash for me while I grab some boxes, do you?"

Mia giggled at the nickname he always called her. "Nope. Baxter is my friend."

She grabbed the dog's leash and petted him, giggling when he licked her.

"What have you all been up to on this beautiful, rare warm December gift of a day we've been given?"

Dani hesitated. She didn't want Frank knowing about Silver's vandalism but she didn't know how to avoid telling him.

Ruben sent her a sidelong look, as if he sensed exactly what was running through her mind.

"Just helping out some neighbors," he said with an easy smile.

Silver frowned and looked as if she wanted to spill the whole story to the veterinarian but she finally looked down at the ground, as if she was too embarrassed to confess to her mistakes.

"What about you?" Dani asked to change the subject.

"My beautiful bride and I went into Shelter Springs to do a little Christmas shopping this morning. I don't recommend it. The stores were a madhouse. But when you have eight grandchildren and four step-grandchildren, you have to start somewhere."

She loved the way Frank always referred to his wife. Myra was just as sweet as her husband and Dani had liked her instantly when they came to town.

"Were you out for a walk or did you stop by for something in particular?"

"A little of both. I won't deny Baxter and I both needed a walk along the lakeshore after all that shopping and those crowds, plus your mother wanted me to come over and remind you about your sister's big concert tomorrow."

"Oh, right."

"And I'm sure I don't need to remind you of this, but your mother is serving churros and chocolate at our house afterward."

"I'll definitely be there for that."

"No concert, no churros. You know the rule."

Ruben made a face. "It's a dumb rule."

"You can take that up with your mother, if you dare." Frank turned to Dani. "You're all invited, too, my dear. In fact, I was heading to your house next to tell you about it. Now you've saved me the trip."

"What concert?"

"My sister sings in a jazz band," Ruben explained. "They're pretty good, actually, and give a fun show, especially at Christmastime."

"That's nice."

"And they're doing a benefit concert at the Episcopal church tomorrow night," Frank explained. "The proceeds benefit the women's shelter. Afterward, Myra always throws a family party with hot chocolate and her famous churros."

Mia's eyes lit up. "I *love* churros," she declared. "Once I had them at school. They were *muy delicioso*."

Frank chuckled. "I've got a wonderful idea. Considering you live next door to each other, you could ride together."

She immediately wanted to protest but Ruben spoke up before she could. "That's a great idea, Dad. What do you say, Dani?"

She wanted to say no. She wanted to tell him to stop being so nice to her, to stop trying to confound her and twist up her insides and make her find him even more impossibly attractive.

"Can we, Mama? I love, love, love churros."

How was she supposed to refuse churros and chocolate with Ruben's family when it sounded so very appealing?

She forced a smile. "Sure. That sounds fun. What time is the concert?"

"It starts at seven, but there's no reserved seating, so you might want to be there early," Frank said.

"I'll pick you up about six fifteen. Does that work?"

"Sounds good. I guess we'll see you then."

She didn't see that she had much choice, when Mia and even Silver looked excited about the prospect.

"Thank you again for all your help today," she said to Ruben after Frank waved farewell to them all and continued on his way with his dog. "We would never have been able to take care of it all without you."

His smile left her entirely too breathless. "I was glad to help, this time. I hope I don't have to again," he said to Silver.

She, predictably, rolled her eyes. "You won't," she said. "I don't want to have to spend another Saturday cleaning up."

"Fair enough. Have fun tree shopping for your Christmas tree. If you need help stringing the lights, give me a call."

She wouldn't. Dani would stay up all night if she had to in order to finish the job. She didn't need to become more dependent on Ruben Morales for help with things she ought to be handling on her own.

"Thanks. Have a good evening."

She handed the box of lights to Silver, gave the tree stand to Mia, picked up the box of ornaments, then ushered her family out of the garage.

She couldn't afford to fall for Ruben, she told herself as they walked across their winter-dead lawn toward home.

Yes, he pushed all her buttons. He was big, sexy, sweet. Irresistible. But she would have to strengthen her defenses and do her best to keep a safe distance from him.

She couldn't risk a broken heart, too, not when her whole life here in Haven Point felt as if it were hanging by some fragile, silvery thread of tinsel.

Ruben knocked on Dani's door the next evening, trying to ignore the restless edge that settled on his shoulders like the gently falling snow that had finally come to Haven Point.

It was stupid to feel any nerves. This wasn't a date. He was simply being neighborly, giving Dani and her girls a ride to a concert. That knowledge didn't seem to take away the anticipation surging through his veins.

She didn't answer the door for a long moment. When she finally did, Ruben completely forgot that he needed to breathe in order to sustain life.

She looked stunning in a wine-colored skirt and a creamy cable-knit sweater. Her dark hair hung in soft waves around her face, unlike the ponytail or messy bun he was used to seeing.

"Hi," she said. Her voice sounded a little raspy, though he wondered if that was his imagination.

He finally remembered he needed oxygen and sucked some into his lungs.

"Hi. I'm a little early, I'm afraid."

He didn't bother telling her he had been watching the clock for the last hour of his shift at the sheriff's office, while he sat at his desk finishing paperwork.

"Not a problem. We're all ready."

Before she finished speaking, cute little Mia peeked around her mother. "Hi, Deputy Ruben."

"Hello, Miss Mia. What a pretty dress. Does Pia have one like it?"

"Not this one," she said with a grin, twirling around to show off the red knit dress and her knee-high boots.

"Guess what? We got a Christmas tree but we can't make it stand up straight. Mom tried all afternoon and finally she said a bad word and threw her gloves at the wall."

"Thanks for sharing that, honey," Dani said, color climbing her high cheekbones.

Ruben laughed. "We've all been there. Don't worry about it. We've got a few minutes before we have to leave for the concert, if you'd like a little help."

"I had to take a thirty-minute shower to get all the sticky sap off earlier. I'm not anxious to go through that again, especially when I'm already dressed for the concert."

"You look lovely," he said, then wished he hadn't when wariness crept into her expression.

He wanted to tell her she was more than lovely, she was

breathtaking. He caught the words just in time. He had a feeling if she had any hint that he dared consider this anything like a date, she would shove him back through the door, slam it in his face and forget the whole thing.

"Let me take a look and see if I can figure out where the problem is. Maybe I can get you straightened out."

"I'm fine," she said tartly. "It's the tree that needs work."

"That, too."

He smiled and after a moment, she sighed and led the way into her living room. The tree they had selected was a smallish Scotch pine with a pretty conical shape. It listed drunkenly to one side and he could see immediately why.

"The trunk on this one is too thin for the tree stand. You need a couple of plywood blocks to keep it in place. Any chance you have a hacksaw?"

"Sure. I keep it in my purse. A girl never knows when she's going to need a hacksaw."

He grinned, delighted with the sense of humor she hid too often. "Around here, you really do never know."

"I guess I'll have to get one, then."

"You can ask Santa to bring you one for Christmas," Mia said.

"Great idea." Dani ran a hand over her daughter's hair with a sweet smile that did funny things to him.

"I have one at home. When the concert's over, I'll stop and grab it."

"What about the churros?" Mia asked, brow furrowed with alarm.

"We won't miss them, I promise. We can fix your tree *after* the churros."

"Whew."

Dani looked at her tree, then back to him. "I don't want you to go to any trouble. I can probably figure it out."

"It will take me five minutes, I promise. Maybe less. And save you all kinds of frustration in the long run."

"You're undoubtedly right. I apparently don't have a high level of tolerance for Christmas tree aggravations."

"Who does?" He smiled. "I hope you've got more tolerance for Christmas concerts."

"Depends on the Christmas concert. But in general, yes. I like Christmas music."

"Good. Should we go?"

She called Silver to come out and the older girl actually greeted him with a smile, which he considered great progress in his relationship with the Capelli females.

Ruben Morales was entirely too appealing.

She watched him interact with his family at the concert, laughing down at his petite mother with the dark hair and bright eyes, at Dr. Morales, at his sister, Angela, who looked like a smaller, more feminine version of Ruben.

It had been a long time since she had been part of a big, noisy family, even on the periphery.

She hadn't really thought this through, the fact that his entire family would be there when she and her girls arrived with Ruben.

She didn't miss the speculative look his mother and

his sister gave her and then each other. They weren't the only ones, either. When she walked into the church with him, she saw a few raised eyebrows coming their direction from other people she had met since she and the girls came to town.

She did her best to ignore them but she wanted to immediately separate from his family and sit on the other side of the church. She really didn't need people thinking the two of them were seeing each other.

Her discomfort didn't ease when the lights dimmed. She found it just as difficult to ignore her awareness of him beside her, big and tough and gorgeous.

"It's nice, isn't it?" Ruben whispered after a few songs, his warm breath tickling her ear and doing funny things to her insides.

"Very," she whispered back truthfully. Did her voice sound as breathless as she felt? "Your sister has talent."

The jazz combo wouldn't have been out of place at the Blue Note or the Village Vanguard in New York, with a smoky sound that added an original twist to the Christmas classics.

"I'm not sure how she ended up with the singing gene, but she's the only one of the four of us who did."

On his other side, Ruben's mother shushed him and Dani winced. She didn't need Myra Morales on her bad side, so she settled back to enjoy the music.

When the concert ended and the performers gave their final bows and left the small stage, the crowd rose and began milling around, with people moving to speak with acquaintances and calling out to friends.

"Wasn't that wonderful?" Myra exclaimed to Dani

when Ruben moved into the aisle to talk to his brothers and Angela's husband, Reed, a lanky cowboy with a slow smile and a clearly defined hat line around his brown hair. "Gets you right in the holiday spirit, doesn't it?"

Dani thought with guilt about how she hadn't exactly been overflowing with holiday spirit the last few years, too busy dealing with her daughters and school. How sad that she had allowed the chaos of her life to steal that joy away from her.

"Yes," she said softly. "It really does. How kind of you and Dr. Morales to invite us."

To her shock, Myra reached out a hand to clasp Dani's. Her hand was warm, soft, and the kindness in the other woman's eyes stirred a lump in Dani's throat.

"I know I've said this before but I'm going to repeat myself. I can't thank you enough for taking a chance and coming here to Idaho to help Frank out at the clinic. I know it hasn't been easy for you and your girls and I wanted to tell you how much it means to me. He's not as young as he used to be. He thinks he can do everything he did when he was your age and he just can't. Having you here to take on some of the load has been wonderful for him."

Frank, she saw, had joined his sons and son-in-law and the men were laughing at something one of them had said. To her mind, he looked pretty hale and hearty, as if he could keep going for decades, but Dani was glad Myra thought her presence had been helpful.

"I'm grateful he took the chance on me," she said.

"From all accounts, you're doing a wonderful job."

She knew that wasn't completely true but she couldn't

politely disagree. Before she could come up with an answer, they were joined by McKenzie Kilpatrick, the mayor of Haven Point.

The other woman was about the same age as Dani. She had always been kind and welcoming, but right now McKenzie was the last person in town Dani wanted to see.

McKenzie would have to know about Silver's little graffiti spree. Dani had the impression the woman made it a point to know everything going on in her town.

Was she coming to tell Dani and her spray paint–wielding daughter to go back to where they came from? Dani drew in a sharp breath and frowned, her shoulders suddenly stiff.

She had been waiting for someone in town to say something about the vandalism. Instead, McKenzie gave her a warm smile, greeted Dani with her usual friendliness, then turned to ask Myra a question about some scarves Ruben's mother was knitting to sell in a booth at the town festival the following weekend.

Dani felt her shoulders relax a little, but the tension didn't completely trickle away.

The easy familiarity between the two women was a firm reminder that Dani didn't quite belong here in this crowd full of people who had known each other for years.

She wasn't sure if she ever would.

A woman could get positively inebriated from that scent.

An hour later, Dani stood in the doorway to Myra's neat kitchen, inhaling the scent of chocolate and cinnamon and frying dough.

She wanted to stand here and simply let the scents flood through her, but she had spent too many years in foster care to be comfortable doing nothing while someone else was working.

"Is there something I can do to help?" she asked Myra.

The other woman looked up from the large six-burner stove where she was carefully piping dough from a pastry bag into hot oil for the churros.

"You're a guest. Guests don't have to work in my house. Sit down and visit."

"This guest would love nothing more than to help you. Please."

Myra shrugged. "You don't have to do a thing except sit back and enjoy yourself, but if you insist, you could roll these churros in the cinnamon and sugar."

"Sure. I can probably handle that."

Dani had learned early how to work in a kitchen in the various homes where she had stayed, though if she were honest, her best skill was washing dishes.

Rolling churros in cinnamon and sugar didn't sound particularly daunting.

She was in the middle of it when Ruben's older sister, Angela, came in. She did a double take when she spotted Dani at the counter. "Wow! How did you get so lucky? Mom usually never lets anybody make the finishing touches on her churros."

"Oh, no pressure now," Dani said. While her words were flippant, she still felt a flutter of nerves, an age-old desire to please that she couldn't shake.

Angela grinned. "I'm just teasing. We're the most casual family around. Mom always told us we couldn't do anything wrong in the kitchen, as long as we were trying. Even if you burn something, it just means you'll know better next time."

Dani had spent several wonderful years in one foster home where a similar attitude had reigned. She had hoped to stay with Betsy Williams forever but the woman had become too ill to care for the foster children she had taken in. Leaving the woman's home had broken Dani's heart, the one she might have thought would have been indestructible by then.

How lucky for Ruben and his siblings, that their mother was so patient and loving.

"Grandma, can we have the first churro?"

Ruben's little nephew Charlie, who belonged to Angela and her husband, Reed, was about the same age as Mia and they had apparently become the best of friends. They leaned against the island, looking longingly at the plateful of churros.

"You can have the first ones," Myra said, "as long as you take the garbage out first."

"I can do that, Abuela," Charlie said.

"Me too, Abuela," Mia said, which made Myra smile, and Dani give a little internal wince at how quickly her youngest child had been absorbed into the Morales family.

Silver, too, seemed to be enjoying herself. Ruben had a nephew and a niece around her age, Angela's son Zach who went to Sil's school and a girl, Esme, who apparently lived in Shelter Springs with her mother, Ruben's brother Javier's ex-wife, and went to school there. Last she had checked, the three of them were hanging out in a corner of the living room. Dani had even heard laughter coming from there several times.

One part of her was delighted that her daughter was making more friends, but she worried about both of her girls becoming too entangled in the family. She couldn't give them this big, noisy, happy family. Not forever. She knew what it was like to yearn for something she couldn't have and she didn't want her daughters to suffer that same pain.

"Thank you," Myra said with a delighted smile as the children returned from taking the full garbage bag out to the trash.

"*De nada*, Abuela," Charlie said.

"*De nada*," Mia repeated with a giggle. "Now can we have a churro?"

"Don't forget the chocolate. That's the best part. There's a perfect spot for churros and chocolate at the table. Have a seat."

Using tongs provided by Myra, Dani rolled two long pastries in the cinnamon and sugar then set them on a plate. Myra ladled the thick, rich-looking hot chocolate into a mug and set it in the middle of the plate and carried the whole thing to the children.

"Here you go. Be careful. The chocolate is still a little warm."

The next few minutes were filled with sounds of exaggerated delight as the children enjoyed the sweet treat that drew the teenagers into the kitchen for theirs, followed soon after by everyone else.

Fifteen minutes later, Dani had dredged a dozen churros in cinnamon sugar and was looking for more when

Myra handed her one on a plate. "This one is yours. Here. I insist. I've saved the best churro of the lot for you."

Dani went easier on the cinnamon sugar for her own. She wanted to eat it standing up there in the kitchen area of the open plan living space but Myra would have none of it.

"You've been on your feet long enough. Go sit down. I'm coming, too."

Dani moved out to the table and was dismayed that the only open seat was next to Ruben, almost as if he had been saving it for her.

He was in the middle of a conversation with his brother Javier, whom she had just met that evening, and his brother-in-law, Reed, but paused to give her a bright smile that nearly made her stumble and spill her hot chocolate all over the place.

Wouldn't that make a lovely impression on the Morales family?

Ruben patted the seat next to him and for a wild moment, she was tempted to race back into the kitchen, throw the dessert into the sink, grab her daughters and flee.

Her heart was in serious danger. She could easily see herself falling hard for Ruben. She might even be halfway there, a realization that filled her with panic.

She drew in a breath, gripped the warm handle of the mug and made herself move forward. She slipped into the chair beside him, aware as she did that it wasn't only the fried churro and the sugary chocolate drink that were bad for her in this family.

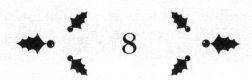

8

"I like your family very much," she said later as he held the door open for Silver and a sleepy Mia to load into the rear seats of his late-model pickup truck.

He smiled down at her and her pulse seemed to kick faster. "They're pretty great. I did okay in the family department."

She hoped he knew his family was much better than okay. Compared to the chaos of her childhood and adolescence, Ruben Morales won the family lottery.

"Did you have fun tonight?" Ruben asked when they were on the road heading the short distance to her house and his next door.

"I did," Mia said sleepily.

"What about you?" he asked Silver.

"The churros were good," she said.

"You seemed to be getting along well with Esme."

"She's nice," Silver said.

"She is. We don't see her as often as we'd like since she's with her mom most of the week. It's always a treat when she can come to family things. Too bad she doesn't go to Haven Point Middle School like you and Zach. I guess you probably know him from school."

"Yeah. I know him. We have English together and his locker is close to mine."

If Dani hadn't been turned around to check to see if Mia had fallen asleep, she might have missed the rather dreamy look on Silver's expression.

Oh, no. Apparently she and her daughter were both susceptible to the charm wielded by the men in the Morales family.

"You probably know he's on the middle school basketball team."

"Yes," she admitted, in a nonchalant sort of voice that didn't fool Dani for a moment. "It's kind of hard to miss since the cheerleaders decorate his locker every time we have a game. Everybody makes such a big deal over the basketball players in the halls and at the pep assemblies."

"Right. He's really busy this year with practices and games. Which actually brings me to something I need to talk to you about," he said as he pulled into Dani's driveway.

"To me?" Silver asked warily.

"All of you, really. But mostly you. Because of Zach's basketball practice and game schedule, I'm running into a little conflict. I think you might be just the person to help me out."

"With what?"

"The last few years, Zach has helped me with a little project my parents wrangled me into, but I think he's going to be too busy for the next few weeks to help me out. You would be the perfect person to step in and give me a hand."

"Again, with what?"

"I'll tell you, but I have to swear you to secrecy first."

"Do we have to take a blood oath or something?"

While Silver spoke with her usual edge of sarcasm, Dani could hear the curiosity underlying it.

"Pretty close."

"What's a blood oath?" Mia asked.

"Don't worry about that. It just means I need you to keep a big secret from everybody. Can you do that?"

Mia gave a sleepy frown. "Mommy says I'm not supposed to keep secrets from her."

"That is a good rule for life, kiddo. You can't go wrong if you tell your mom everything going on in your world."

Silver scoffed a little but hid it with a cough that didn't fool Dani for a moment—or Ruben, for that matter.

He and Dani shared a look, and she knew he was having the same thought. All teenagers kept things from their parents. It was as inevitable as acne.

She wasn't sure she liked these moments when their thoughts seemed synchronized, almost as if they were a united front.

"Here's the thing, Miss Mia," Ruben went on. "Your mother will know this secret. In fact, I probably should have talked to her first before bringing it up."

"Too late for that now," Dani said.

He made a face. "Sorry about that. It's a good thing, I promise."

"Why don't we go inside so you don't have to do the big reveal out here in the car?"

"Good idea."

She didn't want to be charmed further by the man when he opened the rear door of his king cab to let Silver out, then made his way around the pickup to open Dani's door and scoop Mia into his arms.

This was a one-time thing. They were *not* a family unit.

Her house was warm and smelled piney from the frustrating Christmas tree that still leaned crookedly against the wall. Winky greeted them all with enthusiasm, moving from person to person to welcome them home.

Silver plopped onto the sofa and gathered the little dog onto her lap. "All right. What's the big secret?"

"I can tell all of you, as long as I can count on you to keep this under your hat."

"What if we don't want that kind of responsibility?" Dani asked.

"Too late for that now," he said, parroting her words from earlier and almost making her smile.

Oh, she liked him, entirely too much.

"Are you going to tell us or keep dragging out the drama?" Silver finally asked. "We swear we won't tell, okay?"

"All right. Here goes."

He glanced around the room as if checking for listening devices. "Every year, my family picks one or two households in town to be the recipients of a special family tradition."

"What's a tradition?" Mia asked from the floor, where she had settled to pet Winky.

Dani tamped down that darn maternal guilt that tended to creep out entirely too often, even when it was completely undeserved.

Yes, she had been busy trying to support her family and get through school but she still took time to do important things with her daughters, even if she perhaps hadn't articulated the reasons why as well as she should have to Mia.

Mia was just asking what a word meant, she wasn't impugning Dani's mothering skills.

Once in a while, Dani needed to give herself a break—which could be easier said than done.

"It's all the unique things we do together as a family," she said. "You know, like the Capelli Champion blue plate special, where one person gets to eat on the special plate on their birthday or whenever they do something amazing."

"Or how Mom always has you put out cookies for Santa," Silver said.

"And carrots for the reindeer," Mia reminded her.

"In my family, we have a few traditions."

"Churros and chocolate," Mia said.

"Exactly." His smile made Dani's toes tingle. Darn him.

"That's one of my favorites. Another one dates back to when I was Silver's age. Every year for twenty years, my parents have picked a few households in town and we deliver a little treat to them each day for twelve days leading up to Christmas."

"Oh. 'The Twelve Days of Christmas.' I love that song." Mia launched into exuberant song. "Four calling birds, three friendships, two turtlenecks, and a partridge in a pear tree."

Silver snickered at her sister's mangled lyrics, but for once didn't call her out on it.

"That's the one," Ruben said with a smile. "We start on December 13 and end on Christmas Eve."

"The twelve days of Christmas are supposed to run from Christmas Day to Epiphany on January 6. I learned that in, like, the fifth grade," Silver said.

"Technically, you're right. And if we wanted to be strict about it, that's the way we would do it, but ending on Christmas Eve is easier and a little more fun."

"What kind of treats do you leave?" Dani asked.

"Small things, like a hand-painted ornament, a Christmas book, a box of candy. Things like that. My mom does all the shopping for it and she assigns Angie one family and me the other one. Since Javi and Mateo both live in Shelter Springs, Mom lets them pick a family close to them to do with their kids now."

"That sounds like a nice tradition," Dani said. Anything that encouraged children to think about others was good, in her book.

"What does this have to do with us?" Silver asked.

"Usually, I tag Zach to help me out with mine but Angie told me tonight his schedule is packed every weeknight and that I couldn't use Andy, either, her middle boy, because he would be busy making *their* Secret Santa deliveries. I need help this year and it occurred to me I know the perfect person to make my deliveries."

"Me? Why would I want to do that?"

"Because you owe him, after what you did to his boat and all the help he gave you yesterday cleaning up your mess," Dani said sharply. "If he wants you to shovel his sidewalk from now until summer, you'll smile politely and say yes."

Silver didn't roll her eyes this time, but she did fold her arms across her chest and give her mother the skunk eye.

"It's not a tough job. You only have to drop off the gift, ring the doorbell, and hide until after they open the door and pick it up."

That caught Silver's attention and Dani could tell she looked intrigued.

"See?" Dani said. "Nothing all that different from what you and your friends used to do back in Boston. Except you never left a present behind."

Her daughter made a face. "We only did that a few times and only to the jerks in the neighborhood."

"There you go," Ruben said. "You've had practice at knock-and-runs already. This will be a piece of cake."

"Who are you giving the presents to?"

"I can only tell you that if you promise to help me. Otherwise I'll be breaching the strict confidentiality agreement."

Silver was silent for several seconds, looking out the window at the snow now fluttering down in big flakes.

"Okay. I guess I'll do it. I don't have much choice, do I?"

Ruben had a hard time not laughing at Silver's glum tone, as if she were being asked to pick between a week in the slammer or being put in stocks for the whole town to taunt.

He was fairly sure he had never been this dramatic when he was thirteen, but then he'd never had to move to a new town and try to make new friends there.

"I wouldn't say you don't have a choice. I can find something else for you to do but it probably wouldn't be as enjoyable. Cleaning out the cages at the clinic would be the first thing that comes to mind."

She groaned. "That's what my mom always makes me do when I'm in trouble."

He glanced at Dani beside him and she shrugged. "Low-hanging fruit. She hates it, so that's what I give her for punishment."

"There you go. We're on the same page. Helping me out with the Secret Santa project might take longer over the long haul—twelve days, compared to a few hours— but it will be much more fun."

"Can I help?" Mia asked. "I can run superfast."

She was the most adorable thing, one of those kids who couldn't help but bring sunshine into the world.

"I'm sure you do. That would be a big help, especially if Silver's legs get tired one night."

"We have to do this for twelve whole nights?"

"It will go by before you know it, don't worry," he assured her. "And you won't have to do it by yourself. I'll take care of some of the nights and maybe I can persuade Zach to come with us a night or two when he doesn't have practice or games."

Ruben hadn't missed the blush Silver wore whenever his handsome nephew was around. He had a feeling there was a crush simmering there, and if he wasn't mistaken, the interest was mutual. He wasn't above using puppy love for his own benefit.

"So you're in, right?"

"Like I said. I don't have much choice," she said, though much of the grumpiness had left her voice, as he had hoped, at the prospect of Zach helping them along the way.

"It will be fun. You'll see. We're taking it to a family that has had some rough times lately. There are four kids in the family including twins around your age."

"Oh?"

"Yeah. Do you know Ella and Emma Larkin?"

She shoved her hands in the pockets of her coat. "Yeah. I know them."

"Then you probably know their mom is in the middle of her second bout of cancer in three years."

Beside him, Dani made a small sound of distress. "Oh, that's terrible. I had no idea the twins' mom was going through that. Sil, why didn't you tell me?"

"How was I supposed to know? It's not like we talk about our moms all the time. Why would we?"

"I suppose that's true enough," Dani said.

"They've had a rough time," Ruben went on. "It can be scary for kids when a parent is sick."

"Yes, it can," Dani said. Her eyes looked haunted for a moment. Had she experienced something similar? Sympathy washed over him. If she had, he hoped she had someone to help her through it.

"My family figured this is a small thing that might help their holidays feel a little brighter while they're struggling. My mom has a way of finding exactly the right people who need a little lift."

"It's a very nice gesture," Dani said.

"So will you do it?"

"Yeah. I'll help you. It's better than cleaning out dog poop," Silver said. "Are we done? Can I go to my room now?"

Dani nodded and Silver disappeared in a flash down the hall, closing her door behind her.

Her mother gazed after the girl, frustration on her lovely features. "That girl. You'd think she'd never been taught manners. A goodbye and thank-you would have been nice."

"Don't be too hard on her. It's a tough age and she's dealing with a lot."

"That's no excuse. You've done so much for her and she should at least show a little gratitude. I'll make sure she does."

Dani was a good mother. She obviously loved her daughters and was doing her best to teach them how to be decent humans.

"And if she doesn't say it, let me. Thank you again for all your help yesterday and for driving us tonight to join your family. It was a lovely evening."

"You're very welcome." He had enjoyed it, too, far more than he'd expected—in large part because Dani and her daughters had been along.

"We loved the treats, didn't we, Mia?"

"I love churros and chocolate. They're my new favorite thing in the whole world."

"I'm glad you liked it. I'll be sure to tell my mom."

"She's nice. And so is your dad. I wish they were my *abuela* and *abuelo*."

"Mia," Dani said, looking embarrassed. It made him wonder about her family situation. She was so close-mouthed about everything. He knew her daughters had a grandmother on their late father's side, but Dani hadn't said anything about her own.

"I think they'd like to adopt you, too."

"Okay," she said happily, then gave a huge, ear-splitting yawn.

"Bedtime for you, missy. Come on. Say good-night to Ruben, then let's get in the tub."

"Good night, Ruben," she said, stealing his heart completely by throwing her arms around his waist. He lifted her up for a better hug then set her back down.

"Night, Miss Mia."

To Dani, he said, "While you're helping her to bed, why don't I straighten out that Christmas tree for you and maybe hang some of the lights?"

He could see the instant refusal leap into her expression. Was she reluctant to accept *his* help or would she have the same reaction to anyone offering aid? He couldn't be completely sure, though he suspected the former.

"You don't have to do that. I'm sure the girls and I can figure it out tomorrow."

"I promised. I can have a hacksaw and a couple of plywood wedges here in five minutes and be in and out in half an hour."

"Please, Mama?" Mia joined her voice in the plea. "I want to decorate our Christmas tree!"

"Thirty minutes," Ruben pressed.

She gazed down at her daughter then up at him and sighed. "Fine. Thirty minutes. But you're not decorating the tree tonight, young lady. If Ruben hangs the lights, you can put the ornaments on tomorrow after school. Agreed?"

"What if I wake up early tomorrow and do it?" Mia negotiated.

"After school," she said firmly. "Right now it's past your bedtime. You need to jump in the tub and put on your pajamas."

Mia sighed, apparently knowing she had pushed her mother as far as she dared. "Fine."

Dani turned back to him as soon as Mia headed into her room. "You really don't have to do this."

"I want to. Your girls deserve a nice tree and I'm more than happy to help. You could simply say thank you."

"I suppose I can't be too angry with Silver for her lack of gratitude if I don't demonstrate it myself. Thank you. We would be very grateful for your help."

"You're welcome." He smiled. "I'll be back before you know it."

"I'll leave the door unlocked so you don't have to knock, just in case I'm busy with Mia's bath."

"Got it. See you in a minute."

He walked back out into the gently falling snow, unsettled at how relieved he was that the lovely evening and his time with Dani didn't yet have to end.

She did *not* want him in her house.

The entire time Dani helped Mia with her bath, she was aware of Ruben just a few rooms away, almost as if she could smell that spicy, leathery, outdoorsy scent of his soap from here.

How was it possible that his presence managed to fill the entire house? Yes, he was a big man, with strong shoulders and firm muscles. But he was still only one man.

"I'm not brushing my teeth with that!" Mia exclaimed suddenly, and Dani realized with chagrin that she had just squeezed hand lotion from the pump bottle in the bathroom onto Mia's toothbrush instead of the kids' toothpaste.

"Oh, man. I'm sorry. Well, I guess it was time for a new toothbrush anyway." She pulled one from the bottom drawer of the vanity where she kept a few extras and unboxed one for her daughter.

"It's purple! My favorite color! Thanks. You're the best mama ever."

If only. Silver would certainly not agree. Her older daughter thought she was harsh and unfeeling, with arbitrary rules and unrealistic expectations.

Every mother needed a child like Mia in her life, though—one who saw the very best in her and was willing to overlook her mistakes and screwups. She prayed her daughter never grew out of this phase.

"And you're the very best Mia a mama could ever have," she said.

Mia threw her arms around Dani's neck, her hair wet and smelling of cherries from her shampoo.

"And Silver is the best Silver a mama could have, too, right?"

"That's exactly right," she answered. It was a good

reminder. Yes, her older daughter was going through things. As Ruben said, this was a tough age and Dani had thrown her into a hard situation at the very same time she lost her father in a violent manner. They would get through it. She just had to remember the days when Silver was as sweet and loving as Mia.

"Can I go see the Christmas tree? I wonder if Ruben is done yet."

"Since that was the fastest bath on record and he had to go home to get some supplies, I highly doubt it's done, but you can go check the status."

While Mia raced out of the room, Dani took her time wiping up the water, putting away bath toys, cleaning the toothpaste off the sink.

She was stalling, she acknowledged, afraid to face Ruben again. She had a ridiculous crush on the man and was going to have to do something about it. She had no idea what that might be, though.

Finally she could avoid it no longer and made herself walk into the living room where she found the lights dimmed and Mia in one of Ruben's arms. She was gazing at the tree, her eyes soft with wonder.

"Look, Mama," Mia whispered when Dani walked into the room. "We have the most beautiful tree in the whole wide world."

Ruben's gaze met hers and Dani had to catch her breath at the expression in them, soft amusement and a warm tenderness.

"Don't you think it's beautiful?" Mia asked.

One would think they had never had a Christmas tree before. Maybe there was something special about this one, a sweet-smelling little pine in their new house beside a lake. Or maybe Mia was simply excited to have Ruben there.

"It is lovely. Look how straight you were able to get it. And I can't believe you hung all those lights already. That didn't take nearly as long as I would have expected."

"You picked a great tree."

"Except for the spindly trunk."

"Nothing's perfect," he said with a grin. "Other than that, this one is the right height and the branches aren't too thick. That made it much easier to string the lights. I'm not quite done. There's one more string I'd like to use for filling in the empty spots."

"It looks beautiful to me. Thank you."

"My pleasure." When he smiled at her like that, she forgot she had earned a doctorate of veterinary medicine. She forgot she was a single mother of two children and felt as if she were screwing up at every turn. She forgot about the fact that his father held her future in his hands and that ruining this opportunity Frank Morales had given her would be a disaster for her and her daughters.

Nothing else seemed to matter except the thick surge of blood in her veins, the butterflies suddenly swarming in her stomach, her overwhelming awareness of him.

She cleared her throat, appalled at herself. "Mia, now that you've seen the Christmas tree, you really do need to get to sleep. Tell Ruben good-night one more time, then head in."

Mia sighed and rested her cheek against his shoulder for a moment, as if she didn't want to leave him, either.

"Good night, Mia," he said.

"Okay. Good night." Mia threw her arms around his neck and hugged him, then kissed his cheek. "Thank you for putting the twinkly lights on my Christmas tree. It's the most beautiful thing I've ever seen."

"You're very welcome. I'll see you later."

The poor man looked completely enamored and Dani supposed she couldn't blame him. Mia had a great deal of her father's charm when she wanted to use it. The little girl smiled at him, waved and hurried out of the room.

"I need to tuck her in," she said. "You said you are almost done?"

"Yeah. It won't take me long to hang that last string. I can let myself out, if you have to help Mia with her bedtime routine."

"Thank you again for everything."

"I'm glad to help," he assured her with another smile that made her hurry down the hall to the girls' bedrooms with her heart pounding as if she'd never seen a gorgeous man smile.

In Mia's room, she read her daughter a short bedtime story and listened while she said her prayers.

"I sure like Deputy Ruben," Mia said sleepily when she finished.

Dani did, too. Entirely too much. "He's very nice, isn't he?"

"Why doesn't he have any little girls?"

That was an excellent question. Why hadn't the smart women of Haven Point snapped up a gorgeous, kind man like him years ago?

"I guess because he's not as lucky as I am," Dani said.

She kissed her daughter on the forehead. "Good night, sweetie."

"Tomorrow, I get to decorate the tree," Mia said, already half-asleep.

"Yes, you do."

"I can't wait."

Dani couldn't help feeling a little envious as she left the room with Mia still smiling about the prospect. How long had it been since she treated each new day like an adventure?

She did love her job. Working with animals had always been her refuge, from the time before her mother got sick. She used to hide any stray cat and dog she found in her room, smuggling in food to it and making little beds on the floor.

Her mom would always find out and would shake her head.

"I'm sorry, but we can't keep it, *cara mia*," Sofia Capelli would say. "You know the rules about animals in the apartment and we can't afford to be evicted."

The two of them would take the subway to the nearest shelter, where Dani would say goodbye, then cry all the way back to their apartment.

That love for animals had sustained her through what she called in her head the "foster care years." In several of her placements, the families had pets, much to her delight. For reasons she couldn't fully explain, they always seemed to gravitate to Dani.

In her experience, animals could have amazing emotional instincts, sensing where they were needed most. Maybe they could tell she was bruised by life, lonely, afraid, and needed the steady, uncomplicated love of a dog or a cat.

Regardless, she loved caring for them and would always end up taking over responsibility for feeding them and cleaning up after them.

It had always been harder to say goodbye to the animals in each foster care placement than it had the people, even those who were kind to her.

Loving animals and having a calming way with them had led her to getting a part-time job in high school at that same shelter where she and her mother used to drop off the strays she gathered. Every day when she would take the subway, she would remember those trips with Sofia and miss her mother with a sharp, piercing ache.

She pushed away the memories. She no longer wallowed in self-pity, as she might have done when she was Silver's age.

Yes, her mom had died when she was a kid and she had ended up in foster care. That truly sucked. She had caught a bad break, like millions of other kids who found themselves in a similar situation, but she still had managed to create a good life for herself and her daughters.

Silver's bedroom light was out, she could see by the dark crack under the door, but Dani decided to say goodnight anyway. She pushed open the door and, in the small glow from Silver's retro alarm clock picked up at a thrift store in Boston, she could see her daughter's hair and a pale blur of skin.

Silver shifted her gaze sleepily toward the door. "What do you want?" she asked, belligerence still threading through her voice.

Dani sighed. "Just checking on you. Do you need anything?"

"No," her daughter said after a moment, her tone a little less abrasive.

"Good night, then," Dani said softly. "I love you, Silverbell."

"Love you, too," Silver whispered, and Dani had to swallow away the emotions at those rare words that felt like a gift.

When she returned to the hallway, she assumed Ruben had finished and left already, until she heard the low murmur of a man's voice coming from the living room as Ruben said something to Winky.

She caught a hint of his outdoorsy soap above the overwhelming pine scent from the tree and she stood for a moment, eyes closed, trying to ignore the sudden jittery ache inside her.

She could do this. She only had to make it through saying good-night to him, then she could close the door behind him and do her best to push the man out of her head as easily as she did out of her house.

After sucking in a deep breath, she made her way to the living room, where she found Ruben on the sofa, winding an unused strand of lights around a plastic organizer that must have been inside the box from his father.

He had turned all the lights off so that only the Christmas tree glowed in the room, a kaleidoscope of colors gleaming against the walls and reflected in the window.

He smiled when he caught sight of her. "Nice, isn't it?"

"It's beautiful," she admitted, oddly emotional at the

sight—or maybe at his kindness in helping put it up for her daughters.

"I feel as awestruck as Mia right now," she said. "There's something so magical about a Christmas tree, especially the first night or two when it feels new again but somehow familiar."

"Agreed. To me, a beautiful Christmas tree like this one represents hope and peace and the wonder of the season."

"Yet you still don't have one of your own."

"I can appreciate the beauty of something even when it's not mine."

She smiled, moving closer to the tree. "In a week or so, I'll be tired of the needles and the sap and bored with having to water it every day, but right now I will simply enjoy it."

He gestured to the sofa beside him. She hesitated, everything inside her telling her it would be a bad idea, considering this awareness she couldn't seem to fight. She gave a mental shrug. She could live a little dangerously for a few more moments. Besides, she had something she needed to say to him and now seemed the perfect opportunity.

She sat next to him, aware of the heat coming from him. "I've been looking back across the last few days," she said slowly, not meeting his gaze, "and I have the sinking suspicion that, like Silver, I probably haven't acted as…grateful to you as I should have."

"For what it's worth, I don't have that impression at all."

She sighed. He was trying to be nice and she couldn't

take the easy way out. Not when she was trying to teach the same lessons about expressing gratitude to her children.

"It's not easy for me, accepting help. You probably figured that out by now."

She finally dared to look at him in time to catch a slow, sweet smile that made her swallow hard.

"I may have had a hint or two," he drawled.

"I'm sorry. It's an ingrained reflex."

"Like Pavlov's dogs?"

She made a face at his reference to the classic psychological experiment. "Something like that. I've had to do most things on my own on and off for most of my girls' lives. Their father was…not around much."

She didn't tell him why, that the man she had married the day before her eighteenth birthday had spent most of their married life in prison and that even after he came out, he couldn't wean himself away from the life.

"I've had to learn how to do everything, from fixing the garbage disposal to changing oil in my cars to setting up the Christmas tree."

"Seems like you've done a pretty good job so far."

For some reason, his words hit her hard. Dani thought of all her insecurities, all the lonely nights she sat up worrying for her daughters, all the things she couldn't give them, all the mistakes and fears and sorrows she couldn't heal.

She thought of the nights over the last three months where Silver had cried herself to sleep over her father, and her fear the time Mia had influenza, and the loneliness that sometimes had her tossing and turning in bed, longing for something that hadn't been part of her life in years.

Couldn't he see she was a disaster, barely holding the pieces of her life together?

"Sure. That's me. Totally in control. No problems here."

She laughed a little hysterically. The sound horrified her and she tried to cover her mouth with her hand but a sob escaped anyway.

"Are you okay?" he asked, setting aside the light string he had been holding.

"I..." She couldn't lie. Not to him and not to herself.

In the end, she didn't need to. He reached for her and, like Mia had earlier, she sank into the safety of his arms and the undeniable comfort of that wide, capable chest.

How long had it been since someone had offered to take on her burdens, if only for a moment? It felt incredible to push them out of her mind and lay them down for now.

Another sob escaped and then another and before she knew it, her shoulders were shaking as she let out all the stress and turmoil that had been haunting her since the night he had brought Silver over with red spray paint on her hands.

Since much, much longer, if she were honest.

She couldn't have said how long she cried against him while the tree lights sparkled against the window and Winky snored softly at their feet. She couldn't have even said exactly why she was crying. It didn't really matter, she supposed, as reason intruded again and she came back to the reality that she was snuggled against Ruben, practically on his lap, and had just let him see a vulnerability she hid so carefully from the rest of the world. Even from herself.

She sniffled one last time, her breathing ragged, then pulled away slightly, too embarrassed to meet his gaze. "I can't believe I just completely lost it and blubbered all over your shirt. Can we just pretend the last few moments never happened?"

"If that would make you feel better."

She was not one of those lucky women who cried prettily, with delicate, diamond-shaped teardrops leaking out from under their perfect eyelashes.

When Dani cried, her nose ran, her skin went splotchy, her eyes turned as red-rimmed as Christmas ornaments.

"I don't think anything could make me feel better right now." There was a box of tissues on the side table, left there from the last time Mia had a cold when Dani had scattered them all over the house for her, and she reached for it gratefully, dabbing at her face even though she knew nothing she did would help fix what was likely a hideous mess.

"I never lose it like that. Ever. I can't remember the last time I cried."

"Then you were overdue," he said, with such kindness in his voice that she almost started up all over again.

"You must think I'm an idiot."

"I think you're a woman doing her best to raise two girls, trying to make a new life in a new town. I'm surprised you haven't had a dozen breakdowns since you came to Haven Point."

"I'll admit to three or four small ones, after the girls are in bed."

"If that's all, then I would say you're doing fine."

She didn't necessarily agree. If she was doing fine and things were going well, her daughter wouldn't have felt compelled to damage the property of three of their new neighbors.

Still, she appreciated his efforts to make her feel better.

"You're a very nice man, Deputy Morales. I imagine in your line of work you get plenty of experience dealing with irrational people."

"Sometimes. But there's a difference between being irrational and being emotionally exhausted and justifiably stressed. In my professional opinion, you fall in the latter category. There's no shame in needing someone to hold you once in a while."

She was in deep, deep danger of falling hard for this man. How in the world was she supposed to prevent it, when he could be so very sweet?

"Well, thank you. I appreciate you being so understanding."

"Anytime."

He spoke the word gruffly and she gazed at him, that hunger from earlier swirling back.

It had never really left, she realized.

If it felt so good to be held by him, how wonderful would it feel to kiss him?

One little kiss. What could that hurt?

She didn't give herself time to answer, only leaned forward to close the space between them and kissed the corner of his mouth. She told herself it was done only in gratitude, a small, rather insignificant gesture to let him know she appreciated all he had done for her family over the past few days and especially for doing his best to help her not feel like an idiot for the last few moments.

The moment her mouth touched warm male skin, however, she knew that for a lie. She was kissing him because she wanted to kiss him. Because she wanted *him*.

Ruben froze for only an instant and the moment seemed crystallized in time, like a pretty snow globe ornament hanging on the tree, then he shifted his mouth and kissed her fiercely, urgently, as if he had been waiting weeks for just this moment.

She hadn't been with a man since her divorce and only now did she admit how very much she had missed this surge of her blood, the catch in her breathing, the ache deep inside.

Everything she had so carefully stored away inside her after her marriage fell apart came roaring back, all her needs and hungers and aches.

His mouth was warm, firm, and she tasted hints of thick, rich chocolate and cinnamon sugar.

If she thought a woman could get drunk on the smell of his mother's kitchen, the taste of those same delicious flavors on his mouth against hers was a thousand times better.

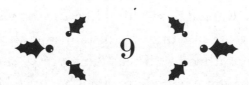

9

She didn't want the kiss to end.

It was magical, delicious, like a hundred dreams come true wrapped up in one heated embrace.

With the snow fluttering down outside and the Christmas tree lights gleaming beside them, the moment seemed perfect. Better than she ever could have imagined.

He didn't seem to want things to end, either. His mouth was fierce on hers, as if he couldn't get enough, and she could feel his racing pulse, his ragged breathing.

She had a wild urge to lead him down the hall to her bedroom, to keep kissing him—and more—all night, but she could never do that with her girls in the house. They risked disaster here, kissing in the front room where Silver or Mia might walk in on them at any moment.

The reminder of her daughters cast a shadow over the

kiss, a shadow that darkened further when she felt a pressure against her leg that didn't feel quite right.

Her mouth still tangled with Ruben's, she shifted her gaze down and found Winky resting her chin on Dani's knee, watching the two of them with interest. They had an audience. Her little dog.

That was the distraction she needed, the one that effectively snapped her out of the heated embrace and back to reality.

She should *not* be doing this, kissing Ruben Morales as if her life depended on it.

What was she thinking?

Yes, he was a kind man. Big deal. She didn't need a kind man right now. She didn't need *any* man, but especially not *this* one, a law enforcement officer and her boss's son.

If she wanted a life for her daughters here in Haven Point, she needed to make it through this yearlong internship. She couldn't allow anything to threaten that. She especially couldn't let down her guard around Ruben.

She couldn't be foolish enough to think she might actually have a future with a man like him. Why would he want someone who had her history of poor judgment, who had been naive and stupid enough to marry a man capable of Tommy's crimes and have not one, but two children with him?

If Ruben knew the truth about Dani and her past, he wouldn't want her anywhere near him or his family.

That didn't change the fact that *she* wanted *him*, that she wanted to stay right here nestled against his hard chest and broad shoulders, where the past and her own mistakes seemed far enough away that they couldn't hurt her.

She sighed. The past always had a way of painting the present with its own ugly brush.

She pulled away, painfully aware of Ruben's ragged breathing, his dilated pupils.

"That was…"

The aroused rasp in his voice rippled down her spine but she firmly ignored it. "Not supposed to happen. I know. I think we're both acting a little irrationally tonight."

"Speak for yourself, Dr. Capelli. I knew exactly what I was doing."

What did he mean by *that*? She couldn't seem to make her brain cooperate enough to figure it out. Her face felt hot, her skin tight, her nerves as frayed as Winky's favorite blanket.

"Then you have to know that was a mistake. I shouldn't have… We shouldn't have… Oh. This is the most embarrassing night of my life."

He stopped her words by the simple yet profound gesture of grabbing her hand. "Would it make any difference if I told you I've been wanting to do that since you moved to town?"

Her fingers trembled in his. "You have not."

"I'm an officer of the law, Doc. I always speak the truth."

She managed to hold back a snort. "I don't believe that's a job requirement for any law enforcement officer I've ever met."

"Well, I'm sorry for that. In this case, I mean everything I say. You might as well know it. I've wanted to kiss you since we met. I'm afraid now that I've done it, I'm only going to want to kiss you more."

He might tell the truth all the time. She, on the other hand, was not only the ex-wife of a man who had been a convicted felon and worse, but she had been a juvenile delinquent in her own right when she had been a wild, angry foster kid lashing out at the world.

She had no such compunction toward honesty, especially when so very much depended on him believing her lie.

"Let's both do our best to forget what just happened. Tonight has been...strange, to say the least."

She rose, hoping against hope that he would get the hint. Dani was suddenly desperate for him to go. She needed time to figure out what had just happened here, how she could have been so stupid as to let him under her defenses, even for a moment.

To her relief, he rose as well and stood watching her for a long moment, the Christmas lights reflected in his eyes.

"I'm afraid I won't be able to forget the taste of you anytime soon," he said, his voice rough, and she had to curl her hands into fists against the urge to wrap them around his neck and go for round two.

What kind of masochistic fool was she?

"I'm afraid you'll just have to be content with your memories, Deputy Morales, because it won't happen again."

"Coming from any other woman, I would consider such a bold statement something of a challenge."

"I am not any other woman. I mean what I say."

Though her voice sounded firm enough, she wondered if he could see her hands tremble. With any luck, it was so dark in here, lit only by the Christmas tree, that he wouldn't have a clue.

To her vast relief, he seemed to take her words at face value. "You do know how to wound a man, don't you? I'll remind you that you kissed me first."

"I know. I shouldn't have."

"Why did you?"

She didn't have an answer for that, at least not one she understood herself.

"It doesn't matter. I'm grateful for all you've done this weekend. It was very kind of you to help us clean up the graffiti yesterday and to invite us to your sister's concert and your family party afterward, and I appreciate you letting me make a fool of myself by crying all over you tonight. Let's just say I let my emotions get the better of me."

His expression told her plainly that he didn't believe her but he didn't press. "Are you still willing to let Silver and Mia help me with the Secret Santa project?"

She had a feeling it would be in all of their best interests to restore a careful distance between her little family and Ruben Morales but she had already told him Silver would help.

She couldn't avoid him. They lived next door to each other and his father was her boss. She tried for a casual tone, hoping to restore things to a more stable footing. "We're both adults here. Things don't have to be…awkward because we shared one little kiss, do they?"

He gave a rough laugh. "Again, you do know how to wound a man."

She wanted to tell him she didn't consider the kiss little, that it had rocked everything secure and safe in her world. She couldn't, of course, so she said nothing.

"Fine," he said after a moment. "If you're still good with Silver helping out, we'll start the Secret Santa campaign on the evening of the thirteenth. As soon as I figure out what time will work, I'll let you and Silver know."

"I'll have her ready. Thank you."

He gazed at her, his expression unreadable. He looked as if he wanted to say something more but he finally sighed. "Good night, then," he said.

"Good night."

He grabbed his coat off the back of the armchair, gave Winky one last pat, then headed out into the snow.

She closed the door behind him and fought the urge to sag against it, desperate for a moment to regain her composure. Instead, she made herself go into the kitchen to replace Winky's water and add a little more kibble to the bowl.

The dog deserved a big, juicy bone. If not for Winky, Dani might have let things go much further and made a terrible mistake.

She had to keep her distance from Ruben, no matter how difficult. The stakes were too great. After tonight and that heated kiss, she could no longer deny this attraction simmering between them. It wasn't only one-sided, that much was obvious. If she gave in to it, if she explored this heat and hunger between them, the results could be disastrous.

She had spent the last three days talking to Silver about how each action had consequences. It was an important lesson for Dani as well, one she couldn't afford to forget.

He couldn't get that kiss out of his head.

As Ruben pulled up in front of the veterinary clinic the following Thursday afternoon, he was uncomfortably aware of his sweaty palms and the low ache of anticipation curling through him.

He couldn't remember the last time a woman had left him so tied up in knots.

That kiss had haunted his dreams. *Dani* had haunted his dreams. Each time he closed his eyes, it seemed as if she was waiting for him, with her vulnerable eyes and her secrets and the sweetness she tried to conceal beneath a thin, crackly veneer of stiff reserve.

She worked so hard to hold herself apart. Why? Was it self-protectiveness on her part? What was she trying to hide?

He had stayed away as long as he could manage, until the need to see her again became too overwhelming, and so he had finally manufactured an excuse to see her again.

Now, as he sat in his patrol vehicle on his lunch hour, he wondered what the hell was wrong with him. She had made it clear she didn't want anything more than friendship with him, so why couldn't he manage to get her out of his head?

He was here now. He might as well go in and talk to her. That anticipation grew stronger as he climbed out of his vehicle and headed inside the clinic.

The reception area was empty except for Gloria

McCoy, his dad's longtime receptionist. She smiled broadly when she spotted him. "Hey, Ruben honey. How are you?"

"Good. Good."

Gloria probably didn't need to know he hadn't slept well since Sunday because of a certain doctor of veterinary medicine who was somewhere in this very clinic right now.

He leaned on the reception counter. "How are you? How's your family?"

"Oh, you know. Hanging in there. Randy's wife is having my third grandbaby in a couple weeks."

"Oh, congratulations."

"And my Jen broke up with her boyfriend. Good riddance, I say. He was no good."

Her oldest daughter, Jen, was a few years younger than Ruben. Though she had grown into a lovely woman, he still always saw her as the pigtailed brat who used to throw snowballs at him and once rear-ended him in the school parking lot a few weeks after she got her driver's license.

"I saw her a few weeks ago at the hospital when I had to take an inmate at the jail in for an X-ray. She's a radiology technician, right? Does she enjoy it?"

"She loves it. She makes a good living, too." Gloria's features suddenly turned crafty. "Now that she's available again and has come to her senses, you may want to think about asking her out. She always had a little crush on you, you know."

He *hadn't* known that—and now he wished she had never told him. Jen probably wouldn't appreciate her mother spilling that particular can of beans. Ruben wasn't sure how comfortable he would be joking around with Jen, the next time he had to take an inmate in for medical care.

"I'll, uh, keep that in mind."

"You do that." Gloria beamed at him and Ruben shifted uncomfortably. He liked Jen but had never been particularly interested in her romantically—unlike a certain other woman he could name.

"If you're looking for your dad, he's not in today. You'll remember, this is one of his regular days off, since the new doc came. I think he and your mom were going Christmas shopping in Boise. Your mom said she needed another present for your brother's girl. Esme, right?"

Gloria always seem to know more about his family goings-on than Ruben did. "That's right. Thanks, but I'm actually not here for my dad. I was hoping to catch Dr. Capelli, unless she's gone home for her lunch hour."

Gloria gestured vaguely to the back rooms of the veterinary clinic. "That one rarely takes a lunch hour, unless her girls are out of school. You're more likely to find her eating a brown-bag lunch while she walks one of the dogs or cuddles a cat."

He couldn't discern from Gloria's tone what she thought about that behavior. He pictured Dani doing both those things and found the image rather adorable.

It suddenly occurred to Ruben that Gloria would likely be an incredibly helpful fount of information about the new veterinarian. She had worked with her since Dani came to town and Gloria wasn't known for being subtle about probing for information about a person.

She probably knew more about Dani than anyone else in Haven Point—including Ruben's dad.

He had dozens of questions he wanted to ask, but they all caught in his throat. He couldn't interrogate his father's nosy office manager, no matter how tempting. That would be inappropriate and intrusive. Right?

"Could you let her know I'm here?" he said instead.

"I'm waiting on a phone call from an insurance company. Do you mind just going on back and finding her? I imagine she's either in her office or in the treatment area. In case you didn't know, her office is right next to your father's."

"Thanks."

He went through the double doors leading from the reception-waiting area to the treatment rooms and offices. The door next to his father's office was open and the light was on but when Ruben poked his head inside, he found it empty. Down the hall, he could hear crooning, a sweet alto voice singing a Christmas carol.

He paused for a moment, enjoying the impromptu concert. Who would have guessed Dani Capelli sang Christmas music? She had a beautiful voice, too. Something gentle and tender unfurled in his chest as he paused there in the hallway. For all her sharp edges, this confirmed his suspicion that Dani was a softy at heart.

He received further proof when he walked farther down the hall to the doorway of the treatment room where animals were kept for observation postsurgery or if they were ill.

Dani sat on the floor in front of one of the cages that lined the wall. In her arms was the biggest bunny Ruben had ever seen, a soft gray with ears that flopped down. She was singing "Away in a Manger" and the rabbit seemed to be enjoying every note.

He had to smile. The woman was making it damn hard to resist her.

She didn't notice him at first, but continued singing to the creature. Ruben wondered for a moment if he ought to slip back out. He didn't want to scare Dani and, in turn, scare the creature.

He waited too long to decide, however. She must have sensed his presence, because she paused in her singing, looked up and gave a little gasp that did indeed have the rabbit jolting in her lap.

"Easy. Easy," she said, in a low, soothing voice that did ridiculous things to Ruben's insides. "I've got you, baby. I've got you."

In one graceful movement, she rose with the huge bunny in her arms and placed him back inside the largest of the cages. "There you go," she said in that same soothing tone, before closing the cage door and turning to face Ruben.

"Sorry I startled you." Taking his cue from her, he kept his voice low, unthreatening.

She moved closer. "It's not me you need to worry about. Cecil can be fierce."

"I'm assuming Cecil is the giant killer bunny."

"Not a killer. He's a particularly big French lop who had a little run-in with a bull terrier yesterday when he was out for a walk with his owner. I think Cecil is still suffering a little PTSD."

Ruben fought a smile, not sure why he found that amusing. Poor bunny. "How's he doing now?"

"Better. He should be ready to return to his family in another day or two."

"That's good. Who wants to be without their giant bunny at Christmastime?"

She made a face as she led him out of the room and into the hallway. "Your father's not here. He and your mother went Christmas shopping in Boise."

"That's what I hear. I'm not looking for my father, though."

"Oh?" He was almost positive he saw her blush. Her gaze danced to his mouth then quickly away and Ruben was instantly hot.

She remembered their kiss as well. He was certain of it.

"Have you had lunch? I was thinking about running over to Serrano's to grab a bite."

She looked briefly tempted, then shook her head. "I can't. I'm sorry. I have appointments scheduled again in twenty minutes."

"Another time, maybe. I should have asked in advance." It was a spur-of-the-moment invitation anyway.

"Guess I'll run home and grab a sandwich, then," he said.

She started to nibble her bottom lip then seemed to catch herself. "I have a turkey sandwich in my office. You can share it with me, if you want."

After more than a decade in law enforcement, few things had the power to astonish him anymore. Dani's lunch invitation would now top that list, especially after the way she had left things between them Sunday night.

"That's very sweet of you. Thanks. I would love to take you up on it."

Looking as if she regretted saying anything, she went to the sink to wash her hands, then led the way back to her office. She gestured to the visitor chair before pulling a small insulated lunch bag out of a minirefrigerator in her office. The bag was decorated in vivid orange and pink flowers, offering a bright little spot of femininity in the otherwise clinical office.

She reached into the bag and emerged with a hoagie sandwich then handed him half.

"All I have to drink are water bottles. Do you mind?"

"It's perfect. I'm on duty anyway."

She handed him a cold one from the refrigerator, grabbed one for herself, then opened the cap and took a long drink.

"Thanks for this," he said. "I probably would have ended up buying fast food before I head back to Shelter Springs. This is a much healthier option."

"You're welcome. Oh, I have hummus and some vegetable sticks, too, if you want"

"Thanks. You're too generous."

She shrugged. "I always make too much lunch and end up wasting half of it."

He chewed a delicious bite, flavored with exactly the right ratio of mustard to mayonnaise, took a swig of his water bottle, then set down the water bottle, reminding himself he needed to get to the matter at hand.

"I really didn't come here for free lunch, I promise."

"I know."

"While this is delicious, I actually stopped by because today is the thirteenth."

She gave him a blank look for a moment before her confusion gave way to understanding. "Oh. Right. The Secret Santa project."

"According to my mother's long-standing tradition, we need to start giving out the gifts for the twelve days of Christmas today if we want to wrap things up by Christmas Eve. Are you still okay with Mia and Silver helping out?"

"I don't think I could stop that particular train now, even if I wanted to," she said ruefully. "They're planning on it. Mia, especially, is excited to help. She's talked about it every day since Sunday night."

Again, her cheeks suddenly seemed to turn a dusky rose and she avoided looking at him, focusing on the sandwich in front of her.

Was she remembering what else had happened Sunday night? He suspected so but couldn't be sure.

He certainly was remembering their kiss, especially when she nibbled on her delectable bottom lip again.

He wanted to be the one doing that.

Memories of those delicious few moments they had spent in her darkened living room pushed to the front of his mind. Her soft curves wrapped around him, her mouth sweet and eager against his, the soft, surprising peace he had found with her in his arms.

Too bad he also recalled so clearly what she had said afterward: *I'm afraid you'll just have to be content with your memories, Deputy Morales, because it won't happen again.*

She didn't want to kiss him again. He would have to

be content with that. Something told him Dani needed a friend and if that was all she wanted from him, he would do his best to respect her wishes, no matter how tough that was to remember—especially when she was sweet enough to offer him half of her lunch.

"It should be fun for them," he said, returning to the real reason he told himself he was here in her office, to discuss the gift deliveries that night. "I'm not as fast as I used to be and it's become increasingly harder for a guy my size to hide behind a tree."

Her gaze danced over his chest and shoulders and, if he wasn't mistaken, she swallowed. "I imagine that's true."

"What time works best for you? I thought I would pick them up around six thirty tonight but I wouldn't want to interrupt your dinner or homework routine. I can adapt, if another time would be better."

"We usually eat dinner early to give the girls time to finish any homework. Six thirty should work fine."

"Do you want to come with us?" he asked on impulse. "When I do this with Zach, I usually drop him off a short distance away from the house we're hitting, then park around the corner or on the next block, where my vehicle isn't as suspicious. While Silver makes the delivery, you and Mia can wait with me, if you'd like."

"That might not be a bad idea, at least for the first night."

"Terrific. I'll pick everybody up, then."

He took another drink from the water bottle, touched again that she would be so unexpectedly generous with her lunch when she could be so prickly at other times.

"How's the Christmas tree?" he asked.

She gave a little laugh. "Completely over-the-top. You'll have to take a look when you come by tonight. I don't think there's a single branch that doesn't have an ornament or two on it. Mia went a little crazy."

"She's a great kid. You're very lucky."

"Believe me, I know." She took a bite of her sandwich, giving him a pensive look. "Why are you still single, Ruben? Seriously. You're great with kids and close to your own family. You're gorgeous that goes without saying—have a good job and appear to have all your teeth. What am I missing?"

He shifted, not sure he registered anything after the word *gorgeous*. Both of them knew he wasn't. Inside, he still felt like the skinny Mexican kid who had been gangly and awkward in high school and didn't grow into his height until after college.

"I don't have a good answer to that. I was almost engaged about seven years ago, until we both realized we were together because it was convenient, not because of any grand passion. She's happily married now and has a couple of kids. I've dated on and off since then, somebody pretty seriously about six months ago, but nothing ever really clicked." He shrugged. "Maybe family life isn't in the cards for me."

The thought left him sad. He was thirty-three and was tired of coming home to a house filled only with his dogs, as much as he loved Ollie and Yukon.

At the same time, he wouldn't settle, not after the great example he had growing up of a loving, supportive family, with two parents who still adored each other.

"What about you? Do you see yourself marrying again?"

She suddenly looked as if she regretted bringing up the topic. "Been there, done that."

"You mentioned the girls' father is dead. I'm sorry."

She set down her sandwich. "Don't be. Mia and Silver are better off without Tommy. He broke their hearts, again and again. We had been divorced for years before he…died a few months ago."

It was recent, then. He hadn't expected that. He didn't miss the way she carefully phrased the sentence. What were the circumstances of his death? There was definitely a story there, one he wanted very much to learn.

He wanted to press her but was afraid now wasn't the time. She had clients coming in soon and he had to get back to work as well.

"I'm sorry," he said again. "Sounds like the guy was a lousy father, but it still couldn't have been easy on the girls to lose him at such young ages."

"They're doing fine. Mia never really knew him. Silver struggles more, but I think she's mostly mourning the father she *should* have had, not the one she did."

"I get it." That didn't make the girl's grief any less intense, he was sure. No wonder Silver lashed out by vandalizing the neighbors' property. Compassion seeped through him.

"He…wasn't a good man, I'm sorry to say. My girls both deserved a father like you had. Someone like Frank, kind and caring," she said, mouth tight. "Unfortunately, that's not the kind of man I picked."

She blamed herself. He could hear the self-recrimination in her voice. It bothered him, made him wish he knew how to comfort her.

"Nobody makes it through this ride called life without making choices he or she regrets," Ruben said quietly.

She gave a raw-sounding little laugh and finally met his gaze. "True enough. You know, when I offered to share my sandwich, I didn't realize I would be rewarded with a bit of wise philosophy."

"It's on the house. Just my little way of repaying you for the food."

Her rueful smile seemed to arrow straight to his heart.

Her late ex-husband sounded like a royal bastard. Was he the reason Dani was so guarded, why she maintained such careful barriers between them? It seemed the logical conclusion. Ruben was angry on her behalf, both for the previous mistreatment and for the way her ex seemed to have left her bruised.

"Thank you," she said. "I enjoyed the philosophy *and* the company. It's nice to eat lunch with someone who doesn't have four legs and a tail."

Before he could respond, Gloria appeared in the doorway. She looked startled to find them both there together. He had the feeling by her sudden dark look that she wasn't particularly pleased about it.

"Sorry to interrupt, Dr. Capelli, but your one o'clock is here. That Chihuahua with the runs."

Dani winced a little and set down the rest of her sandwich, from which she had maybe taken three total bites. "Thank you, Gloria. I'll be right out."

The receptionist headed back to the front office and

Dani gave him an apologetic look. "Sorry about that. Gloria isn't always the most tactful person."

"You don't have to tell me that. She's worked for my dad since I was a kid. I know just what she's like."

"Of course." She rose and he had no choice but to do the same.

"Thanks for sharing your sandwich. I don't know when I've enjoyed a lunch more."

"So did I." She paused, nibbling that lip again. "Ruben, I…"

He had a feeling she was about to tell him all the reasons they shouldn't share lunch—or anything else—again. He didn't want to hear it, so he cut her off. "I'll see you tonight for the top-secret project."

"I… All right. Six thirty."

She suddenly looked so adorably flustered, so unlike her usual reserved composure, he couldn't help himself. He leaned down and kissed the corner of her frown.

"Have a good afternoon," he murmured, then turned and walked down the hall already counting the moments until he could see her again.

10

For the rest of the afternoon, Dani refused to let herself dwell on the strange interlude with Ruben or the weird, incongruous combination she felt around him, a mix of nervous awareness and a soft, seductive peace.

She was too busy taking care of the Chihuahua with abdominal distress, a black Lab who needed some porcupine quills pulled, Cecil the traumatized lop bunny and three Maine coons in need of checkups.

By the time she showed out her last patient and his human, she was exhausted. She finished her paperwork, grabbed her bag, put on her coat against the December chill and walked out to the waiting area to say goodbye to Gloria.

"That was a crazy afternoon. Thank you for helping

everything to run smoothly. I don't know what I would have done without you."

"You're welcome." Gloria reached to shut down her computer for the evening, then returned a couple of files to the drawer to clear off her desk.

"Good thing you found time for a lunch break in there," she said. "By the way, I didn't realize you and Dr. Morales's son were such good friends."

There was a slight question on the end of her words, as if Gloria were trying to ascertain just how friendly the two were.

"We live next door to each other. It's impossible to avoid each other in a town as small as Haven Point."

"I suppose that's true." She paused. "He's a good guy, Dr. Capelli."

"I agree," she said, not liking Gloria's tone or her own defensive reaction to it. Why was it any of Gloria's business if Dani was friends with Dr. Morales's son?

"He's always been a hard worker, even when he was a kid who would come around here to make extra spending money. I thought maybe he would become a veterinarian like his dad, he was that good with the animals, but he had other ideas I guess."

"Kids often do."

"He's a good guy," she repeated. "I sure would hate to see him get hurt."

Was Gloria warning her away from Ruben? The idea would have been laughable if it wasn't so astonishing.

"Are you saying you think I would hurt him? Why would I do that?"

"I don't know. Maybe you'll decide things aren't working out for you here and you need to go back to the East Coast."

Did *Gloria* believe what she said, that things weren't working out here for Dani? All her doubts and insecurities seemed to crowd through her psyche, all the voices that told her she was better off staying a waitress instead of thinking she could ever build a solid future for her daughters doing something she loved.

"I appreciate the advice. I'll keep it in mind," she said stiffly.

She had thought Gloria liked her. The woman had been kind to her and was always more than patient with the girls. It hurt to know she questioned Dani's staying power.

"You should be relieved to know, then," she said, still in that tight voice, "that I'm not dating the man and I have no intention of changing that. Put your mind at ease. We're friends who happened to have lunch together today, that's all."

At her tone, Gloria looked regretful. "That didn't come out the way I meant. Sometimes my mouth blabs things before I really think them through. I've just known Ruben since he was little and, I'll admit, I've always thought he and my Jen would make a cute couple. I guess I was surprised when I saw you together earlier. Forget I said anything."

"It's forgotten." Dani forced a smile. "I'll see you tomorrow, Gloria. Have a good evening."

"Do you have any fun plans?" the woman asked, obviously trying to make up for her tactlessness of earlier.

I'm going to hang out with Ruben. You got a problem with that?

She almost said the words but decided not to pour fuel on the fire. Some day her own smart-ass mouth was going to get her in trouble here in this town full of nice people who might not expect it from her.

"Homework, dinner, bed. That's about it."

"Well, give those cute girls of yours a hug from me. Good night."

Dani tried not to dwell on Gloria's concerns as she followed that outline for her evening and helped Mia get in her nightly reading practice and hounded Silver about her math worksheet, then threw together one of the girls' favorites for dinner, her version of pasta *e fagioli* soup.

"When are we going? I can't wait. I can't wait," Mia said as she dried the dinner dishes while Dani washed. "When Ruben gets here, can I be the one who takes the present to the door?"

Dani frowned down at her daughter. "Why are you asking again, honey? We have talked about this all evening. Silver is going to do it this first time and check out the situation at the Larkin house. She's a really fast runner and should be able to figure out the best places to hide. After that, we can decide if she thinks you can do it."

Mia was too excited about the evening ahead of them and didn't appear dejected. "That's okay. It will be fun to wait in the truck with Ruben."

Dani wished she could agree. Instead, her stomach was in knots, worrying about spending even a few moments in a vehicle with the man, especially with this soft, tensile connection that seemed to have formed between them when she wasn't looking.

Gloria's words kept ringing through her head. *He's a good guy. I sure would hate to see him get hurt.*

Gloria's unspoken message was that Dani was not the right kind of woman for him. She couldn't agree more. Both of them knew Dani was not the sort of woman who could make someone like Ruben happy.

She had no room in her life for any man right now, but especially a man who was a complete mismatch for her. Ruben was an officer of the law, for crying out loud. A squeaky-clean, make the world-a-better-place kind of man.

The moment he found out about Tommy, about his life of misdeeds and the chaos he had left in his wake and especially his last terrible acts, he wouldn't want anything to do with Dani or her girls.

There was a chance he already knew. She had told Frank right after it happened. She hadn't felt right about keeping something like that from the kindly veterinarian, even knowing it might ruin the opportunity for her.

Frank had assured her none of that mattered to him, which had only endeared the man more to her. She didn't *think* he would have told his son, but she couldn't be completely sure.

If he knew, would Ruben have been so kind and understanding to her and her girls?

Headlights suddenly flashed in her driveway before she could come up with an answer to that. He was about fifteen minutes late, which seemed unusual for him.

Nerves fluttered through her and Mia's sudden squeal didn't help matters any.

"He's here! He's here!"

"Why do you always have to repeat everything you say?" Silver groused. "Do you think we didn't hear you the first time or something?"

"Enough, Sil. Will you just try to stow the attitude for five minutes tonight? I'll remind you, we're doing all of this because of you."

Silver slumped back into her chair, her mouth in a tight line. Dani wanted to think her words had some impact on her daughter, but she doubted it.

Had she been so difficult when she was thirteen? She didn't think so. Of course, that had been during the three relatively peaceful years she had lived with Betsy in that big brownstone in Flushing.

Though the woman had taken in three other girls around Dani's age, they each had their own rooms, a rarity during her years in the system. That big house by far had been the most comfortable of her placements and she had been on her best behavior during those years, until Betsy became ill and could no longer care for her charges.

All in all, thirteen had been a pretty good year. Maybe that's one of the reasons she had so little patience with her daughter at the same age, who had so much more than Dani had.

She didn't have time to dwell on the past, especially not when the doorbell rang out through her house and Mia raced to it, her features glowing. At least one of them was excited about the prospect of a little holiday mischief.

"Hi, Deputy Morales" Dani heard her say cheerfully.

"Hey, Miss Mia," he answered.

Something was wrong. Even before she walked into

the foyer to see his face, she could tell by the tone of his voice.

Seeing him only confirmed her suspicion. This afternoon when he had left her at lunchtime he had seemed cheerful, happy, his smile easy and warm. Now there was a closed-in quality to him, a tightness around his eyes and a deep sadness that seemed to have settled over him.

What was wrong? What had put that sudden bleak look in his eyes? It was all she could do to keep from asking and she had to fight the urge to place a comforting hand on his arm.

"Are you ready to go?" he asked.

"Yep." Mia beamed at him. "I can't wait!"

He didn't smile back. "Silver? Still up for this?"

Dani waited apprehensively for her teenager to make some sarcastic comment. *Not now, Silver,* she wanted to say.

To her vast relief, Sil was uncharacteristically subdued, almost as if she had picked up on Ruben's unspoken turmoil as well.

"I just need to put on my coat," her daughter said.

"Make sure it's a black or dark blue one, if possible. That will make it easier to hide in the bushes or behind trees, if you have to."

"I can't believe a sheriff's deputy is telling me to wear dark clothing, the better to skulk around the neighborhood. What is the world coming to?"

This earned Silver a small smile, but it contained none of his usual warmth.

What was wrong? And how disconcerting, to realize how very dependent she was becoming on that smile and his usual cheery good humor. She was coming to crave it just as much as she yearned for a good plate of her favorite lasagna from Il Bambino's in Queens.

She had a horrible thought that left her cold. Had he somehow found out about Tommy? Had he gone back to the sheriff's department and put in a little research?

They didn't have the same name anymore so connecting the dots wouldn't be easy but it wouldn't be impossible.

There was also the chance he might have asked his father. Would Dr. Morales keep her secrets? She wanted to think so but couldn't be sure.

No. She gave him a closer look. Something told her his strange mood had nothing to do with her or her girls.

"You'll be skulking around this time for a good cause," he reminded Silver. "I wouldn't ask otherwise."

"What about us?" Mia asked. "Do we need dark clothes, too?"

His heavy mood seemed to lift a little as he smiled down at her youngest daughter. "You should be fine just the way you are."

"Good. I only have one winter coat, and it's this one."

She twirled around to show off the pink-and-purple coat she adored.

"It's very nice," Ruben said.

"Here, kiddo. Let's get your hat." Dani helped Mia put on the matching purple-and-pink beanie a friend back in Boston had knitted for her.

"I think we're ready now," Dani said after Silver joined them and Dani had the chance to put on her own coat.

"Great." He mustered a smile that again didn't quite reach his eyes.

What had happened?

"I've got tonight's gift in the truck already. It should be easy this time. The first few deliveries, the family won't be expecting you. After about the third night, they'll be on the lookout. Once, we delivered Secret Santa to a family that had six kids. They staked out the yard one night, trying to catch Mateo making the delivery. Fortunately he was a star on the track team and they could never see him."

"Silver is superfast, too," Mia said. "You should see how fast she runs. I can't even keep up with her. Neither can Mama."

"That's good." Ruben's smile seemed a little more genuine.

"You sure you're ready?" he asked Silver.

"As I'll ever be," she answered. To Dani's relief, she actually *did* look excited—from the anonymous gift-giving or from the risk involved, Dani didn't know but she supposed it didn't really matter.

"We'll use my pickup tonight since it's dark and unobtrusive," Ruben said. "But after a few days, we may want to switch things up, just to keep them guessing, in case somebody notices a strange vehicle in the neighborhood."

"Good heavens," Dani exclaimed. "I never realized this was more complicated than making a ransom drop."

"It can be, but the Morales family has had lots of experience, so you're in good hands."

The shiver rippling down her spine was due to the falling snow as they walked outside, not because her imagination was suddenly busy going off in all kinds of inappropriate directions.

After the previous unseasonably mild weekend, a storm system had moved in. Though it had only dropped a few inches, the snow was falling steadily, the kind of storm that could lay down a heavy blanket in only a few hours.

"Look how pretty the snow is, Mama." Mia lifted her face to the snow as she always did and held her tongue out to catch a snowflake.

"You're such a goon," Silver said, though it was said with more affection than malice.

"You are," Mia retorted.

"You both are. Get in Ruben's truck and let's do this," Dani said.

The girls climbed into the back row of his king cab again and Dani slid into the front seat. The vehicle smelled of him, that indefinable woodsy, sexy, masculine smell that did such ridiculous things to her insides and made her want to lean her head against the leather and inhale for a few hours.

"I guess you know where the Larkin girls live," Ruben said as he backed out of the driveway.

"I've been there a few times," Silver said.

Something had happened between Silver and the girls. Until a few weeks ago, the twins, Emma and Ella, had been among Silver's small circle of friends in town. Now whenever their names were mentioned, Silver behaved oddly, with a fine-edged tension Dani couldn't quite understand.

Ruben didn't appear to notice anything unusual. "Great. I'll drop you off at the end of their street and then pull down the road a little bit, where I'm out of view from their house. All you have to do is knock on the door or ring the doorbell—your choice—then hide around the side of their house or behind their shrubs until they answer. After they pick up the gift and go back inside, you can slip away and make your way around the corner to find us. You good with that?"

"I think I can handle it," she said drily.

"I have no doubt at all. I really appreciate your help with this. I'm getting a little too old to be hiding in the bushes and, as you put it, skulking around the neighborhood. If they're not home, by the way, just leave it."

His headlights illuminated the snow falling thickly as he drove to his destination. The street was quiet. Everyone with any sense was tucked in at home by the fire, safe from the increasing intensity of the weather.

Through the windows, she could see Christmas trees glowing through the winter night and several houses had lights outlining their windows and following their rooflines.

Inside, she could see shadows moving behind closed curtains and blinds. She wasn't a Peeping Tom but she did like to see houses all closed up against the night. It made her wonder about the people who lived inside. What they cooked for dinner, what they were watching on television, if they were laughing or having a party or playing video games.

When Silver was small, after Tommy went upstate the first time, Dani had left her with a babysitter in the evenings so she could go to night school after caring for her all day. She used to take the city bus to campus and back through a few quiet suburban neighborhoods.

She remembered coming home from class completely exhausted but with just enough energy to gaze at those houses and those closed curtains and the filtered blue light from the television screens. As she imagined people in their safe little cocoons, she would vow that she and Tommy would give their little Silvia a better childhood than their tiny fifth-floor walk-up apartment where they shared a bathroom with the apartment next door.

Through hard work and sacrifice and plenty of help along the way, she had come further than she'd ever dreamed. She was a veterinarian. They lived in a three-bedroom house on a beautiful mountain lake, something she couldn't even have imagined back then, when she had never been quite sure if she would have enough to feed her little girl.

Things weren't perfect. She would be the first one to admit that. She could be abrupt with the girls, more impatient than she wanted to be. But they knew, above all else, that their mother loved them.

She remembered hearing once that a person had two chances to be part of a good parent-child relationship, once when they were children and once when they were parents. She had missed out on the first chance for a big portion of her childhood after her mother died, but she was doing her very best to make sure the second phase was filled with joy.

An important element of that was teaching her daughters to care about others, and participating in this little

Christmas tradition with Ruben would help in that department.

"Here we are." He pulled to the side of the road in front of a vacant lot in a place where his pickup would not attract undue attention. From the console, he pulled out a small, neatly wrapped box and handed it to Silver in the back seat.

"Cute. Did you wrap it yourself?" she asked, with only a hint of sarcasm in her voice.

"My mom did this one, actually. She's done most of the prep work of buying and wrapping the gifts, since she knows her sons probably won't get to it."

Silver paused there, her glove on the door handle.

She was nervous, Dani realized.

"Nothing to worry about." Ruben gave a reassuring smile, picking up on Silver's apprehension, too. "Just go to the door, set the present down, ring the bell and run like he—, um, heck."

"Got it." Silver pushed open the door and stepped out into the snow.

Bundled in her dark coat, hat and the tightly wrapped scarf Dani had handed her before they left the house, Silver was all but unrecognizable, a blob of wool and down and GoreTex as she trudged to the corner and then out of sight.

"She's a good kid," Ruben said, watching after her.

His words warmed her far more than the heater of his pickup could. People couldn't always see past Silver's purple hair and attitude.

"She is," Dani murmured.

"I wish I could go with her." Mia's sigh from the back seat was deep and heartfelt.

Ruben turned around to smile at her. "Another night, okay? We'll make it happen for you."

"Promise?"

"Yes. Now, I'm going to turn off the engine and the lights so we don't look so suspicious sitting here. Are you okay with that?" he asked Dani. "It's only for a moment."

"We'll be fine, won't we, Mia?"

"I'm not cold one bit," she declared.

Ruben turned the key, plunging them into darkness and quiet. Outside, the snow fluttered down onto the landscape.

"This is fun," Mia said.

Ruben didn't answer and Dani frowned as he gazed out the windshield at the snow that began to pile up quickly.

"What's wrong?" she murmured softly. Something about the intimacy of the cab here in the dark gave her the courage to ask him. She didn't want anything that might tighten the growing bond between them, but she couldn't bear that he was obviously upset about something.

"What makes you think something is wrong?"

Though she felt stupid for presuming she knew the man, she wanted to think she had gained a little insight into him, especially over the last week or so.

"Instinct, I guess. You seem very different right now than you were at lunch. You're upset about something."

Did you find out about my ex-husband and what he did?

The words hovered on her tongue but she didn't dare ask him.

He was quiet for a long moment, so long that she thought he wasn't going to answer. Finally he gave her a searching look across the width of the pickup truck, then sighed.

"Let's just say it's been a long afternoon. This time of year can be tough on some people."

"And tough on those charged with looking after us," she answered.

"Unfortunately, that can be true." He was quiet again, listening to Mia humming Christmas songs softly in the back seat, always happy to entertain herself.

"I don't imagine you were all that thrilled about coming with us," he said after a moment. "But I'm selfishly glad you did. I needed this tonight."

"To sit in a cold pickup truck in the dark, waiting for my daughter to finish a knock-and-run?"

He smiled a little, and she wanted to think it was slightly more genuine. "That, yes, plus to have the chance to sit for a moment and think about some of the good things the holidays bring. The little kindnesses and the family time and the peace of a Lake Haven December night." He paused. "Too many people find this time of year lonely and sad. It breaks my heart sometimes."

Her own heart seemed to break a little and she wished that she could be the sort of woman who had the courage to hold him close and take away some of his pain, as he'd done for her the other night.

Gloria's words seemed to ring in her ears. Ruben was a good, caring man who deserved far better than somebody with her kind of baggage.

"I'm sorry your afternoon was hard." She didn't have any other words that seemed adequate.

"Nothing like a Chihuahua with diarrhea."

"Ew. Gross. You said *diarrhea*," Mia piped up from the back seat, making both of them smile.

That intimacy swirled around them again, that sense that they were alone here in the dark.

"I have to admit, I'm a little sad to find out you have to deal with rough things over the holidays. I'd like to believe a place like this is immune to that kind of thing."

"Believe me, Lake Haven County has its troubles, just like anywhere else. Otherwise, I wouldn't have a job."

"I suppose that's true. It doesn't make it any less sad."

Before he could answer, the back door opened and Silver jumped in. "Okay, that was fun!"

Ruben chuckled. "Did you get caught?"

"Almost. All the lights were on inside and I could tell they were home, but I was like a freaking ninja. You should have seen me. I crawled up the front porch steps and stayed low so they couldn't see me, then put the thingy down, rang the doorbell and took off as fast as I could around the side of the house. I thought for sure they were going to come looking for me, but then a minute later I heard the door close. After another minute or two, I peeked around the house and they had gone back inside."

"Did they take the gift?" Dani asked, struck by how long it had been since she had seen this kind of enthusiasm and excitement from her daughter.

She wanted to lean across the pickup truck cab and plant a great big smooch on Ruben Morales's cheek for giving her this little glimpse of the Silver she remembered from a few years earlier.

"Yeah. It wasn't there anymore, at least. I waited a few more moments to make sure no one was going to come back out, then I sneaked away and hurried back here."

"That sounds so fun!" Mia exclaimed. "I want to do it."

"Maybe we could both go tomorrow night," Silver said. "If I'm there with you, I can show you where to hide and wait for me while I go up to the door. You have to be fast."

"I can be. I promise. I'll run as fast as I can."

"That sounds like a plan." Ruben started up his pickup truck, turned the lights on and slowly drove back toward their houses. "From here on out, you'll have to be more careful. They'll be watching."

"Maybe we should mix up the time we go, just so they're not expecting us, watching for us."

"I was going to suggest exactly that," he said. "Let's go about seven thirty tomorrow, if that's not too late."

"Works for me," Silver said.

"The way this snow is coming down, you may have to run in boots."

"No problem for me. I went to school in Boston. You don't know snow until you've seen what we used to get."

By the time they reached Dani's house, another inch had fallen atop the two or three from earlier.

Ruben let them out and walked them up to the house. "Where's your snow shovel? I can clear some of this away. We're supposed to get a few more inches so you'll need

to clear it again in the morning but I can at least start
things off and take care of what's here now."

"That's totally not necessary. Silver and I can do it."

"I know you can, but you'll be doing me a favor. After
my afternoon, I could use some kind of physical outlet."

She again wondered what had happened and wished
she could ask him. If he could find a little release by clear-
ing her driveway, she didn't see how she could refuse.

"The shovel is in the garage. Silver, will you show
Ruben where it is while I get Mia to bed? You can leave
it on the porch when you're done. And thank you. That's
one more way I'm in your debt."

She was busy for the next twenty minutes with Mia's
bath and bedtime routine. By the time her lights were out
and Silver was in the shower, Dani figured Ruben would
have been long gone. When she looked out the window,
however, she spotted him leaning on her shovel handle,
gazing out at the lake and the mountains that gleamed in
the pale moonlight filtering through the storm clouds.

He looked so very desolate. On impulse, she grabbed
a mug from the cupboard, heated some water in the mi-
crowave and mixed in some of her favorite gourmet hot
cocoa, threw on her coat and boots, and walked out into
the night.

He looked over when she approached him and the an-
guish in his eyes tore at her heart. He quickly schooled
his expression.

"What's this?"

"Cocoa. It's not much, but you look like a man who
could use something sweet."

She felt the chill from his ungloved hands as he took it from her. "Thanks. That's very thoughtful of you, Doc."

"You're welcome."

She thought about slipping back into the house but he had been extraordinarily kind to her the other night and she didn't see how she could walk away and leave him to his distress.

"Do you want to talk about what happened after you left the clinic? Just so you know, I'm tougher than I look. I've probably heard worse."

He gazed at her for a long moment, the steam from the cocoa curling between them. Finally he sighed. "I got a call about ten minutes after I left your clinic. I was there all afternoon and into the evening. A murder-suicide north of Shelter Springs."

"Oh, no," she murmured.

"It was an elderly couple in their eighties, both with health trouble. She had Alzheimer's and he was in heart failure."

"Did you know them?"

"Not really. They used to bring their little dogs to the clinic when I was a kid and I remembered seeing them. My folks would know them better than I did. That didn't make it any easier. They had a daughter and she's the one who found them."

"Oh, poor thing."

"Right. I guess Al was getting sicker and could no longer take care of his wife's needs. He knew he was dying and he didn't want to leave her alone to go into a nursing home when something happened to him. That was all written in a note to his daughter. He shot his bride of more than sixty years, then laid down beside her, grabbed her hand and killed himself. I was first on the scene after the daughter called 911. It was…rough."

She ached at the raw, ragged edge to his voice.

"Oh, Ruben. I'm so sorry."

She reached a hand out to touch his arm through the soft down of his jacket. Before she even made contact, he set the mug of cocoa on the ground and wrapped his arms tightly around her. He needed this, the comfort of human contact. It was a small thing she could do. She hugged him close, wishing she could absorb all the cold of his skin and return it with heat.

He shuddered a little against her, not from the cold, she realized, but from being able to lean on someone else for a moment.

Some part of her had always considered law enforcement the enemy. Dani knew that probably traced back to her childhood, to the time when her mother died and the authorities came to take her away. A police officer enlisted by child welfare had dragged her away from her apartment, screaming for her mother. From then on, she had equated the police with loss and pain and unfeeling bureaucracy.

Then later, after she hooked up with Tommy, his choices and lifestyle had meant that any police officer posed a potential threat.

She felt stupid to realize how wrong she had been. They were human beings, doing a job. Some skated through, yes, and wielded the power of their position like a billy club. Others, like Ruben, were caring, dedicated, passionate law enforcement officers.

She held him for a long time while the snowflakes spit from the sky and the wind blew off the lake.

When he pulled away, he looked adorably embarrassed. "Thank you. I guess I needed a little human contact."

"There's no shame in needing someone to hold you once in a while, Deputy Morales. Somebody wise once told me that."

"Somebody should smack that know-it-all right in the mouth."

"Good idea," she murmured. Before she thought it through, she kissed him gently, intending only to offer comfort and solace. He seemed to catch his breath against her mouth and then he pulled her back into his arms and kissed her fiercely.

11

Somehow Dani's kiss pushed away the darkness that had hung over him all afternoon, since he had walked into that heartbreaking scene. He couldn't say she kissed him and made everything better, but at least he could focus on something else for now.

Her mouth was cold and tasted of chocolate. He wanted to savor every inch of it. It was crazy to kiss her out here, with the snow settling on his hair and his shoulders, and his feet cold in the snow, but he didn't care about any of that. She was here, in his arms again, as he had dreamed about all week.

She gave a soft little noise and wrapped her arms more tightly around him and Ruben pulled her close, wishing he could absorb all the cold and give her back only heat.

He was falling for this woman. He never would have

expected it, even a week ago, but Dani and her curious mix of vulnerability and defiance were somehow managing to wriggle into his heart.

He knew he couldn't keep her out here all night, not when the temperature was dropping and even now a fine layer of new snow covered where he had just shoveled, but he couldn't make himself end the kiss.

She was the one who finally pulled away after several long moments. Her nose and cheeks were rosy from the cold and she looked completely irresistible.

"I probably shouldn't have done that."

"You don't see me complaining, do you?" The only thing he wanted to complain about was that she had stopped.

She made a face. "You should be. I'm being completely irrational. I told you not even a week ago that we shouldn't kiss again, yet here I am breaking my own rule."

"You know what they say about rules. The only reason to make them is to break them."

She didn't smile, only continued looking at him with those shadows in her eyes. Was it really such a terrible thing that they had kissed again?

She shivered and he couldn't resist pulling her into his arms again, if only so he could steal a little more peace from having her in his arms. She nestled against him with a little sigh, her arms going around his waist and her cheek resting against his chest.

"Don't worry about it," he murmured. "That was a sympathy kiss. It doesn't count. I had a rough afternoon and you were only trying to help, which you did perfectly. I needed the reminder that I'm still alive and the world still contains magic and wonder, like Christmas trees and kisses from beautiful women. Thank you."

She gave a small half laugh he felt through the layers of his clothing. "Nice spin."

He did feel better. That heartbreaking scene would still haunt his dreams for nights to come, but she had helped counterbalance the tragedy through a bright, shining moment he would never forget.

He kissed the top of her head and she stayed there a few minutes longer, her arms around his waist while the snow swirled around them.

"I need to go inside."

"You do. It's freezing out here. I'm sorry I got distracted and didn't finish the hot cocoa you brought me."

She reached down and picked up the mug, already covered in a thin layer of snow. When she straightened, she gazed at him, eyes solemn and the wind tangling strands of her hair.

"I don't make smart decisions where men are concerned. I never have. I can't afford to let you be yet another mistake, Ruben. I have too much to lose here in Haven Point."

This wasn't the place he would have chosen for this conversation, outside in her driveway in the middle of a storm—especially not after the day he'd had, when his emotions were raw and exposed.

"What makes you think we would be a mistake?"

"Years of experience. Let's leave it at that. Look, I'm very attracted to you, Ruben. That is probably obvious. I'm having a very hard time resisting you."

"Good. For the record, I'm having a hard time resist-ing you, too."

She sighed. "We both have to try harder. I'm not good at relationships. Trust me when I say I'm not the kind of woman you need."

How could she know what kind of woman he needed, when he was only now beginning to realize it for him-self?

She was shivering and he wanted to tuck her against him again, to keep her warm and safe against the ele-ments and against those shadows in her eyes.

"We don't need to talk about this right now. Why don't you go inside and we can have this conversation another time?"

"I'd rather finish it now."

He didn't like the hard finality of her words. "Fin-ish it?"

"I want to make a life here in Haven Point with my daughters. They deserve so much better than I've been able to provide to this point. Your father has given me a chance at a future for them I never imagined. I can't screw that up. I *won't* screw that up."

"You're saying a relationship with me would have the potential to damage your future."

"I'm saying I can't take that risk."

"I sure would like to know who hurt you so badly."

She gave a ragged-sounding laugh. "I could probably come up with a long list, but at the top of it would be myself and my own choices. I'm trying to make decisions with my head these days, not with my heart."

"We've all made poor decisions, Dani. At some point

you might want to think about not beating yourself up about them any longer."

She gazed at him, the wind tangling her hair. When he saw she was shivering, he knew he couldn't push her about this now.

"Go on inside. I'll finish up out here and leave your snow shovel by the door."

"I… Thank you."

Gripping the mug of cocoa she had so sweetly fixed for him, she fled, leaving him outside in the cold.

Dani was absolutely the world's biggest sucker.

All day long, she had been telling herself she didn't need to go along with Ruben and the girls while they made that night's Secret Santa delivery. Her presence wasn't necessary anyway, and she really didn't want to be alone with him in his pickup truck.

Despite all that self-talk, here she was, trying her best to avoid Ruben's gaze while she put on her coat and gloves, Mia dancing around her.

She was the reason Dani was doing this, when she wanted to stay home where she would be safe. All afternoon, her daughter had begged and begged Dani to come with them.

You have to come, Mama. You have *to.*

She really didn't, but Mia was so excited at the prospect of helping her sister with the gift drop-off, she was practically bouncing off the walls. She had spoken of nothing else all day.

Dani didn't want anything to spoil Mia's joy in the

small act of service. If that meant Dani had to endure Ruben's company, she would figure out how to survive it.

"I can't wait," Mia said.

"You're going to have to be quiet, though," Silver reminded her. "I'm not sure you can do that."

"I can! I promise I can!"

"If you don't, you'll blow everything. They'll see us and the whole thing will be ruined."

Nervousness suddenly flitted across Mia's features, replacing any trace of excitement. "I think I can be quiet," she said, though her voice didn't seem remotely confident about the possibility.

Ruben knelt down to her level. "I have faith in you, sweetie. I know you can do it. You're going to be *great*."

Mia's exuberance returned and she threw her arms around his neck. Ruben gave a surprised laugh and hugged her back for a moment before he stood up.

"Everybody ready?"

No. Dani wasn't at all ready, but she had promised Mia.

"Let's go," she said, doing her best to ignore the simmering tension between them.

When she again climbed into his pickup truck, the familiar scent of him seemed to surround her like an embrace. She wanted to close her eyes and lean against the seat and simply savor it.

"I'll take you to the same place as last time," Ruben told Silver as he started up the truck. "Follow the same route you went last night. As I've said, from here on out, we'll probably have to mix things up a bit in case they're watching for you but I don't think you'll have trouble tonight, especially since we staggered the delivery time."

"Don't worry about this. We got it," Silver said, nudging her sister in the back seat.

Now that she had done it one night, Silver seemed to consider herself something of an expert. She was also more excited than she'd been the night before.

When Dani had asked her earlier if it had been difficult to keep quiet around her friends about the Secret Santa project, Silver had shrugged.

Not really, she had said. *I'm not hanging out with the twins much right now.*

Dani had tried to press, but Silver had become evasive, almost cagey.

They're busy with other friends right now, she'd finally said. *You're the one who told me friendships sometimes come and go at my age.*

Dani had said that, but she had also liked the twins and considered them a good influence on her daughter.

Oh, the capriciousness of teenage relationships. She had certainly seen that in her own life. It hadn't helped that she had moved schools so many times, with each different placement in the foster care system.

With luck, this would be Silver's final move during her school years. Her daughter would have plenty of time to make good and lasting friendships—unless Dani screwed everything up and they ended up having to leave Haven Point.

The storm of the night before had dropped about five inches of snow on Haven Point. Everything looked festive and charming, with icicles dripping off eaves and Christmas lights sparkling under a layer of white.

The sidewalks had been shoveled, which would make it easier for the girls to walk across the landscape.

"Good luck," Ruben said after parking in the same spot as the night before and turning off his lights.

"Here we go," Mia exclaimed as she climbed out of the vehicle.

"Remember," Silver said. "You have to zip your lips and keep up."

"I will," Mia promised.

Dani watched until they were out of sight, wishing she had gone with them. The time she dreaded was here. For the next ten minutes or so, she would have to be alone with Ruben.

She often had heard people say the phrase *the silence was deafening* but she had never really considered what that meant until right this moment. Usually she liked quiet moments of peace and reflection, but she would have described the hush inside Ruben's pickup truck at that moment as heavy, oppressive and excessively awkward.

She curled her fingers inside her gloves and was just about to say something banal about the weather when he spoke.

"Tell me about the girls' father."

The question coming out of the blue hit her like a punch to the gut. "Excuse me?"

"I don't even know the guy's name. I've been wondering all day about him and what he did to leave you so gun-shy about even kissing another man."

She caught her breath, not at all prepared for the question, for the world of pain and guilt it sent churning through her.

"He is not the reason I can't have a relationship with you, Ruben. At least not the only reason."

"But he's part of your past. A big part. What did he do to hurt you? Was he abusive?"

"I don't see how that's your business."

"You're putting something between us. If it's your husband, then it's my business."

"Maybe I just don't want a relationship right now. That's not a crime, Deputy Morales."

"No, it's not. But you've kissed me twice. There is something between us. I'd like to know the reason you're fighting it so hard."

"So because I kissed you twice, you think that gives you the right to know my entire life story?"

"Only the parts you want to tell me. I would like to get a clearer picture. You could at least tell me his name and how he died."

If she told him that, he would undoubtedly know everything—or at least could do an internet search and find the entire ugly picture.

She had legally changed her name and Silver's for a reason after her divorce. Mia had been born after that, so she had always been a Capelli.

Even then, she had worried that Tommy's choices, like toxic seaweed, would tangle up her and her girls and drag them under along with him.

Tommy had done nothing to support them. In fact, his choices had virtually guaranteed that he wouldn't be around to help raise his daughters, that he would be once more back in prison, paying for his crimes.

In her fury and hurt and fear, she had acted to protect

herself and her daughters from being tarnished by their father's actions. Why should he have the right to share his name with his daughters?

It had seemed one more way to put distance between them. She had wanted no connection with him after he broke parole and was returned to prison. It had seemed easier for her and the girls to share the same name.

How grateful she had been for that fortuitous decision, especially after the events of three months earlier. It made it that much harder to trace a connection between Mia and Silver and their father. She didn't want them growing up under the cloud of having such a notorious man for a father.

She looked at Ruben now. She didn't want to tell him. It reflected so poorly on her and her own lousy judgment, that she had once been naive enough to fall for a man who turned out to be capable of such terrible things.

Ruben was a dogged investigator. Something told her he wouldn't rest until she told him. He would wrangle the information out of her, one way or another.

Somehow she knew he wouldn't interrogate the girls, but she also knew Silver might let something slip. Despite Tommy's poor choices, Silver had loved her father and missed him. Dani could envision a scenario where she mentioned his name, then Ruben would find the information out anyway.

Maybe it was better for her to tell him herself—not to control the narrative, but to be clear with Ruben about just how very bad she was for him.

She didn't want to tell him. Some part of her wanted to hold on to the last few moments of his good opinion, before he knew the truth. That was cowardly, though. She owed him honesty. He had been kind to her and to her daughters. She also trusted that he wouldn't spread the information around.

She let out a breath and gathered her courage.

"His name was Tommy," she said. "And he was—"

The rear doors of his pickup opened before she could complete the sentence. Mia and Silver climbed in, both out of breath and laughing, and the moment was gone.

12

Her husband was *what?*

Ruben ground his teeth in frustration. What had she been about to tell him before the girls came back?

It was his own fault for bringing up the subject during a time when he knew they would only have limited opportunity to talk. What choice did he have, though, but to steal time when he found it? After the night before, she had been more than clear that she wasn't going to allow many private chats between them.

He felt as if he knew even less than he had before. All he had was a name, Tommy—and what the hell kind of grown man used a name like that, instead of Tom or Thomas?

He pushed his frustration aside for now. Maybe he would have an opportunity to suss out more information later.

"How did you do?" he asked Silver and Mia.

"That was the most fun *ever!*" Mia exclaimed.

"Did they see you?"

"Nope. Silver had me wait at the hiding place behind the bushes, then she went up and rang the doorbell, and ran so fast back to me. You should have seen how fast she ran!"

"That's great," Ruben said. "Good job."

"What did we give them?" Silver asked. "I forgot to ask you."

Ruben had to think back to the present his mother had showed him. "I think it was a CD of classic Christmas music to set the mood."

"Who even has CD players anymore?" Silver asked.

"I hope they do or they won't have any way of listening to it."

"Can I do it again tomorrow?" Mia asked.

"Well, here's the thing. Tomorrow night's going to be a busy time in Haven Point. It's the boat parade, if you'll remember, so I was thinking I would take care of tomorrow's delivery. Maybe I'll run over late tonight and leave it on their porch without ringing the bell so they find it first thing tomorrow morning when they go to get the newspaper."

"Who even gets a newspaper anymore?" Silver asked.

"You're killing me here," he said, which earned him only a grin in return.

She was, he thought as he started up the pickup and pulled away from the curb. When he wasn't looking, all of the Capelli females seemed to have wormed their way under his skin.

Silver was funny and smart, with a compassionate heart underneath all her brashness. Mia was completely adorable, with a joy for life and a generosity of spirit that he found completely irresistible.

And Dani.

He couldn't stop thinking about her. She haunted his dreams and his days. He looked forward to every moment he spent with her.

Yeah, he was falling hard for the woman and she was doing her very best to keep him at arm's length.

"I might do the same thing late Saturday night for Sunday's delivery, then we can get back to normal for Monday night. What do you think?"

"I guess," Mia said, disappointment threading through her voice. "I wanted to take their present to the door and ring the bell one time."

"We can see about that next week, okay? Anyway, you'll be having too much fun tomorrow at the boat parade to miss it too much. You're going, right? Trust me, this is something you don't want to miss."

"We're going, right, Mama? I want to see all the boats."

"I imagine we'll stop by at some point."

Dani had been subdued since she had told him the first name of the girls' father. Was what had happened to her marriage so very painful for her that she grieved at the mere mention of the man?

Ruben glanced across the cab as he pulled into their driveway. He took a chance, though he had a feeling she wouldn't be happy with him. What was the difference? She was already doing her best to push him away.

"Here's a crazy idea. Do you guys want to be *in* the parade?"

"In the parade?" Mia exclaimed in an awed voice, as if he had just asked her if she wanted to move permanently into Cinderella's Castle at Disneyland. "Yes!"

"One problem," Silver pointed out. "We don't have a boat."

"Problem solved, then. I have one, as you may recall. A big one, with room for at least fifteen people. I'm signed up for the big parade. My nephews are helping me decorate *The Wonder* tomorrow and they'll be riding along as well as my brothers and possibly my mom and dad. There's plenty of room, if you'd like to join us."

Dani stared at him and Ruben met her gaze steadily. This was the sort of thing friends and neighbors did with one another. They hung out and went on boat rides and had fun together.

She opened her mouth to respond. He could tell before any words even came out that she was going to come up with an excuse. Before she could, Silver piped up.

"I wouldn't mind being in the parade," her daughter said in a deceptively casual tone. Dani shifted her stare to her daughter, her mouth sagging a little more.

"Great. That's two of you," Ruben said cheerfully. "Dani, I guess it's up to you. What do you say?"

It really wasn't fair to gang up on her but he figured it was for a good cause. The girls *would* have fun participating in the boat parade and he would enjoy the chance to spend more time with them. Maybe he might even have the chance to find out a little more about this mysterious Tommy and the reason Dani looked so troubled when she spoke of him.

"Why would anybody want to take a boat ride in December with five inches of snow on the ground?" she asked.

"I have a good heater on the boat, with a cover that keeps out the elements. Plus, if it gets too cold, you can go down into the cabin, which is always toasty."

"Please, Mama? Please!" Mia begged.

"It really does sound fun." Silver added her voice.

Dani gazed at her girls in the back seat then sent him a sidelong look that told him she wasn't particularly pleased with him right now for dangling this possibility in front of her daughters before speaking with her about it.

"I don't know how I can say no. Even though I still think you're all crazy to want to be out on the water this time of year."

Anticipation curled through him, rich and delicious. "Great. Just make sure you bundle up. I owe you some hot cocoa so I'll make sure I have plenty on hand."

It was a deliberate reminder of their kiss the night before and he was rewarded by her delectable mouth tightening.

"What about churros?" Mia asked hopefully.

Ruben laughed. "I can't promise that, but I'll see what I can do about providing some kind of warm treat. The parade goes from the marina in Haven Point up to Shelter Springs. I'm going to shuttle my pickup and boat trailer up there with Javi so we won't have to ride the boat back. I can drive you home afterward."

"This is the best Christmas ever," Mia exclaimed. "I can't wait!"

"I hope you enjoy it," Ruben said.

And I hope your mother can find some way to forgive me for roping you all into it.

Despite Dani's promise, Ruben wasn't sure she and her daughters would show up.

The next night as the sun began to slide behind the Redemption mountain range, he moved around his boat, checking that all was in order before the parade.

"Maybe they're not coming," his brother Javier said.

"Maybe not." He tried not to show his disappointment. He assumed Dani would at least call to tell him she wasn't coming, but maybe she got tied up with a weekend emergency at the clinic.

"The first boats are going to be taking off soon," Javi said. "How much longer do you want to wait?"

"A few more minutes. We still have to wait for Mom and Dad anyway."

He checked his watch and the dock where he had told Dani to meet him. Maybe she had decided her girls were better off watching from the shore at their first Lights on the Lake Festival. He couldn't blame her for that.

Suddenly he spied three figures racing toward them and the tension in his shoulders instantly released.

"There they are," he told Javi.

"We're coming," Silver called. "Don't leave yet."

Ruben couldn't hide his grin as the three of them hurried down the dock.

"Careful," he called. "Grab the rope railing. It's icy in spots."

Dani reached a hand down to grab Mia's hand and said something to Silver, who used the rope as well to make her way to the boat.

"Sorry we're late," Dani said, rather breathlessly. "Traffic was crazy and then I couldn't find a place to park."

"No problem. I should have warned you. Actually I should have had you ride with my mom and dad so you didn't have to park. Sorry I didn't think about it."

"We're here now. That's the important thing."

It was. While he was thrilled his family was coming along on this inaugural parade entry for *The Wonder*, he was aware of a deep joy that Dani and her girls were here, too.

Javi helped them aboard.

"Oh," Mia exclaimed, clapping her mittened hands together. "Your boat looks so pretty."

"Thanks. I had help from Esme, Zach and Andy. They're all hanging out below deck where the food is, if you want to join them," he said to Silver.

She seemed to blush, confirming his suspicion that she had a little crush on his nephew Zach. "Okay. I'll do that."

He gestured to the stairs that went down to the tiny cabin below deck. The space was barely big enough for a small galley, a table with two bench seats that folded down to a bed, a little closet-sized toilet room and a berth the size of a double bed.

The Wonder was a wild extravagance, but he figured his brothers could take it out with their families if they wanted. His father might even get in on the fun, once he was officially retired.

His family lived on a huge lake. It seemed only natural to have something more substantial than a few kayaks, paddleboards and his dad's small fishing boat. His nephews couldn't wait for him to take them out on overnight fishing trips.

"Are you sure you're ready for this?" he asked Dani now.

"You should know I'm not a fan of boats."

"We'll be fine. I have life jackets for everybody. We'll be cruising just offshore so the parade watchers can see our lights and we'll be going slowly."

Another boat went past them, causing his to sway a little in the water, and Dani wobbled slightly. He caught her before she could fall. Heat kindled between them, even through her layers, and it was all he could do not to pull her into his arms.

Too bad they had an audience consisting of most of his close family members and hers.

"Your boat does look very nice. This must have taken some time." She took in the colored lights that outlined every angle and curve of the boat.

"Everybody came over early and helped me with the lights. Mateo is the one who insisted we bring along his light-up inflatable penguins."

"They're the perfect touch," she assured him. If he wasn't mistaken, that might almost be a smile he saw dancing there around her mouth. It made him want to kiss her again.

This was going to be a long boat ride if he had to spend the whole time keeping a tight rein on his impulses.

"I hope we all don't feel like we're in the North Pole, out on the water."

"Don't worry. Everything's warm below deck and inside the enclosure."

"Where do you want us?"

He had a feeling she wouldn't want to know the answer to that. "Let's grab you some life jackets, then you can choose where you want to sit. Wherever you're comfortable. We're only waiting for my parents."

"They're on the way," Javi said a moment later as Ruben was finding two life jackets in the right sizes that would fit over their outerwear. "Dad texted and said they were on their way from the parking lot. And here they are now."

Ruben saw his mother and father heading down the dock and had to sigh. Despite his repeated assurances to them that they needed to bring only themselves, his mother was carrying two large grocery bags in one hand and his father had a cooler. Ruben climbed down to help them onto the boat.

"Grab a seat, everybody," he said once they were on board, before taking his spot at the controls.

"Can I sit by you?" Mia asked. Without waiting for an answer, she plopped onto the seat next to his. "Mama, sit by me."

Dani looked at the other available seating some distance away, then back at her daughter. With an almost audible sigh, she took a seat just on the other side of Mia.

Ruben didn't miss the way his mother did a double take when she spotted Dani and Mia sitting by him.

"Hello, Dr. Capelli. Miss Mia. How fun that you're joining us!"

"Darling Dani. Hello," his dad said. "I do hope there's no animal emergency in Haven Point, with both veterinarians on board for the next few hours."

Dani looked stricken. "Oh. I didn't even think of that. Maybe I should get off."

"I was only joking," his father said. "You are not getting off, young lady. The animals will be fine. We have good techs. I'm not sure which one is on call tonight, but I'm sure whoever it is can handle things so you can enjoy yourself tonight. If there's an emergency, they can always call the vets in Shelter Springs."

"Have you eaten?" Ruben's mother asked. "I've got all kinds of snacks. Popcorn, licorice, sugar cookies."

"I love sugar cookies," Mia said, with no attempt at subtlety whatsoever. "They're my favorite."

"Then you better grab the first one. Here you go, sweetie." Myra reached into one of her bags and pulled out a container. She opened it and passed it around.

Ruben reached for a cookie just as his radio went off with instructions for the parade.

"It's showtime," he said. "Everybody ready?"

"As I'll ever be," Dani muttered.

He gave her a reassuring smile and started up *The Wonder*.

Her girls were having the time of their lives.

Mia hadn't moved from Ruben's side all evening. Every once in a while he would let her take the steering wheel or helm or whatever it was called on a boat of this size. She would grin at her mother and then wave exuberantly at the parade watchers along the shoreline.

When Dani had checked on Silver and Ruben's niece and nephews, she found them all laughing hysterically while they played card games below deck. They weren't really getting into the spirit of the holiday event down there, but she supposed that didn't really matter. They were socializing in their own way. Silver was enjoying herself and actually having fun. Dani couldn't ask for anything more.

"This is wonderful, isn't it?" Myra said, pitching her voice loud enough to be heard over the low rumble of the boat.

"It really is."

"Can I let you in on a secret?"

"Um, sure."

"I've always wanted to ride on one of the boats during the light parade. For years, we've watched from the shore and it's been great fun to see all the decorations the boat owners put into the parade, but I secretly wanted to be out here on the water. I have a sneaking suspicion that might be one of the reasons Ruben bought this thing. There's a chance I may have mentioned it to him last Christmas."

A soft warmth unfurled inside her. "That's very sweet."

"He has always been a wonderful son. One day, he's going to make some lucky woman very, very happy."

Myra gave her a meaningful sort of smile and any warmth inside her seemed to crystallize and shatter. That lucky woman would *not* be Dani. It couldn't be. His mother had to see that, didn't she? Why on earth would she ever think Ruben might be interested in *Dani*—a divorced woman with two children, who was barely holding her life together?

His mother seemed to be waiting for her to answer. Dani shifted uncomfortably. "I'm sure that's true. He's a very kind man."

"He's wonderful with children, too."

She looked over to where Ruben was showing Mia something on the control panels of the boat. She caught her breath, more charmed than she wanted to admit by the sight of the two of them together, Ruben, tough and masculine, Mia so sweetly joyful.

Oh, she wanted something like this for her daughters. A man to care for them, watch over them, love them.

Her chest ached. How could she take that chance again, with her lousy track record?

"There's only one problem with riding in the parade," Myra said, interrupting her thoughts.

"What's that?"

"Now I can't decide whether it's more fun to be *in* the parade or to watch the parade."

"Maybe you can alternate," she suggested.

"Great idea. Next year, you and I can sit on the shore and wave to all the boats as they pass by."

Dani loved the idea of being there a year from now, after so many years of feeling as if her life was on hold. Wouldn't it be wonderful to throw down roots, to adopt some of these traditions for her own family? Maybe she would start a Secret Santa project for her girls next year, drawing upon the experience they were gaining this year through helping Ruben.

Where would they be a year from now? If they were still in Haven Point, she couldn't imagine they would be riding on *The Wonder* again. The thought filled her with an odd sort of loss. She shook it off, annoyed with herself. Even if Ruben never invited her out on his boat again, she and her girls were here now.

How ridiculous, to squander *this*—the people, the food, the magic of the season—because she was worrying about some nebulous future. She wouldn't do it, she decided. At least not tonight.

When they arrived in Shelter Springs, the scene at the marina was noisy and chaotic, with boats queuing up to be loaded onto trailers at the ramp or floating up to the docks to let out their passengers.

"It might have been faster just to take *The Wonder* back to Haven Point on the water," Frank said.

"I should have realized the backup we would face here," Ruben said. He gave Dani an apologetic look. "This might take a while. I'm sorry. I can let you off and you can ride back to Haven Point with my parents. They shuttled my mom's SUV here earlier."

"You can't load the boat onto the trailer by yourself," Frank reminded him.

"No, but Javi is here. He and I can do it together."

"That's a good plan. We can let everybody off and they can drive down to the festival while we take care of the boat." Ruben's normally quiet brother Javier spoke up.

He had said little on the boat ride. The man was obviously going through something rough.

"Mama, can we go to the festival?" Mia said.

She should have thought this through better. Her car was parked at the marina in Haven Point, as Ruben had said he could give them a ride back to town after the parade. "I'm not sure if we'll be able to, by the time we're done helping Ruben with the boat. We'll see. If not, we'll make it next year."

"If you trust us to keep an eye on them, we could take your girls with us," Myra suggested.

Mia clapped her hands to show her approval of that idea and Dani didn't miss the way Silver nudged Esme with a grin and looked under her eyelashes at Zach.

"Are you sure?"

"Positive," Myra said. "We will *love* having them along with us. I only wish we had room to take you along, Dani, but we only have seat belts for seven in my SUV. I do hate for you to miss your first Lights on the Lake Festival."

"We still might make it in time," Ruben said. "Depends how long it takes to put out and drop the boat off at my place."

"Looks like there's a dock there where boats can let off their passengers. The queue is shorter there," his father suggested.

A few moments later, Ruben motored next to the dock and Javi jumped out to tie the boat and lend a hand while the passengers climbed out.

Dani's girls didn't seem too concerned about leaving

her behind, too excited at the fun ahead of them. "Bye, Mama," Mia said.

"You have to promise me you'll behave yourselves and stick with Dr. and Mrs. Morales."

"I will and Silver will, too, won't you?"

"Sure thing," Silver said.

Her older daughter seemed actually...happy. Happier, at least, than she had been since they came to town. A tight band around Dani's heart seemed to ease a little and she smiled at Silver.

"Keep an eye on your sister, okay? Here's some spending money, if you need it."

"Thanks." Silver shoved the twenty she gave her into her pocket then bounded off the boat.

"They'll be just fine. I promise, we won't let either of them out of our sight. You have my number, right?" Myra asked.

"Yes. I have yours and Dr. Morales's, plus Silver's."

"If you make it to the festival before it closes, call and we'll let you know where we are. If not, we can drop the girls off at your house or they can wait at our house, whichever you prefer."

She waved them off, then settled back on the boat.

Javi was going to climb back on, then pointed to the lineup of boats still waiting for the ramp. "That's a good hour of waiting in the water. You could make it back to the marina in Haven Point in about half that. Want me to drive your truck and trailer back and meet you there?"

Ruben turned to Dani. "We'll let you decide. Are you tired of the water or can you handle another half hour in *The Wonder* back to Haven Point? It will be faster now that the parade is done and there's not so much traffic on the water."

"I'm game for a return trip. Sounds like that would be the easier course. My car is at the marina in Haven Point anyway."

"Good plan. I guess we'll let you out here, then, Javi."

His brother hopped onto the dock, untied the rigging and tossed it back onto the boat. "I'll see you back in Haven Point, then."

Ruben waved, maneuvered the boat away from the dock then slowly made his way around the other boats in the marina and out to the open water of the big lake.

The moment they were clear of everyone, Dani suddenly realized just what she had signed up for. Thirty minutes alone with Ruben on a romantic moonlight ride on his boat.

Heaven help her.

"The parade was fun, but I have to admit, I like this better."

The boat seemed much quieter now as Ruben motored steadily back to town. There was an intimacy under the moonlight. A few other boaters had opted to make the return trip so they weren't alone on the water, but they all seemed to keep their distance.

"Are you warm enough?" he asked her. She had moved up to sit beside him, much to his delight.

"I'm fine. You were right, it's cozy here with this all-weather cover."

"That was one of the selling points. When you live

on a mountain lake, you've got a short boating season. Having a cover extends that, at least by a few months."

In the glow from the boat instruments, her features were a blur. What was she thinking? Did she think he had somehow arranged all of this to be alone with her? He hoped not—although he had to admit, he might have, if he'd been that smart.

"The girls seemed to have fun tonight. I think I even saw Silver laugh a time or two."

"Don't say anything," she said, "but I think my daughter has a crush on your nephew."

He smiled, remembering those innocent, uncomplicated days when liking a girl meant holding her hand between classes and maybe slipping notes into her locker.

"Zach is a good kid. Don't worry. Even if he likes her, too—which I think he does—he'll be respectful."

"Your family is pretty hard to resist."

"Then why keep trying so hard? They like you, too. As much as you let anybody like you, anyway."

She gave him a long look. "What is that supposed to mean?"

Now he'd done it. Opened his mouth, when he meant to simply enjoy the ride with her. "Never mind. Forget it."

"No. I'd like to know."

He sighed. "Only that you seem to go out of your way to keep people at a careful distance, almost as if you're afraid to let anybody get too close. My family. The women of the Haven Point Helping Hands. Andie told me they've invited you to join them, but you're really good at making excuses. I just wonder why you're trying so hard."

She gripped her hands tightly together in her lap. "I didn't grow up in a nice, safe place like Haven Point, where they have light parades to celebrate the holidays and everybody knows everybody else."

"I know. You grew up in Queens. But there are good people everywhere. Surely you had plenty of nice people around you there. Teachers. Neighbors. Friends. Your own family."

Her hands curled in her lap and she gazed out at the boat lights cutting through the water. "I'm not like you, Ruben, with a wonderful, warm, loving family that gets together on Sundays and spends holidays together and does nice things for neighbors, just for the fun of it. That's a completely foreign way of life to me. I'm…struggling to adjust."

"What was your childhood like, then?"

She looked out at the moonlight slicing across the cold lake. "Not pretty. I went into the foster care system when I was eight years old and stayed there until I got pregnant with Silver at seventeen, mostly to escape."

That explained so many things about her. Ruben's heart ached and he fought the urge to turn off the motor, float there in the water and just hold her, as she had done for him only a few nights earlier.

"What happened to your parents?"

"My father walked out when I was two. I have no idea where he went or why and to be honest, I don't care. He lost the right to be considered any kind of father a long time ago. Mom tried her best to keep things together until she got sick. Hepatitis C. It hit her hard and she died before she could get a liver transplant."

"I'm so sorry," he murmured.

"One day she wasn't at the apartment when I came home from school and a neighbor told me she collapsed on the stoop and was taken away in an ambulance. Social services came right after that and a cold stick of a woman told me my mother, my only remaining parent, had died. She told me to gather a few things I cared about so she and a police officer could take me to a new house."

His throat ached and he finally couldn't resist following up on his earlier impulse. He reached out a hand and pulled her closer to him. He thought she might yank away but after one frozen moment, she stayed there, cradled under one arm while he maneuvered *The Wonder* through the dark waves with the other.

"Was it...rough? Foster care, I mean." He had to ask.

"There was no physical or sexual abuse, if that's what you're wondering. I know that can happen but I suppose I was luckier than some. I had a few close calls in the latter area but I knew enough to sleep with a kitchen knife close by and nobody tried anything twice."

His hand tightened on the wheel as a mental picture emerged of her, slim and dark and pretty, sleeping with a kitchen knife. He hated even thinking about it.

"Some of it was good. I spent three years with a wonderful woman who loved the foster children she cared for, until she became too frail to continue."

"It's good you had that, at least."

"It's tough on a kid, always knowing every situation is temporary. Wondering when the call would come and you'd have to grab your garbage bag of belongings and head to the next temporary place. With every new family, I would vow that I wouldn't cause trouble, but somehow it never quite worked out."

"Oh, Dani. I'm so sorry."

This glimpse into her past was both heartbreaking and illuminating. So many things about her made more sense now. She had a hard time making connections because deep down in her psyche some part of her was in a constant state of worry that they would be yanked away.

She had trusted him enough to tell him this part of her past, something he didn't think she shared very easily.

"You said you got pregnant with Silver at seventeen, mostly to escape."

Her shoulders tensed beneath his arm and she slipped away from him. Cool air rushed in to take her place.

"I was…looking for a happy ending. The safety and security I lost when I was eight."

"I take it you didn't find it."

She laughed, a sound without amusement. "You could say that. I might as well spill all my secrets. You want the ugly truth about me, Ruben. Fine. Here you go. I married an ex-convict."

He glanced over, sensing that wasn't the worst of what she wanted to tell him.

"Did you?" he said mildly.

"Tommy had served six months in jail for grand theft when we married. I knew that. He told me it was a misunderstanding, that he had made a mistake and trusted the wrong people, and I believed him. Mostly because I needed to believe him."

He had seen that in the loved ones of people who ran into trouble with the law. They convinced themselves all the evidence was wrong, that their loved one had a bad rap and the system was rigged against them.

Ruben knew there were cases where innocent people were convicted of crimes they didn't commit. They were the outliers, though. As a law enforcement officer, he wanted to believe that the system usually worked the way it was supposed to and those who committed crimes ended up right where they belonged.

"Tommy and I had two good years after Silver was born. I thought he had put the past behind him. He had a steady job as a mechanic and we were happy, I thought—until the day he was arrested along with three of his friends for organizing a luxury auto theft ring and chop shop in Jersey. Two members of the crew made the mistake of carjacking a Mercedes belonging to the wife of a federal judge, so this time Tommy was sent upstate. He wasn't actually part of the carjacking but because this was his second arrest as an adult after numerous juvenile offenses and because he was considered the leader of the enterprise, the one calling the shots, he was sentenced to five to ten years."

Not a small chunk. The charges must have been serious. "That's a stiff sentence."

"I tried to tell myself we could still make things work. That he would change and be the sweet man I knew when he got out again. I stayed married to him. I wrote to him every week while I was struggling to survive as a mom on my own, desperately trying to hang on to my scholarship and stay in college. Every Sunday, I would pack up Silver and we would take the train upstate to visit him."

He could picture her, defiantly resilient, trying to make the best of things. His heart ached for all the things she didn't say, the sacrifices she must have had to make and the loneliness she must have endured.

"He served four years. When he got out, I thought things would finally be different. That's what he promised me, over and over. He had vocational training as an electrician in prison and was going to make a new start."

"But he didn't?"

"You probably know how hard it is for felons on the outside. I think he tried for a while, but…something had changed in him. Or maybe I had changed during that time on my own. I don't know. Six months after he got out, I discovered he was hanging with his old crew, staying out late, being evasive about where he'd been. I kicked him out. I filed for divorce and left New York for Boston and vet school. Two months later, I found out I was pregnant with Mia, but by then Tommy was in trouble again and had been found in violation of his parole."

"He went back to prison?"

"For four more years." She was quiet. "He came to visit the girls once when he got out and I barely recognized him from the man I had once loved."

"That must have been tough, being on your own with two little girls while going through graduate school."

"Somehow the girls and I survived. During my second year of school, I started corresponding with your father and eventually he offered me this internship when I finished, with the potential to purchase his practice if

I liked it here, so we moved here right after graduation. This was my chance to give the girls the life I always dreamed about."

"You're doing exactly that."

"I thought I was. But somehow the ghosts of our past mistakes never quite leave us alone, do they?"

He thought of his own mistakes on the job, the moments when he hadn't been fast enough to react or had misjudged a situation or underestimated a suspect.

"They don't. But life has a way of helping us eventually make our peace with them."

"I hope so. But I'm not there yet."

She was quiet. "I don't want to tell you, but I think you need to know the rest of it."

The rest of it? What more could there be? Judging by the way she twisted her hands in her lap and wouldn't meet his gaze, it had to be something she considered terrible. On impulse, he turned the boat engine off, wanting to focus on her without the distraction of having to maneuver the boat. They floated there on the water, rocking gently on the waves.

Under other circumstances, he would have found it restful and beautiful there on a cold December night, being safe and dry here inside the shelter, but the tension shimmered between them.

"There. Go ahead. Now I can give you my full attention."

"It's bad, Ruben. So bad."

"Tell me," he urged. He reached out for her hand and after a startled moment, she entwined her fingers through his.

"After that last visit a few years ago, I severed contact with Tommy," she said slowly. "I didn't know where he was until I heard his name on the news three months ago."

Three months ago. Right after she had come to Haven Point, around the time she began to shut herself off from participating in community events and started turning down invitations.

Her hand was trembling, he realized. All of her was trembling.

"Why was his name on the news?"

"You heard it, too, Ruben. Everyone in the country did. One lovely September afternoon, he walked into a bank in Brooklyn and pulled a gun on the tellers. He ended up killing a guard and two police officers in a shoot-out as he tried to escape, before he was eventually gunned down."

Ruben's gut clenched. He remembered that case, though it happened across the country. Every member of law enforcement grieved when any of their own died in the line of duty and these deaths had seemed particularly senseless.

"Tommy DeLuca," he said.

"That's right. My ex-husband—the father of my beautiful girls—is Tommy DeLuca."

13

As she might have expected, Ruben went rigid at her words.

Three months earlier, Tommy's name had been bandied about on every news channel. He had been talked about in the same disgusted tones people used when discussing mass shooters, white supremacists, violent dictators.

He had become the current face of evil, a representative of everything wrong in the world—until the next newsmaker did something heinous and wiped him from memory.

Ruben remembered. She could tell by his reaction and the sudden tension that seemed to vibrate from his skin to hers where they held hands.

"DeLuca. Not Capelli," he said, his voice gruff.

She pulled her hand away and curled her fingers into a fist, wishing she could hold that heat inside. "I legally changed my name and Silver's back to my maiden name during the divorce proceedings, before Mia was born. I can't tell you how many times I've been grateful for that decision. Never more so than three months ago."

Water lapped against the boat. Normally the sound would have been calming, but not at this moment when her emotions were raw and exposed.

"I told your father the moment I heard the news, of course. When he first offered me the internship, I felt I had to tell him about Tommy—that he had served time during our marriage and some of the things he had done—but I don't know if I ever mentioned his name. I had to tell him everything after…after Tommy killed those men, who were only doing their job."

"What did my father say?"

That was yet another reason she adored Frank Morales, for his steady, kind support while she had been reeling in shock.

"He said I couldn't take on the burden of what my ex-husband had done. They were his choices, not mine. As far as your father was concerned, none of it mattered."

"Sounds about right."

"What else could he say? I was already here and had started working at the clinic."

"That wouldn't matter to my father. He says what he means."

"He is wonderful, yes. I was beyond grateful for his support, but he is the only other one who knows. You understand why I don't want this to get out. Imagine how people would treat the girls if they knew about their father."

He stared. "Why would anyone treat them any differently? They had nothing to do with Tommy's actions. None of it is their fault. Or yours, either."

"There you go, wearing those rose-colored glasses again. Of course people will treat me differently!"

"You've been divorced since before Mia was born. At least six years ago. And you've said he hasn't been part of your life in that time. How are you responsible for his actions?"

"You're being irrational if you don't think people will think less of my judgment for having married and had two children with a cop killer. Of course they will!"

He jaw hardened. "Then they're idiots. Idiots you don't need in your world. No one should blame you for your ex-husband's bad acts. If they do, they're not people you need in your life."

He couldn't really be that naive. He was in law enforcement. He had to know that even baseless whispers and finger-pointing about a person could ruin lives.

She had married Tommy. That fact was indisputable. She had been married to him for almost six years, together almost eight, though he had been in prison for more than half of that time. They had created two amazing daughters together.

No matter how she tried to excuse it in her own head by telling herself she was too young to know better, by comforting herself with the reminder that she had divorced him as soon as she realized he wasn't going to change, a grim fact remained.

She had once loved a man capable of terrible things.

"You and the girls are not responsible for what Tommy DeLuca might have done," Ruben said again.

"That's easy to say. You've never had people fire you from a job when they find out your husband was in prison. Or mothers in your apartment building not allow their children to play with yours. That was only when his crimes involved robbery. This is so much worse. He killed three people. Of course people will judge me and the girls for that. I don't sleep at night, worried if the next day will be the day someone figures it out and tells the…the world."

Her voice wobbled a bit on the last sentence, much to her chagrin. Ruben stepped closer, his expression intense.

"Small-minded people might want to tarnish you with the same brush. It's a natural hazard of living in a small town that one of the favorite pastimes is talking about your neighbors. I can't promise you or the girls won't ever face hurtful gossip, but I can promise it won't come from anybody you need in your life. No one should ever blame you or Silver or Mia for what their father did. My family won't. I certainly don't. Come here."

Before she realized what he intended, he pulled her into his arms, tugging her against his chest. She wouldn't let herself cry again, but thick, heavy emotions clogged her throat.

He was such a good man, kind and warm and generous. If everyone in Haven Point were like Ruben and his family, she would have no worries about telling people about her past. Some were, she knew. She had met other kind people here and wanted to give people the benefit of the doubt.

She was afraid. She knew it and was ashamed of it but couldn't seem to help it. She had spent so many years in foster care trying to be perfect that she was afraid to show people her imperfections, real and perceived.

What about those who could only see her ex-husband's crimes when they looked at her? She didn't want her girls to carry that stigma.

She let him hold her for a long moment, knowing this would be the last time she could allow it. His heat seeped through her coat and his arms enfolded her in strength and comfort.

How she wished things could be different, that she had made other choices at seventeen and didn't have this dark cloud hanging over her now because of those decisions.

"Ruben," she began, but whatever she intended to say was lost when he leaned down and silenced her with his mouth pressed against hers.

She should have immediately pulled away but she didn't have the strength. How could she possibly resist the temptation to kiss him one more time?

The boat rocked softly on the waves, pushing her toward him then away again, and she could hear the distant sound of other boats. Some part of her knew they needed to be heading back to Haven Point so she could find her children at the festival.

She pushed the knowledge aside for now. She could have this moment, couldn't she? A tiny slice of time to kiss this man who made her feel things she thought she had put away forever.

He deepened the kiss and she pressed herself against him, lost in the delicious sensations that pushed away the darkness.

They could make love, out here on the water.

The thought tangled her breath and left her light-headed.

There was a bed in the berth down below. She had seen it when she checked on Silver earlier. They could go below while the waves rocked the boat and she could be with him fully, as everything inside her ached for.

And then what?

They couldn't be together beyond this moment. It would be hard enough to push him away, as she knew she must. She couldn't make things harder on either of them by deepening their intimacy.

She closed her eyes, hating what she had to do but aware she had no choice. She wrenched her mouth away, though it was just about the hardest thing she'd ever done.

"Stop. Please, Ruben. Stop. We can't do this."

"Why not?"

"I told you. I make terrible decisions where men are concerned. Now you know just how terrible those decisions are. I can't drag you into my mess."

"I'm in it, like it or not. I care about you, Dani. I'd like to see where this goes between us."

She closed her eyes. "You have to be realistic here. Put away those glasses and look at me. What would the sheriff or others in the department think if they found out you were seeing a woman whose ex-husband had killed two of your own?"

That seemed to soak in. He let out a heavy breath

and straightened. "I hope they would be smart enough to know you can't be held responsible for the actions of someone who hasn't been part of your life for years."

"What if they don't see it that way?"

He gazed at her. "You're really going to let this come between us?"

"There is no *us*, except for a few kisses." Her hands were shaking and she folded them together, her heart aching. "That's all we have. All we'll ever have."

"Why? Because you made a mistake once and gave your heart to the wrong man?"

When she didn't answer, he reached for her hand, trapping her fingers before she could pull them away.

"Would it make a difference if I tell you I'm falling in love with you?"

His low words burst through her like Roman candles trailing a shower of sparks. She wanted to reach for them and hold on tight, to tuck them against her where she could treasure them forever.

Reality splashed over her just seconds later as if someone had doused her with that cold lake water.

"You're attracted to me. You're not in love with me."

"I'm thirty-three years old, Daniela. I've been attracted to plenty of women. I've never been in love with a single one of them, until now."

She wanted to believe him, to throw herself back into his arms right here on *The Wonder* and stay forever.

She couldn't do it. She didn't dare take the chance.

She never should have kissed him that first night. She had somehow known this man had the potential to break her heart—not because of anything he did but because she didn't have the strength or courage to reach for the future they might have together.

She swallowed, hating herself all over again. "I'm flattered, believe me, but I... I'm not interested in a relationship," she lied. "Not with you and not with any man. You've been very kind to me and my daughters and I'm so grateful but...it has to end. I thought we could be friends but I can't see how that's possible. Not with this...this heat between us that we can never act upon."

"It's more than attraction and you damn well know it."

"I can't, Ruben. I'm sorry. Can you just take me back to Haven Point now? I need to find my daughters."

He gazed at her for a long moment. She couldn't see his expression through the dim light but she could feel the tension radiating off him.

She wanted to tell him she was sorry, that she didn't mean any of it. She wanted to step back into his arms and kiss him again until nothing else mattered. Instead, she forced herself to move away from him, to the other seat on the boat.

He opened his mouth to say something but closed it again and started up the boat, pulled up the anchor and headed back to Haven Point in silence.

Ruben usually enjoyed his regular visits to Haven Point Middle School, but he wasn't looking forward to this one.

If he could have passed the emergency call off to someone else, he would have, but he was the school's liaison with the sheriff's department. It was his responsibility.

With only one more school day before Christmas vacation after this one, the anticipation at the school was as noticeable as the smell of corn dogs coming from the cafeteria. A big Christmas tree dominated the entryway, paper chain garlands were draped around the interior doorways and white paper snowflakes dangled from the ceilings.

He must have just missed the bell going off between classes, since the halls were clogged with students laughing, looking at their phones, shoving each other.

He saw at least a dozen Santa hats and as many ugly Christmas sweaters.

As he made his way to the office, he waved at several students he knew and fist-bumped a couple more. He was just about to push open one of the double glass doors into the office when Silver Capelli walked past.

"Oh!" she exclaimed. "Hey, Ruben." She actually smiled at him, which he considered amazing progress, considering where they had been a few weeks earlier.

He let the office door close again and moved out of the way of people going in and out so he could talk to her. "How's it going?"

"Pretty good. School is almost out for Christmas break. Only three periods and one day left, then we're off for two weeks."

He remembered that jubilation leading into a long break from school. Nothing else compared to it. How did grown-ups lose that excitement somewhere along the way?

Ruben looked around to make sure no one else was in earshot. "And only five more nights of our little project. How's that been going?"

She gave the same furtive scan of the area before shifting her gaze back to him. "Pretty good. I haven't been caught yet, if that's what you're asking. Mia and I are pretty sneaky."

Ruben had been shut out of his own Secret Santa deliveries a few days earlier, though he wasn't sure if the reason had more to do with his schedule becoming more chaotic leading up to the holidays or because Dani was purposely avoiding him.

He only knew that earlier in the week he had to work a late shift to cover for another deputy and asked if Silver could handle the delivery without him. Dani had suggested he leave all the gifts at their house so they could make the deliveries when it was convenient for her family's schedule, instead of his.

He couldn't manage to come up with a good argument. She was right, his work shifts had become crazy.

It made sense to hand it over to her and her girls. At least this way, the secret gifts his mother had prepared didn't all have to be delivered in the middle of the night when he was done with work.

Despite the logic, he couldn't help feeling excluded.

"Good job," he said to Silver. "My schedule should be a little more regular from now until Christmas Eve. Do you want me to take over now? I can probably handle the rest."

"No. I've got it," she said. "Mia would be heartbroken if we couldn't finish out the whole twelve days. She gets a real kick out of it."

He had a feeling Mia wasn't the only one. "Well, let me know if you change your mind. I can take a night or two."

"I think we're good. I need to get to my English class

before the tardy bell rings. I'll see you later, Ruben." She flashed him a quick smile. "Merry Christmas."

"Bye."

He watched her meet up with a couple of girls and start walking down the hall. She seemed to be talking and laughing with them, a far cry from the sullen girl she had been a few weeks earlier.

She had her mother's smile. He hadn't noticed it before, but now it made his heart ache.

He now knew what it felt like to bang his head against a wall again and again.

While her daughter was becoming friendlier and more comfortable around him, Dani had moved in the opposite direction. After their night on his boat during the Lights on the Lake Festival almost a week earlier, she had gone out of her way to avoid him. The warm, caring woman he had come to know over the past few weeks had once more become prickly and unapproachable.

He sighed. His life had seemed uncomplicated a few weeks ago. Now he was so tangled up over Dr. Daniela Capelli, he wasn't sleeping well, he was short-tempered, and he seemed to have lost any anticipation and joy for the upcoming holidays.

"Ruben. There you are."

The assistant principal at the middle school marched toward him, his features tight and his belly hanging over his belt.

Todd Andrews was around Ruben's age and they went to school together. Ruben remembered him as a sanctimonious jerk even in elementary school, when Todd used to volunteer every week to be the hall monitor so he could write up infractions committed by anybody he didn't like.

As far as Ruben was concerned, he hadn't changed much. If anything, a little power had made things worse.

"Hey, Todd," he said casually.

"I called in a report nearly forty minutes ago. What took you so long?"

The temper that seemed on a knife's edge these days threatened to flare. He had been working sixteen-hour days all week and was deep in the middle of an ugly domestic abuse case that was particularly heartbreaking this time of year. Not to mention that the middle school was a fifteen-minute drive from Shelter Springs in good weather and right now a storm was slowing traffic.

Apparently when the assistant principal of the middle school called, Ruben was supposed to speed over with his lights and siren blaring.

"Things are a little hectic this close to the holidays, Todd. I was on another call. What's going on? The dispatcher said you wanted to report another theft."

The middle school had been experiencing a rash of thefts, with the PE lockers being particularly hard hit since students often didn't bother to lock up their belongings.

"This is a little more than a missing cell phone! We have a serious situation. Maybe I need to speak to Sheriff Bailey."

"You could do that," Ruben said slowly, "but since I'm the department liaison to the middle and high schools in Haven Point, I'm afraid he would only pass your call on to me. You might as well start where you're going to end up. With me."

They had been over the subject of protocol and lines of authority before. It didn't seem to make any difference. Todd had always disliked Ruben and seemed to think going over his head to Marshall—someone he *also* disliked—would somehow solve all his problems.

"Since I'm here," Ruben said, "you might as well tell me what's going on, then I can consult with Sheriff Bailey."

He could tell by the other man's pursed lips that Todd didn't particularly like that idea. Too bad. Ruben had more important things to worry about than the man's ego. He was here to do his job.

Todd glowered. "I can't stress enough the gravity of this matter. The spirit club has been raising money to send to victims of the latest hurricane. We keep a jar in the office and people have been dropping off their extra change all month, until they had collected more than $250 in donations."

"That's impressive. Good for the spirit club."

"I would agree, except right after third hour, the whole jar disappeared. It was here before that, then it was gone. I thought perhaps a member of the spirit club leadership might have taken it to count the donations, since their fund-raising campaign ends today. They're supposed to talk to me first before handling the jar but students don't always follow procedure."

Much to Todd's dismay, Ruben was certain.

"I'm assuming you checked with them all."

"Of course I checked with them all! I called each one out of class and they assured me they hadn't seen the jar.

Someone took it. Someone unauthorized. You need to move fast. I would suggest you put the whole school on lockdown until you find the culprit."

Ruben gave an inward groan. He couldn't put the whole school on lockdown over a missing jar of change. The very idea was ridiculous.

"Let's hold off on that while I ask a few questions first," he said. "Do you have any suspects?"

"I have four hundred suspects. They're called students."

Yeah. This was the reason he didn't like the guy. Todd always saw the bad in people, which Ruben considered a lousy character trait when it came to dealing with middle school students.

"Any chance you could narrow that down a little? You have security cameras in here, don't you?"

The other man's lips thinned further. "We do, but unfortunately they've been malfunctioning since last week and we haven't been able to get the district IT person in to take a look. Principal Garcia tried to call before she left town earlier this week and couldn't get anyone. Everybody seems to be backed up this time of year. Believe me, if the cameras were functional, I would have looked there first before involving the sheriff's department."

Ruben found this disheartening on several levels, especially the part about the principal being gone. Vicki Garcia was far more reasonable, with a kind heart and bucketloads of patience.

"That's too bad. I was hoping for an easier resolution."

"We need to search everyone. If you won't authorize a full lockdown, I think we should at least start a locker-by-locker search until we find the missing jar. It's a little big for students to hide under their shirts."

Ruben could think of several problems with that suggestion. While the law was vague about whether students had any expectation of privacy or protection from law enforcement against searches on school property and the school district had its own rules, the sheriff's department policy was clear. Without a warrant—or in this case, four hundred warrants—he could only search school lockers if he had strong and compelling evidence of wrongdoing.

Not only that, most of the students he knew kept all their belongings in backpacks and carried everything from class to class. He suspected half of them didn't even know their locker combinations.

Ruben tried to head off Todd's exuberance. "Let me do a little digging before we jump the gun. I need to talk to the office staff and see if they can give me some names of people who might have been in the office around the time the jar disappeared."

"Don't you think I've already asked the secretaries?" Todd demanded. "They don't know anything."

If he spoke to them with that kind of derogatory tone, Ruben completely understood why no one would want to tell the man what they knew. "I have to follow procedure. You, of all people, should appreciate that. Protocol demands I interview potential eyewitnesses myself, even if they have already been interviewed by school staff. I know it's a pain, but I can't break the rules."

The vice principal looked torn between his deep and abiding love for rules and his insistence that his way was the best. "It's a big waste of time, if you ask me," he fi-

nally said. "You would do better to at least search the
backpacks and lockers of the ones we've had the most
trouble with this year. The likeliest suspects. For instance,
I hear you had some vandalism at your place a few weeks
ago and that our new student from the East Coast was
involved. Maybe you should start there."

Okay, now Ruben wanted to punch the bastard.

"Why would you think that?"

"There's a rumor going around that her family is connected—organized crime."

"Mafia? Really? Because she has an Italian surname?
That's a little xenophobic and racist, don't you think,
Todd? I'm surprised at you."

The other man flushed. "Setting aside the rumors I
have picked up about her past and that her father was the
leader of a crime syndicate, there remains the fact that
she vandalized your home and that of one of our most
beloved faculty members. Gertrude told me all about it.
I don't think it's a coincidence that Miss Capelli moves to
our school and suddenly we have a rash of thefts throughout the school year. And now this."

"I think you're jumping to conclusions with no basis
in fact. Let me do my job, Todd. I'll start by talking with
the office support staff and we can go from there."

He turned away without giving the man a chance to
argue his point, hoping against hope that Silver Capelli
had been at the exact opposite end of the school building when the jar of money disappeared.

"Any progress?" Marshall asked when Ruben called
to check in an hour later.

"Nothing. I'm stumped. How do you want me to proceed?"

"Not with a lockdown and not with a person-by-person search, that's for sure. Your instincts are right on. Call in Todd's prime suspects and see if you get any hint of anything that doesn't feel right. These are kids. It should be pretty easy to tell if they're lying."

"You have kids. Can you always tell when Christopher isn't telling you the truth?"

"Good point," Marshall said. "Not always, but he usually has a tell or two. Watch for those who won't meet your gaze and also the overlong and too-complicated answers. You know the drill."

"Yeah. Thanks. I'll keep you posted."

He hung up from Marsh and looked over his list of suspects. He had spoken with all the staff and student office helpers, taking down names of everyone who had been in and out of the office around the time the jar had disappeared.

One name stood out. Silver Capelli. She had come in between classes during that time frame, claiming she had a verbal message from another student that one of the counselors wanted to speak with her about her schedule. That message, if it really had been given to Silver, appeared to have been a mistake. None of the three counselors claimed to have summoned her.

He had a grim, tight feeling in his chest. He had to find another suspect. If Silver had taken the donation jar, it would devastate her mother. He couldn't imagine having to be the one to tell Dani that Silver was on the hook for this.

With renewed determination, he headed out front to speak to the office staff one last time before he started going through the list of suspects and calling students back to speak with him.

Before he could reach the desk, the vice principal shoved open the double doors, carrying a large jar in one arm and dragging Silver behind him with the other.

"Ha! I found it," Todd declared, giving Ruben a triumphant look. "I haven't had time to count it but I hope it's all there, all $250 and change. And guess where I found it? In Miss Capelli's locker, where I suggested we look an hour ago, if you'll recall."

Ruben's heart dropped. She looked terrified and confused, but with that come-at-me defiance he had been used to seeing until lately.

"Sil," he said slowly. "Tell me you didn't do this."

The vice principal snorted "Of course she did it! The evidence was right there in her locker!"

"Did you have a warrant to search my locker?" she demanded.

"I don't need a warrant." He gave her an evil grin. "School administrators can search students' lockers and belongings at will, as long as they can show credible evidence of wrongdoing."

"What was your credible evidence?" Ruben asked calmly, trying his best to keep his temper contained. "This is the first I'm hearing of anything beyond suspicion."

The Silver he had come to know over the last few weeks wouldn't do something like that. Sure, she had vandalized *The Wonder* and a few other places. But she had also pitched in to clean up her mess. He sensed Silver used brashness and attitude to hide her inherent insecurities, like her mother did.

"While you were busy talking to the secretaries, I received an anonymous tip telling me exactly where to look for the missing money. Apparently someone saw her hiding it in her locker."

"How did you receive this so-called tip?" Ruben asked.

"A phone call in my office. And before you ask, no, I don't know the number. It was blocked. All I know is that the caller was a female student, obviously trying to disguise her voice by speaking in a false lower octave."

"It doesn't matter who called you," Silver said, her expression a mix of anger and fear. "They were lying. I didn't steal that stupid jar and I have no idea how it ended up in my locker."

Todd snorted. "So it just mysteriously appeared there and you had nothing to do with it. We're supposed to believe that?"

"I don't care what you believe. It's the truth. I didn't do it. And whose dumb idea was it anyway to leave a big jar full of money out in a public area full of middle school students? You should have just put a sign on it saying Take Me."

Ruben had to agree she had a point but Todd apparently saw things differently. His features turned an ugly shade of purple.

"That's quite enough out of you, young lady," he said, fierce dislike in his voice.

Why the hell did the man get a job in education when it was clear he couldn't stand the students? Todd was a bully, plain and simple. A clean-cut, by-the-rules bully. The only trouble was, with the more reasonable principal gone, this particular bully was calling the shots and Ruben didn't know what to do about it.

"I don't know how they did things where you came from," Todd said, "but here in Haven Point we don't tolerate this kind of behavior."

Silver folded her arms across her chest and gave him a scornful look. "Really? In my whole life, nobody ever told me it was against the rules to steal things. Back in Boston, we got extra credit for it."

"Silver, your sarcasm is not helping," Ruben said.

She turned a pleading look in his direction. "I didn't do this. I would *never.* I'm telling you, somebody had to have planted that in my locker."

Ruben was beginning to believe the same thing. He found it highly suspicious that she had been given a mysterious summons to speak with a counselor who never asked for her, right around the time the jar went missing.

Coincidences in his line of work were rarely that.

"Why would somebody set you up? Do you have any enemies?"

She gave him a pitying sort of look. "I'm new to the school when everybody else has been here their whole lives. I have an accent that's somewhere between Boston and Queens, I have purple hair and I wear clothes that won't catch on here for at least three years. Of *course* I have enemies!"

"If you have enemies, it's because you haven't tried to make friends," Todd said in a snide voice. "Face it, Miss

Capelli, you've had a bad attitude since the first day you arrived at Haven Point Middle School."

Silver gave a little shuddering breath and Ruben knew instinctively she was close to tears. Damn it. She would *hate* crying in front of the vice principal, as much as her mother had hated crying in front of him.

He wanted to wrap his arms around her and promise her everything would be okay, that he would do everything he could to figure out a way to make this right, but he was helpless in the situation. All evidence pointed against her and at this point, Ruben had no proof someone else was behind the theft.

"Can you narrow that list down a little?" Ruben said. "Are you sure you can't identify the person who told you a counselor wanted to see you earlier?"

She shook her head. "I think it might have been a seventh grader. I didn't know her. She just said someone told her to tell the girl with purple hair that she had to go to the office, so I did."

"That's quite a convenient story," Todd said with a sneer.

"Ask Mrs. Hobbs, the counselor. I showed up and she didn't know a thing about me coming in, since she never asked anyone to get me."

"How do we know you didn't just make up the whole thing? It's more likely that you came up with some farfetched story about someone telling someone to get you for Mrs. Hobbs, all so you could have an excuse to be in the office and steal the jar of money."

"But I didn't," she said. "Ruben, you believe me, don't you?"

He could say nothing, not with Todd there ready to jump on his every word.

"It looks pretty bad, kid."

"Stealing is grounds for immediate disciplinary action. Automatic suspension, at the very least, while we determine what charges will be filed in the criminal court."

"Criminal court? But I didn't take anything!"

"The proof was in your locker."

"I told you, someone else must have put that in there. It wasn't me."

Ruben believed her, without question, but he knew Todd wouldn't see things the same way. It was up to Ruben to prove her innocence, which was always much harder than proving guilt. He just had to find the person who set her up and convince them to admit to the truth.

No problem. Ha.

"Any idea who might have been able to do that? Who else would have your locker combination?"

For the first time, he saw her falter. She looked down at the ground then at her fingernails.

"I don't know," she finally said, her voice subdued, giving him the distinct impression she wasn't being completely truthful. "Maybe someone watched me get into my locker once and, I don't know, figured out my combination from that."

"Is there a master list on the computer of students and their combinations? Could someone have hacked into that?" Ruben asked Todd.

"That's ridiculous. Why would anybody do that?"

"To frame Silver, maybe."

"Highly unlikely."

"But not impossible."

"Nearly." The vice principal scowled. "We keep that information in a folder on the secretary's desk. But I can't imagine how a student could have access to that without being seen snooping, especially under my watch."

Someone had managed to steal a jar of money off the counter without being seen under his watch but Ruben decided it might not be very politic right now to remind Todd of that.

"This is all a waste of time. Miss Capelli obviously stole that money. I am not surprised." He turned to her. "I'm just shocked that you would bring your ways to our school and think you can get away with it. We got you, didn't we?"

He grinned maliciously and Ruben again had to fight the urge to deck the little bastard. He could take him out with one good punch, but that would solve nothing and the paperwork would be a nightmare. He just had to figure out how he could fix this for Silver and for Dani.

Silver seemed to shrink in her chair and Ruben could see tears forming in her eyes.

"I am ordering suspension for the remainder of today and of course tomorrow, then I will consult with Principal Garcia during the break and we will determine the correct course of action from this point."

"The correct course of action would be to pull your head out and accept that I did not do this," she insisted.

Ruben wanted to tell her to stow it, that she was only making things worse for herself, but he could say nothing under the circumstances.

"I'm calling your mother right now. I'm sure Dr. Capelli will be shocked that her daughter could stoop to such terrible behavior."

"My mom? Why do you have to call my mom?"

"Because she needs to come and get you. As of this moment, you're suspended."

Silver sat back in the chair and covered her face with her hands and Ruben's heart broke for her.

"Given the seriousness of the situation, I don't think this is something that should be done in a phone call, Todd. I'm sure you agree with me on that."

The vice principal looked confused. "What are you suggesting?"

"I know Dr. Capelli. She works with my father, as I'm sure you're aware. Right now she's at the clinic. I think the best course of action would be for me to take Silver to her mother and speak with her there about what has happened today."

"I think it would be best if we call her in so I can tell her what kind of trouble Silver is in."

The anticipation in Todd's voice curdled his stomach. *So you can bully Dani, too, just like you're doing with her daughter? No chance in hell*, Ruben thought.

"Because of the seriousness of the matter, this is really a matter for law enforcement now. I'm afraid I need to take her into custody."

"What?" Silver said. She looked completely betrayed. He again wanted to assure her that everything would be okay but he couldn't say anything in front of the vice principal. Besides, he wasn't sure he could promise her anything of the sort, not when the evidence was so damning against her. It was hard to argue her innocence when the missing money was found in her locker.

"It would be best if I talk to her mother in person. Thank you for your help with the investigation but I'll take care of things from here." He met Silver's gaze, hoping she could see he was on her side. "Do you have everything you need? Your coat, your books?"

She lifted her backpack without meeting his gaze, her face crumpled as if she had lost faith in everything good and right in the world.

"Okay," he said in his most stern voice for Todd's benefit. "Let's go talk to your mother."

"You haven't finished your Christmas shopping yet? I've been done for *months*."

Dani cringed inwardly at the chiding tone from Gloria. Yet one more thing for her to feel guilty about. She had been a little busy the last few weeks trying to keep up with her work at the clinic and juggle being a mom to a troublesome teenager and an energetic six-year-old.

"I did most of mine online, which took so much hassle out of it," Gloria went on. "I'm afraid you're too late for online delivery now, though, especially up here in Haven Point. I always figure it takes things at least an extra day or two to make it over the mountains from Boise."

"You're probably right," Dani murmured. "I'm mostly done. I was thinking I would make a late-night trip to the big-box store in Shelter Springs after the girls are in bed tonight."

"You better finish before the weekend," Gloria advised. "I wouldn't be caught dead shopping on the last

Saturday before the holiday. The crowds will be *insane*. People think Black Friday is the biggest shopping day of the year, but it's not. It's the Saturday before Christmas."

She had lived in metropolitan areas all her life, first New York then Boston. Somehow she had a feeling her version of insane crowds and Gloria's version would be significantly different.

"I'll keep that in mind," Dani said. "Can you find my notes from my last appointment with McKenzie Kilpatrick's poodle? She's bringing her in again this afternoon for a follow-up appointment and I want to go over what we talked about last time."

The clinic door opened before Gloria had a chance to respond. Both of them turned to greet the newcomer but Dani's automatic polite smile of welcome never even had time to sprout at the sight of Ruben, in full, forbidding uniform complete with Stetson and coat, walking in with a subdued-looking Silver.

Dani's stomach plummeted. She could only think of a few reasons her daughter would be escorted home by a deputy sheriff, none of them good.

Oh, Silver. What kind of trouble are you in this time?

She straightened her spine, vertebra by vertebra. "What's going on? It's the middle of the school day. Are you sick?"

To her astonishment, Silver burst into tears and rushed through the door to the reception area. Dani barely had time for the shock to register before her daughter threw her arms around her, sobbing words she couldn't understand.

"Honey, it's okay. Whatever it is, it's going to be okay. We'll fix it."

"You can't fix this. I hate it here. Please, Mom, can I go back to Boston or New York? I could stay with Chelsea's family or…or Grandma DeLuca said I could live with her. Please, Mom."

There was no possible way on earth she was going to let Silver live with a friend or with Tommy's mother. "What's going on, Ruben? What's happened?"

Ruben glanced at Gloria, who was watching the whole proceeding avidly. "Can we go back to your office to discuss this somewhere more private?"

"It doesn't matter where we are," Silver said, her voice vibrating with emotion. "You can tell Gloria and everyone else. I don't care."

"Tell us what?" Dani asked, her sense of foreboding increasing.

"I've been suspended from school and now Ruben is going to arrest me."

14

Dani wasn't sure which was louder, her instinctive gasp or Gloria's sudden curse word, which wasn't at all fit for children's ears.

"Sorry. What?" She couldn't have heard Silver correctly. She *couldn't* have.

"Why don't we move this to your office," Ruben suggested again.

Through her shock, Dani looked at Gloria and then toward the front windows, where she could see a car pulling into the parking lot. Most likely it was McKenzie Kilpatrick with her beautiful standard poodle Paprika. Dani did *not* need the mayor of Haven Point hearing about Silver being in trouble, at least not until Dani herself knew what was going on.

"Gloria, will you please tell Mayor Kilpatrick I've been delayed but I'll be with her momentarily."

Dani's stomach curled with nausea as she led the way back to her small office. As usual, Ruben filled any space he occupied, but she didn't have time to focus on that.

She shut the door behind them all. "What is this about? Will someone please tell me what's going on?"

Silver only sobbed into her hands and Dani put an arm around her daughter's shoulders, giving Ruben an expectant look.

He sighed, his expression difficult to read. "Someone took a collection jar intended for disaster relief from the front office today. After the vice principal received a tip, he searched Silver's locker and found the jar there. I'm afraid she has been suspended for now and will likely face other disciplinary action when the principal returns after the New Year."

Dani felt as if someone had just touched dry ice to her insides. Everything seemed to shrivel and burn. First graffiti, now stealing a collection jar for charity. What was happening to her child? Was this the way Tommy had started? A poor choice here, a disastrous one there? First stealing spare change from school then moving on to a bank robbery and an eventual shoot-out with police?

The thought left her nauseous, grateful she was sitting down.

She thought when she came to Haven Point she was doing the right thing for her children, trying to carve out a happy, warm life for them. Now everything was falling apart.

Dani looked at Silver's downcast head against her, the

purple of her colored hair in vivid contrast to Dani's white lab coat.

No. No, she couldn't believe it. Emotions rose in her throat and as they did, she had a sudden unmistakable assurance.

Her daughter would not have done this.

She didn't care what kind of evidence Ruben thought he had against her. She knew her child and knew without any measure of doubt that Silver would not have stolen a collection jar intended for charity.

She would never believe it.

It wasn't simply that her daughter had a generous heart and always tried to help those in need, though she did. Silver was always the first one to make sandwiches and hand them out to the homeless or to empty her piggy bank to help out a cause she was passionate about.

Beyond that, Dani couldn't believe it simply because her daughter was entirely too street-smart to be part of something so ridiculously stupid, to think that she could get away with that kind of half-assed crime in full daylight, in a crowded school.

Dani had never wanted to be one of those parents who would never think ill of their own child and believed the whole world had it out for her. But in this case, she had to stand by Silver. She just couldn't accept it.

Her gaze shifted to Ruben and initial shock and dismay began to transform into something else—a deep sense of betrayal. He knew Silver. He had to know she would never be involved in something like this, no matter what kind of evidence he found.

"Honey, I need to speak with Deputy Morales out

in the hallway," she said, careful to use his official title, not Ruben.

This man with a badge on his chest was not their sweet, kind friend who had taken them on boat rides and held her while she cried and delivered gifts to neighbors in need. This was a hard, immovable law enforcement officer.

Would it make a difference if I tell you I'm falling in love with you?

He had obviously come to his senses, as she had fully expected. He wouldn't be here, otherwise.

Pain and loss, her old familiar companions, sliced through her but she did her best to ignore them for now.

He followed her out into the hallway, his features remote.

Dani closed her office door with Silver on the other side and tried to keep her hands from trembling as she faced him. "You think she did this."

A muscle in his jaw flexed. "It's a little hard to defend her to the vice principal when the jar and the money were found in her locker."

"I can't believe you would let this happen."

"What was I supposed to do?" His voice had a bite to it but she ignored it and plowed forward.

"Have a little faith! You know Sil. You know she would never do this. This is exactly what I was afraid would happen! I should never have told you about her father."

On some level, she knew she was being unfair, taking out her fear and frustration on him because she didn't know what else to do. In some strange way, his uniform had come to represent everything that seemed out of reach to her.

Security. Comfort. A safe haven.

She wanted that here in the aptly named Haven Point, but, as usual, she had screwed everything up. She was in love with Ruben and her heart ached at the impossibility of it all, the happiness that apparently would always remain just out of reach.

"I get it." Her voice sounded as cold as the rest of her felt. "Her dad is the worst sort of criminal, so of course Silver must be, too. She must have bad blood."

He continued to look down at her with stony features. "I never said or implied that."

"You didn't have to. I'm sure that's what you're thinking. The first moment anything goes wrong, it must be Silver's fault. Who else could be responsible?"

"You have a damn chip on your shoulder as big as Idaho, Dani. This has nothing to do with freaking Tommy DeLuca. The stolen money was in her locker. That's tough to explain away. Even you have to admit that."

For a moment, doubt flickered through her. Was it possible Silver had staged the whole thing knowing she would be caught? Was this some convoluted, underhanded way she had come up with to force Dani's hand and make her send Silver back to Boston or to New York and her grandmother?

No. She couldn't believe it. Sil would never do something like that. Her daughter was *not* her father, trying to manipulate every situation to her advantage.

Dani would never believe it and it hurt more than she ever imagined to discover that Ruben could.

"I know. You're only doing your job. I get it. The evidence was against her, plus there's the minor little matter of her father being a vicious cop killer. Why would you believe her when she said she didn't do it?"

"Can you just put down that chip and trust me for five freaking minutes?"

If her emotions weren't such a tangled mess, she might have laughed. Trust him. He had no idea what he was asking of her. She had spent her entire life trusting people, only to face betrayal after betrayal.

She couldn't have this out with him right now. She had a patient waiting. Unfortunately, McKenzie would simply have to wait a few moments longer. First, Dani had to do her best to comfort her heartbroken and frightened daughter.

"Thank you for bringing Silver here. I'm sure you didn't have to. I could have gone to the school to pick her up."

"The vice principal wanted you to, but I thought it would be better if I broke the news to you first myself."

She wanted to be grateful to him for that, at least, but she couldn't manage anything more than a stiff nod. "You've done that. Thanks. You can go now. I'll deal with things from this point."

"Dani—"

She didn't want to hear his apologies or explanations. Not now. He should have stood up for her daughter. He had assured her that her past didn't matter a bit to him but at the first opportunity, Ruben was as quick as everyone else to judge and condemn.

"Under the circumstances, I'm afraid you'll have to take care of your own Secret Santa tradition tonight. My girls and I will be busy with other things."

Oh, she sounded like a bitch. She heard her own clipped words and wanted to call them back but this was for the best. Better to cut ties with him now, once and for all.

"I'll have Mia run over the rest of the gifts for the Larkin family and leave them on your porch. Excuse me, Deputy Morales. I have to focus on my daughter now."

She walked into her office and closed the door, feeling as if her heart had been sliced to pieces and was now lying on the floor under his boots.

A dark cloud seemed to have descended on their little house by the lake.

Silver had stayed in her room since the previous afternoon, periodically coming out like a shadowy wraith to use the bathroom, pick at her food, grab a drink, then return.

Mia didn't quite understand what was going on. Neither Silver nor Dani felt like she needed to know, but it was clear she sensed something serious was wrong. She was subdued, quiet, without her usual excited Christmas chatter or the songs she had been singing nonstop since her school program the day before.

Dani didn't sleep well, tossing and turning while she tried to figure out what she could do to clear her child's name. Silver had told her all she knew, that someone she didn't know had told her a counselor wanted to see her. She had gone to the office, only to find out the message had been in error. Next thing she knew, the vice principal had been yanking her out of class and hauling her to the office to find Ruben there.

For reasons Dani didn't understand, her daughter didn't seem upset at Ruben. Far from it. She said he had tried to reason with the vice principal but the school had stood firm.

Perhaps Dani had been too hard on him. She remembered her bitter words and the abrupt way she had kicked him out of her office. He had asked her to trust him but she still didn't know how she could possibly do that.

She only knew this was the worst possible thing that could happen to Silver when she was trying to adapt to a new school. Guilty or not, she would be the subject of gossip at school. It was inevitable. She would be tried and convicted by all her peers. Dani was certain of it.

Maybe they would be better off picking up and going somewhere else. She was licensed to practice veterinary medicine anywhere in Idaho. They could move to a large community like Boise and she could practice there—or she could take the necessary licensing tests in another state and start over somewhere completely new. Maybe somewhere warm and beachy like California would be a nice change.

Some part of her was very much afraid that wouldn't do any good. How could they ever escape Tommy De-Luca's grim legacy? The past would follow them wherever they went.

She finally rose well before sunrise. After letting

Winky out to do her business and then opening the door so she could come inside again, Dani sat with her dog in her lap next to the Christmas tree Ruben had helped them put up.

There, alone, she wept for the mistakes she couldn't change, the decisions she couldn't undo and the ripple effect those choices continued to have in the lives of those she loved.

At last, she brushed herself off, dried her tears and rose. Her daughters needed her and she needed to focus on that.

After sending Mia off to school, Dani persuaded Silver to go into the clinic with her while she worked her Friday half day.

Silver wanted to stay home and hide away by herself but Dani didn't feel like that would be the best option for her. Better to give her something constructive to do and help focus her attention outward, so she told Silver she would pay her to walk and cuddle some of the dogs and cats they were boarding over the holidays.

It seemed to work. Animals always had a way of working their calming magic and Silver was in a much better frame of mind by the time they left the clinic.

As she and her daughter were driving home through the snow-covered pines and firs that lined the road beside the lake, inspiration struck. "Mia will be getting out early today for Christmas break. I think we should drive to Shelter Springs, finish our Christmas shopping, have a nice dinner somewhere in town and then go to see *The Nutcracker*. I believe tonight is the last night we can catch the amateur ballet troupe's production there. What do you think?"

"I guess, as long as we won't see anybody from my school."

Dani briefly shifted her gaze from the road, her heart breaking all over again for her daughter. "I can't promise you that. I'm sorry. There's a good chance we might see someone from school. I understand why you would want to avoid everyone. Never mind. We can go to the ballet next year. Tonight, let's just stay home and watch a movie or something."

Silver chewed her lip, a habit Dani knew her daughter had picked up from her. "No," she said after a moment, her voice resolute. "I didn't do anything wrong, so I shouldn't be the one hiding at home like I'm ashamed or something."

"Good call," Dani said around the lump in her throat. "We'll go and have a great time together, just the three of us. Anybody who has a problem with it can take it up with somebody who gives a rat's ass."

Silver giggled, the sound so sweet that Dani didn't even feel guilty for swearing.

As Dani might have expected, Mia was thrilled with the idea of dinner and the ballet, especially as it meant dressing up a little more than usual.

Dani had just finished putting on her favorite red sweater and piling her hair up into an easy updo when the doorbell rang.

"Who could that be?" Mia asked, dancing to the door with her best ballerina pirouette. She opened it before

Dani could make it to the door herself to check the peep-hole first.

Mia beamed at the person on the other side. "Hi, Ruben! Guess what? We're going to see *The Nutcracker.* I watched it once on TV but now we get to see the real thing, with real people dancing. Like this."

She did another pirouette, twirling her doll around in her arms.

"You're both very good. May we come in? We need to talk to your mom and to Silver."

We? Who was here with him? Dani moved farther into the living room, sticking the last pin in her hair. Her hands froze and slowly lowered when she spotted two girls with him, Emma and Ella Larkin.

They were the friends of Silver whose mother had cancer, the family who had been receiving all the Secret Santa gifts delivered by Silver and Mia for Ruben over the past week.

The girls didn't meet her gaze, just looked down at the ground, and Dani frowned in confusion.

Why were they there? Had they found out about the gifts? Oh, she hoped not. Silver and Mia had taken such care to avoid discovery. It would be too bad if the surprise had been ruined.

It must be that. What else would bring them here, in Ruben's company? They were certainly having an odd reaction, though.

"We need to speak with Silver, too," Ruben said. He glanced at her, his features so grim and remote that her heart ached. He was wearing his uniform again and the silvery badge at his chest reflected the lights of the Christmas tree he had helped them with.

She wanted to tell him no, that Silver was unavailable, but her daughter popped her head out of her bedroom before Dani had the chance.

Silver had the same reaction Dani had to the twins' appearance. She froze, then frowned in confusion. "Oh," she said. "Hi."

Dani could detect no warmth whatsoever in her voice, which surprised her. Until the last few weeks, the three girls had been friends.

"Silver, could you come in here and sit down?" Ruben said. "Emma and Ella have something they need to tell you."

"It doesn't matter," Silver said quickly.

"Yes, it does."

Though she looked as if she wanted to flee back into her room and slam the door, she finally moved slowly into the living room, her hands curled at her sides and her features tense. She perched on the edge of the sofa and Dani sat beside her.

"What is this about?" she asked.

"Go ahead, girls," Ruben said, in that same solemn voice.

Dani couldn't tell the girls apart. She thought Silver had once told her Emma had a mole on her cheek. Or was that Ella? Either way, with their fine blond hair and blue eyes, the girls looked so much alike, Dani wondered if their own mother knew which was which.

Today, they both looked as if they had been crying, she

realized. Their eyes were red, with little makeup streaks on their splotchy cheeks.

What on earth was going on?

One of them stepped forward a little. "We…we owe you an apology," she said, speaking quickly as if the words were being forced out of her. "Emma and I were the ones who stole the spirit club's donation jar. *I* stole it, anyway. It was easy, since I'm an aide in the office. I just put it in one of those empty boxes of paper reams from the copy machine, when the secretaries were back in the staff room having a treat. Then I offered to take all the empty boxes to the recycling outside."

"Except she didn't," the other girl said. "El made up a fake note so she could call me out of class and I opened your locker and we put it in there. And we're sorry."

Dani stared at the girls, completely astonished. She had always thought them such nice girls. They had been kind to Silver since they moved to Haven Point, the two girls Dani had considered Silver's closest friends.

Why would they do something like this?

She looked over at Silver and was further shocked to realize her daughter didn't seem particularly surprised, almost as if she had been expecting something like this.

"How did you know my combination?"

Emma spoke up. "You gave it to me that time when I needed extra space to put all that stuff for my country presentation in Spanish class about Mexico, remember? The piñata and the sombrero and the sodas we bought at the market."

"She still had the combination on her phone," Ella

confessed. "We just opened your locker before third hour and stuck it in there."

"And then I called Vice Principal Andrews with the anonymous tip," Emma said, her voice breaking a little. "It was a dumb thing to do and we're really sorry."

"Super sorry," Ella said. She looked at her sister's distress and tears began to leak out of her eyes, too. Their reactions appeared genuine, but Dani was still so stunned, she couldn't be quite sure.

"We thought maybe you would get detention and that's all."

"We never thought you'd be suspended," Ella said. "When I heard Vice Principal Andrews telling the secretaries this morning that you would probably have to go to juvie after the New Year, I thought I was going to throw up."

"Is that when you decided to tell the truth?" Dani asked, still reeling.

The girls looked at each other, then at Ruben. "N-not exactly," Ella admitted.

"But we probably *would* have told the truth, even if Officer Morales hadn't pulled us out of class after lunch and took us into the office so he could tell us he knew we did it."

"He gave us a big lecture about how bad it was to let somebody else suffer for something we did. It was really scary."

"He said how disappointed our mom would be in us to know that while she is fighting for her life, we are doing bad stuff with the life we've been given and blaming other people." Emma started to cry again and her twin squeezed her fingers.

"He said how, if we had any character at all, we would tell the truth about stealing the money jar and…and everything else."

"Everything else?" Silver looked stunned and, if Dani wasn't mistaken, guilty.

Emma sniffled. "Yeah. He said we should tell him everything. We had to, if we wanted to make things right."

"We didn't want to but…but it was the right thing to do. So we told him we were with you that night with the spray paint and that it was our idea in the first place."

Dani sat back, not sure she could take any more surprises. "Ella and Emma were the girls out with you that night."

Of course. She should have realized. She remembered Silver telling her they weren't hanging out anymore. Maybe they felt guilty that Silver had been caught while they had gotten off scot-free.

"It was all our fault, Dr. Capelli," Ella said.

"Sil didn't want to go, but we made her. We told her she was a baby if she didn't and we…we were going to tell everyone at school about her dad."

Her dad. Silver had told them about Tommy and the girls had used the truth about his crimes as a weapon against her.

Dani closed her eyes and cursed a blue streak in her head, the words she didn't say anymore. This was worse than she could have imagined. Far worse.

She opened her eyes and realized Mia was sitting on

the chair closest to the Christmas tree, watching the whole proceeding with a kind of baffled interest.

Dani didn't want her here for this discussion. She was only six years old, an innocent who still believed in Santa Claus and Christmas miracles and happy endings. She didn't need this kind of ugliness in her world.

"Mia, honey, would you go in your room and play with Wink and Pia for a little while?"

Her chin jutted out. "But I want to talk to Ruben."

"I really need you to watch Wink. Just for a minute, pumpkin, okay?"

She huffed out a breath but picked up her doll. "Come on, Winky," she said, and dragged both doll and dog to her room, where she closed the door.

When Mia was out of earshot, Dani turned to her older daughter. "You told them about your father."

Silver's chin trembled and her eyes looked guilty. "I know you told me I shouldn't tell anyone, but I was at their house one day and the TV news was on and they did a story about one of the kids whose dad was killed going back to school and...and I felt so awful and...and sad it all slipped out. But they promised not to tell."

"We didn't," Emma assured her. "We only said that so she would come with us that night, but we would never tell, I promise, Dr. Capelli."

The word would get out. They might think they weren't breaking a confidence by telling one girl. And then that girl would tell another and that girl would tell another, and in a flash the entire school would know the horrible truth.

Dani tried not to panic. This wasn't the time for it.

Some part of her wondered if it would be better to come clean with everyone in town about Tommy and take their chances about how people might react. Getting in front of the truth might be better than this constant fear of exposure.

She suspected Ruben was right. There would certainly be people in town who would inevitably think less of her, who would lump her and her daughters in with Tommy and his horrible final acts. To certain people, like perhaps the vice principal at the middle school and others like him, Silver would always be considered poisoned fruit dangling from a criminally inclined tree.

Dani accepted her own culpability in ever hooking up with Tommy in the first place when she was a needy, starved-for-love teenager, but she absolutely hated the idea of anyone thinking less of her daughters, who were truly innocent of the entire situation.

She wanted to think most people would be like Frank and Myra Morales. They wouldn't blame her or her girls for the actions of a man who hadn't been part of their lives in years.

It wouldn't be a universally held position, she knew, but maybe they were tough enough to handle the whispers and gossip of the few.

She could worry about that later. Right now, she needed to hear what these girls had come here with Ruben to tell them.

"All right. So you were there that night on the little graffiti spree. I still don't understand why you stole the money jar and tried to pin it on Silver."

The girls started to cry again, so hard that Ruben

placed a hand on each shoulder. Just as it did for Dani, his presence seemed to steady them, even when he was being stern and forbidding.

"It was so stupid and mean and *wrong* and we should never have done it," Ella said through her sobs.

"We thought she had told on us for the vandalism, especially when we saw your family with Deputy Morales at the boat parade."

"We kept thinking you were going to come and arrest us," Ella said with another sniffle.

"We…we thought that if Silver got in trouble for something else, nobody would believe her if she said the graffiti was our idea."

"We just didn't want our mom to know we did such a bad thing. Dad made us promise we wouldn't do anything to upset our mom, so we could have the best Christmas for her."

"It might be our last one with her and we…we didn't want to get caught," Emma said. "But we just made everything worse."

Dani swallowed. Their convoluted reasoning made no sense, but then, she wasn't thirteen years old, dealing with a seriously ill parent.

She wanted to be furious with the girls, and some part of her was, but she couldn't help a deep sense of sorrow for the hard times their family was going through. She had been younger than Emma and Ella but she vividly remembered that terrible, helpless feeling as her mother grew more and more ill.

"Here's the thing, girls," Ruben said, his voice solemn. "Silver never once told me who was with her the night of the vandalism. She took all the blame and did all the cleanup by herself."

If possible, the girls looked even more guilty.

"I asked her a dozen times and she would never say a word," he continued. "She protected you. She insisted she was by herself, even though I heard you guys that night and knew she wasn't alone."

"We're so sorry, Sil," Emma said.

"Really, really sorry," her sister added.

"We shouldn't have said that about your dad, that we would tell people. We would never do that, I swear."

"I still don't know why you care if people know, though," Ella said. "It's not like what he did is your fault. I mean, you're just a kid and you barely knew him. How can anybody blame you?"

"It's not your fault, any more than it's our fault our mom has cancer. It might make you sad and stuff, and that's okay, but it's not your fault."

Dani felt as if Emma's words suddenly unlocked a door in front of her, showing her something profound and simple on the other side.

Ruben had tried to tell her but she hadn't let the truth seep in. Somehow hearing it from these young girls made her see the situation with stronger clarity.

Tommy's choices were not *her* fault and they weren't Silver's. She didn't want her daughters to carry guilt over them for the rest of their lives, to forever feel as if they were somehow tarnished because of their father's actions.

She didn't want it for her daughters and she didn't want it for herself.

And if she wanted them to be free of Tommy forever,

she couldn't hide in fear from the things he had done as if she—or they—were somehow responsible.

She wasn't.

Silver wasn't.

Mia certainly wasn't.

Part of being free of the past meant owning it. Not hiding in fear but being open with those who cared about them, trusting that they would accept that inviolable truth as well.

Since coming to Haven Point, Dani had been so afraid to trust anyone. She could blame it on her insecure foster care upbringing or her own bad choice in relationships, but the result was isolation and loneliness.

At some point, she would have to take that leap, as much as it scared her.

"We're really sorry," Emma said. "After we told Deputy Morales the truth, we told Vice Principal Andrews. He didn't want to believe us at first."

"Yeah, he said we were only covering up for our friend."

Emma grinned a little through her tears. "But then Deputy Morales yelled at him and told him he was a small-minded swear word and if he didn't do everything possible to clear your name, Deputy Morales would personally see to it that he was demoted back to teaching health class."

"You did that?" Silver looked stunned.

Ruben shifted. "You were innocent and he refused to accept it. I couldn't allow him to continue smearing your reputation at school."

"Wow. Thanks." Silver smiled at him with the same kind of adoration her sister might have offered.

Ruben cleared his throat. "Okay, girls. You've apologized. Your dad is waiting out in the car for you."

"What's going to happen now?" Silver asked.

"It's a little too early to say for sure. I don't believe the county attorney will want to charge them with anything, especially because the money was all accounted for and has already been sent to the charity for hurricane relief. I'll talk to him and see if we can avoid charges, as long as you girls agree to community service for the vandalism, the theft of the donation jar and your attempts to pin it on an innocent friend."

"Yes, sir," they both said together. The girls appeared contrite, chastened by the reality of what they had done. Dani hoped they were.

"Will…will you ever forgive us, Silver?" Emma asked.

Beside Dani, her daughter gave a little shrug. "Probably. For now, I still want to be mad and hurt for a couple of days."

Ruben's gaze met hers and Dani saw an amusement that matched her own over Silver's honesty. His amusement quickly faded, replaced by something stark and unbearably sad.

She ached, knowing she had caused that look.

"Our dad took our phones for, like, ever when he had to pick us up at the school," Ella said. "We can't call you, but maybe we could come over during Christmas break and hang out and stuff. We can try to borrow our dad's phone and call you."

"Maybe," Silver said, with little enthusiasm.

The girls seemed to accept that. "Okay," Emma said. "I guess we'll see you later."

Ruben walked them to the door and watched as they climbed into a waiting vehicle in the driveway before turning back to Silver and Dani.

"How did you finally figure out it wasn't me?" Silver asked after the door closed behind the Larkin twins.

"I *never* thought it was you. Not for a single second," Ruben said. "You told me yesterday you didn't do it and I believed you. That's what I said on the way to the vet clinic, remember?"

"I thought you were just saying that." Silver looked as if reality still hadn't sunk in.

"I wish you had trusted me. It's kind of my job to get to the bottom of things, remember? I told you I would figure out who really stole the jar."

Dani felt sick inside all over again, remembering how she had accused Ruben of jumping to conclusions because of Tommy.

"I should have believed you," Silver said.

"You should have. It's never a sign of weakness to trust somebody to help you out when you need it."

Silver reached out and hugged him tightly. "Thanks."

He hugged her back, eyes soft. "You're welcome, kiddo."

"Seriously. How did you know it was them?" Silver asked.

Ruben gave a rough-sounding laugh. "If you want the truth, I didn't have any idea who was behind it yesterday, I only knew it wasn't you. Then something happened last night."

"What was it?" Dani had to ask.

He gazed at her, his expression guarded. "Because somebody was mad at me, I had to do the Secret Santa delivery by myself. While I was out there lurking about, I happened to notice that the Larkin's mailbox was spray painted red. The exact shade of red I cleaned off *The Wonder* a few weeks ago. I couldn't believe I hadn't noticed it before, but maybe it was because I wasn't the one doing the deliveries this year."

"I never even noticed that," Silver admitted.

"Again, it's my job to notice things. I knew it couldn't be a coincidence. I guessed that they were the ones who provided the spray paint. I imagine they found it in their garage or something."

Silver flushed a little. "I didn't want to do the graffiti. I thought it was dumb but they really wanted to, for some reason. They were mad at Miss Grimes because she sent Ella to detention. I thought that's all we were going to do, then they wanted to do the other places and I… I didn't say no. So that makes it my fault as much as theirs. My mom always says going along is the same as saying yes."

"Your mom is right about that," Ruben said gruffly. "I also remembered your strange reaction when I told you the Larkins would be the family we planned to help with the twelve days of Christmas. You mentioned something about how you weren't really hanging out with the twins anymore. With that kind of response, I had to suspect something must have happened between you and them."

"They were afraid I was going to tell on them, even though I didn't. I thought they were just being wussies.

I didn't even think about how maybe they were worried about upsetting their mom."

"Even though you guys were mad at each other, you stepped up to do the Secret Santa deliveries for them anyway. That took guts, kiddo."

Dani thought she had been proud of her daughter for holding her head up against unjust accusations earlier, but that paled in comparison to this moment, knowing her daughter had been willing to do a kind thing for two girls who had treated her abominably.

Silver had taken the high road, focusing not on her own hurt feelings but on the tough time the Larkins were going through because of their mother's illness.

Dani hugged her and for once, Silver didn't pull away but leaned her head on her mother's shoulder.

"So you figured out Ella and Emma were likely involved with the graffiti. I still don't understand how you were able to make the leap from the spray paint to them stealing the collection jar," Dani said.

"Last night when I couldn't sleep, I went over the list the school had given me of all the students who had been in the office around the time the money disappeared. I discovered Ella was an office aide the hour just before the disappearance, which gave her plenty of access and opportunity. I told you before, I don't believe in coincidences. I couldn't figure out a motive at that point, but I thought if I talked to the girls, I could maybe get there."

He gave a slight chuckle. "For the record, Vice Principal Andrews was not in favor of me taking the girls out of class and questioning them, but I went ahead and did it anyway. I don't think I'm going to be on his Christmas list this year."

Silver and Ruben grinned at each other and Dani felt emotion swell up in her throat.

She wanted to throw her arms around him, to thank him from the bottom of her heart for believing in her child when he had every reason not to. They owed him so much. She couldn't even hope to find the right words.

"Ruben, I..."

Before she could complete the sentence, she heard Winky's claws on the hardwood floors of the hall and a moment later the dog came into the room, trying desperately to shake off the Santa hat Mia must have put on her.

"Can we come out now? We've been in there *forever*."

Oh. Poor Mia. "Yes. I'm sorry. You can come out."

Ruben seemed to take that as his cue. He shoved on his Stetson. "I've got to run. We're shorthanded this time of year and I've been gone long enough. Have fun at *The Nutcracker*."

"We will now," Silver said.

"If I don't see you again before the holidays, merry Christmas."

That reserve was back in his gaze, Dani saw. She had put it there and she didn't know how to fix things. She desperately missed the warmth she had become used to seeing.

"Merry Christmas," she murmured. She wanted to say so many other things but now didn't seem the time. He didn't give her a chance anyway. He patted Winky, who had taken the Santa hat off by now and was chewing on the pom-pom, then gave Mia a quick hug, smiled at Silver and walked out the door, without even looking at Dani.

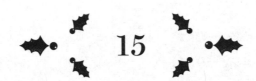

15

"That was so fun, Mama. Thank you for taking me."
Dani smiled at a sleepy Mia cuddled in her bed
with her dark-haired doppelgänger doll beside her and
the handsome new nutcracker she had purchased at the
play tucked in beside Pia. Mia hummed a few bars of
the music they had enjoyed, lilting and lovely and clas-
sically familiar.

"You're welcome, honey. I'm glad you had fun."

"Can we go see the ballet again next year? Maybe it
can be our family tradition."

"What a terrific idea."

"All families need traditions. That's what you said."

"We do need them."

"And can we do our own Secret Santa next year to
someone? That was Silver's idea and I want to do it, too."

Her heart softened at these girls who liked the feeling of reaching out and helping others and wanted it to continue.

"I think that's an excellent idea. We don't have to only do nice things in December. We also need to think all year long about people around us who might need something happy in their world."

Mia smiled, already almost asleep and Dani hugged her one more time then turned out the light

Traditions were necessary, she thought as she walked out into the hall. Her girls needed that sense of continuity. Would they find that if she picked up and moved to a new state to practice veterinary medicine?

For too much of her life, she had been focused on the next thing. Getting out of foster care and being on her own. Having a baby. Tommy's release date. Final exams, the next semester's classes, earning her degree.

She wasn't working toward anything now, except being the best veterinarian, mother and *person* she could be.

It was past time she stopped thinking everything would be perfect at some point in the future—when she could afford a better house, when her student loans were paid off—and started focusing on how she could make this moment the best possible.

She needed to commit to Haven Point, to building a life here and fully integrating into the community. Tonight, she had bumped into several families from Haven Point at the ballet and everyone had been more than kind to her. She and the girls had even been invited to a family New Year's Eve party at Eliza and Aidan Caine's house in Snow Angel Cove.

Dani had given a vague, noncommittal answer at the time, but she would call Eliza the next day to accept, she decided. It seemed like a monumental step, but one she felt good about.

When she walked into the living room, she discovered Silver, hair wet from her shower and in her pajamas, lying on the floor and gazing at the Christmas tree. Winky rested on her stomach, perfectly content.

Silver had turned on Christmas music and it played softly in the background. The tree seemed particularly fragrant tonight, its piney scent capturing the magic of the season perfectly.

Dani tried to imprint the sweetness of the moment in her mind so she could take out the memory to enjoy during those times when Silver inevitably tested her patience.

She sat beside her on the floor, leaning back against the sofa. "Are you okay?"

Silver nodded. "Just enjoying the Christmas tree. It's so peaceful here, watching all the colors. Remember how I used to do this when I was a little kid back in Queens, in our crappy apartment? We had that ugly little fake tree but I still always wanted to lie on the floor and dream about Christmas."

Those early Christmases had been meager indeed, with Tommy in prison and Dani in school and working various part-time jobs. She had felt like such a failure as a mom, unable to provide more for her daughter, but when she reflected on it now, she remembered only the joy on Silver's face at whatever few small presents she found under that ugly fake tree.

"Did you enjoy the ballet? It was fun to see Ruben's parents there, along with his nephews and niece."

Silver moved to a sitting position, her back against the sofa like Dani's, and settled Winky into a more comfortable spot on her lap. "Zach said their grandparents take them every year to see *The Nutcracker* during the holiday season."

"Ah. Another Morales tradition." She sent Silver a sideways look. "What else did Zach have to say? You talked to him for most of the intermission."

"He asked me what was going on, why I wasn't in school today. He said a kid in his geometry class told him I had been arrested, so Zach got all up in his face and told the kid to stop telling lies about me." Silver grinned a little but quickly hid it by turning her face away.

"That's sweet of him to stand up for you. Did you tell him what really happened?"

"No. It didn't seem right to rat out Ella and Em. I told him it was just a misunderstanding and I would be back after Christmas. He seemed happy about that."

Dani smiled. "I think he likes you."

This time Silver didn't bother to hide her grin. "Maybe."

They sat in a companionable silence, listening to a jazzy version of "Silent Night."

"Ruben's pretty great, isn't he?" Silver said out of the blue. "He believed in me the whole time."

The torrent of emotions Dani had done her best to dam up all evening seemed to break free and she had to close her eyes at the sheer force of them. "Yes. He is pretty great."

"If he didn't keep investigating, I might still be suspended." Silver sent her a sidelong look. "You know why he went to all that effort to clear my name, right?"

"Because he's an excellent judge of character," Dani replied.

Her daughter grinned. "Well, yeah. But also because *he* likes *you*."

Would it make a difference if I tell you I'm falling in love with you?

She thought of those moments in his arms on the boat, the sheer joy of being with him. Had she ruined everything between them? How could she make it right?

"I need to ask you something," she said to Silver. "Something serious. Do you really hate it here? If you do, I can look into practicing somewhere else. I would like to stay in Haven Point and build our future here, but not if you're going to be miserable."

Silver pulled Winky higher in her arms and tucked the dog's little head under her chin. "I'm sorry I've been unhappy. It was…everything with Ella and Emma, plus missing my friends back in Boston and stuff. I don't really hate it here."

"But could you ever love it?"

"Yeah. I think I could. It's pretty here. There's maybe not as much to do as Boston or New York, but we can always go back and visit those places when we want."

"That's right. I'm okay with you going back to stay with your friends on a visit. Maybe you can start saving your money for a plane ticket by doing extra work at the clinic."

"That would be good." Silver paused. "I have friends

here. There are good people everywhere and there are jerks, too. Ruben told me the trick is to surround yourself with the first kind of people and do your best to ignore the second."

Yet more wisdom from the man. How could she help but love him?

"And don't forget, you have to start by *being* a good person yourself, instead of a jerk."

Silver was quiet for a moment and seemed content watching the Christmas tree and petting their fluffy dog. "Hey, do you think Ruben might let Mia and me do the last few Secret Santa deliveries?"

"You still want to, after the trouble Ella and Emma caused you?"

"I like taking the gifts. It makes me feel good inside and it's a small thing I can do for someone else. Besides, their mom might die. I think they made some stupid choices because they're afraid, which I would be, too, I guess, if there was any chance I might lose you."

Oh. Just when Dani thought she had her emotions under control, her daughter had to go and say something like that. Emotions clogged her throat and her eyes welled up with tears.

Yes, the bulk of the teen years were still ahead of them, but Dani hoped she never lost sight of how amazing her daughter was.

"I'll talk to Ruben. I don't think he'll mind. You should probably get to bed now. It's late."

"Yeah. I'm tired."

They both rose and to Dani's delight, her daughter wrapped her arms around her waist. "Merry almost

Christmas, Mom. I think it's going to be our best one ever."

That Silver could say those words after the trauma of the last three months and the final horrible, desperate choices her father had made filled Dani with joy.

After Silver went to bed, taking Wink with her, Dani sat for a long time there in the darkness illuminated only by the Christmas tree.

She knew what she had to do—she needed only to find the courage for it.

It was nearly midnight when she saw the lights of a vehicle pulling into the driveway next door. Ruben must have worked a late shift, after doing his best to clear her daughter's name all morning.

She needed to speak with the man and suddenly she knew it wouldn't wait another moment.

Heart pounding, she pulled on her boots. She didn't bother with her coat, just grabbed the knit throw from the chair and draped it around her shoulders like a wrap before heading outside.

The December night felt like a precious gift. It was snowing gently, big, puffy flakes that landed in her hair and on the wrap. In the moonlight, she could make out the vastness of the lake and the steep mountains rising up on the other side. The hushed beauty of the scene humbled her and made her infinitely grateful she could witness it.

She was nervous about talking to Ruben, but there was also a sense of...*peace*. That was the only word she could use to describe it. Silver had described the experience of gazing at the Christmas tree using that same word and it fit here, too.

She felt a deep sense of peace.

At his door, she didn't hesitate for an instant, simply knocked softly. From inside, she heard a well-mannered deep-throated bark she recognized as Yukon's and another little yip from Ollie and then the door opened.

Ruben looked as if he had been in the process of taking off his uniform when she knocked. He wore the dark khaki pants but only a white T shirt and none of the other things that always hung on his belt—his weapon, his radio, his Taser. All the things that made him appear so dangerous.

She had a feeling they probably weren't far away, though. He wasn't the sort of man who would answer the door in the middle of the night without being ready for anything.

His eyes widened in shock when he spotted her. The dogs rushed out, tails wagging to greet her.

"Dani! What are you doing here? Come in."

As she went inside with Yukon and Ollie sticking close to her, she realized she had never been in his house in all the months she had lived next door to him.

Now she looked around with interest. It was comfortable, masculine, with Mission-style furniture and photographs of Haven Point and its surroundings on the walls. It smelled like him, too, that outdoorsy, cedary scent she found so delicious.

His house seemed to fit him, somehow.

"What's going on? Are the girls okay?"

"The girls are fine. Everyone is fine." She petted

Yukon. Maybe she should have waited until morning. What had seemed urgent to her might not appear the same to him when he was tired from a long day at work.

"I came for two reasons. Three, really."

He studied her and some of his tension seemed to seep away. "That sounds serious. Sit down."

He gestured to the sofa but she shook her head. "I won't take long. The girls are home alone. They're in bed, but I probably should have told Silver where I was going."

Her daughter might figure it out, given their conversation earlier. She wasn't sure how she felt about that.

She hadn't really thought this through, intent only on sharing some of the thoughts running through her mind.

"She's one of the reasons I'm here. Silver would like to finish up the Secret Santa deliveries to the Larkins and I told her I would ask you about it."

He blinked those incredibly long eyelashes. "After everything the twins did to Sil, she still wants to be part of that?"

Dani laughed a little. "I know. I had the same reaction. She says she likes giving the presents and likes the way it makes her feel to be doing something nice for them."

"She's a great kid."

"She is. I sometimes forget that in the day to day. It's important that I don't lose sight of it. I'm trying to do better."

He smiled and her knees turned suddenly wobbly for some reason. She thought about taking a seat, but decided she felt a little more in control on her feet, wobbly or not.

"As I said, Silver is only one of the reasons I'm here."

"Oh?"

"I think I was so stunned this afternoon that I didn't properly thank you for going to bat for her like you did."

His T-shirt rippled as he shrugged his shoulders. "What else could I do? I knew Sil wouldn't have taken that money. She said she didn't and I believed her. None of it made sense. I'm just glad I could figure it out before the school moved forward with pressing charges."

She was, too, more appreciative than she could ever tell him. She would have hated knowing her daughter had a juvenile record.

"I didn't say it this afternoon but I'm deeply grateful for your instincts and your investigative skills. We would have been lost without you."

"I'm glad it worked out the way it did." He gave her a careful look. "You said you had three reasons for stopping by. What's the third?"

The peace she felt earlier seemed to have evaporated now. For one crazy instant, she was tempted to tell him she had miscounted and her work here was done.

That would be cowardly, though. If her daughter could show such strength and grace, Dani could do nothing less. She drew in a deep breath for courage and stepped forward. "I... I would like to give you something."

He raised an eyebrow, looking so gorgeous that everything inside her seemed to sigh.

"An early Christmas present?"

"Something like that."

Gathering her nerves, she took another step, raised up on her toes and pressed her mouth to his.

At once, all of her nerves fled and that peace returned.

This was right. *They* were right. She was so foolish to have doubted it for a moment.

After a heart-stopping moment of hesitation when she began to wonder if she was too late, he wrapped his arms tightly around her and kissed her with a ferocity that stole her breath.

She gave a little laugh and entwined her own arms around his neck, loving the taste of him and the overwhelming sense of joy exploding like those Roman candles again.

Love coursed through her, sweet and beautiful, like a cleansing storm.

He kissed her until her knees were weak again, until she couldn't think straight and her breathing was ragged and she was a quivering, aching bundle of desire.

"Have I mentioned before how much I love Christmas presents?" he murmured against her mouth.

It took her dazzled brain a moment to make the connection back to what he had said earlier. She laughed, loving him more than she ever imagined possible.

"That was more an apology than a Christmas present, I guess."

"You don't owe me any apology."

"I do. You bared your heart to me last week. At the time, I wasn't in a good place to hear it. But I haven't been able to think about anything else since then and… I'm sorry for the way I reacted."

"You're forgiven," he murmured.

"You make it too easy." She stepped away a little, knowing she had to get through this, no matter how difficult, and she couldn't seem to string together a coherent thought while she was in his arms. "When you told me you were falling in love with me, I...panicked."

"I'm sorry."

"It's not your fault. I wasn't looking for this when I moved to Haven Point but I think I fell hard right around the time we met. I was sure of it that day you held me when I had a breakdown, when you were so very kind to me, and I've been fighting it ever since."

"How's that working out for you?"

She made a face and took one more deep breath for courage. "Terribly. I don't want to fight it anymore. I love you, Ruben. I love how kind you are with my children, I love seeing you with your family, I love the way I seem to lose my head completely when you kiss me."

He seemed to take that as incentive to kiss her again and Dani wanted to sink into him, to stay here forever in the shelter of his arms.

"Yes. Like that," she said, her voice thready and aroused.

He smiled and kissed the corner of her mouth and she had to wonder just why she had been fighting this for so long.

"I had long ago told myself I would be better off forgetting about romance entirely and only focusing on my girls and my career. And then I met you. You made me laugh and cry and feel things I thought I never would again. You helped me realize I still have so much love inside me to give to the right man."

He held her and she listened to his heartbeat, knowing she didn't want to be anywhere else in the world except right here. "You are the right man, Ruben. Good, decent, caring. The kind of man I think I've finally managed to convince myself I deserve. More than that, the kind of man I need."

This time, she kissed him and the fierce emotion in his eyes was all the answer she needed.

They kissed for a long time, until they were on the sofa, wrapped together under the throw she had brought over. The snow was falling gently outside the window and she could see the Christmas tree he had helped set up gleaming through the night from her house next door.

He had brought light and color to her world, in so many ways.

"I can't stay," she said with deep regret. "I have to get back to the girls."

"I know." He kissed her again then stood up and pulled her to her feet, rearranging the sweater he had been in the process of tangling.

He wrapped the woven throw back around her shoulders with a soft tenderness that stole her heart all over again. "I love you, Daniela Capelli."

She laughed a little. "Nobody calls me Daniela. How did you even know that's my full name?"

"My dad mentioned it long before you came here. He told me years ago he had met a lovely veterinary student with a beautiful name to match. I could never have imagined during that passing conversation that one day I would be completely enamored with that woman—and with her daughters, I should add."

What would her girls think about the idea of her and Ruben together? She felt a tiny flutter of misgiving but pushed it away. Silver and Mia both loved him and would be thrilled.

"I'll walk you back," he said.

"You don't have to."

He raised an eyebrow in answer, grabbed his down coat from the closet by the door and reached for her hand.

Ollie and Yukon came with them, their advance guard, sniffing every patch of the sidewalk as Dani walked hand in hand through the falling snow toward her little house along the lakeshore with the man she loved.

Epilogue

Ruben started up *The Wonder*, the thrum of her motor familiar and beloved to him now after the past year.

"Here we go." Beside him, Dani gave a smile that was even more familiar and beloved.

"Last chance. Are you sure you don't want to stay on dry land and watch the parade with the girls and my parents? I still feel a little guilty that you haven't seen the whole Haven Point Lights on the Lake boat parade in all its glory."

She shook her head. "I'll have other chances to see it. Right now, I'm exactly where I want to be."

Though it was almost time for the parade to start, he couldn't resist stealing a moment to kiss his beautiful bride of three months, there at the Haven Point marina on a cold December night.

"I'm glad you're here with me."

"So am I. I've been looking forward to it for weeks. I still can't believe everybody bailed at the last minute and it's just the two of us."

After the big party of the previous year, everybody in his family had ended up staying on shore for various reasons. Angie had obligations with the Haven Point Helping Hands booth, Silver had been invited to ride on a friend's boat and his parents had been persuaded by Mia to watch the whole parade from the park in town.

He didn't mind. Between his job, the girls and her increased responsibilities at the clinic now that his father had officially retired, these moments alone together were as rare as they were cherished.

"The dogs are ready," she said, laughing at their trio of canines who were sprawled out on the foredeck, waiting for the fun to begin.

Okay, they weren't completely alone. Ollie, Yukon and Winky—who had formed their own little pack over the past year—never missed a chance to go out on *The Wonder*.

The dogs, like Dani and the girls, had become seasoned sailors after a summer spent out on the water every chance they could find.

The past year had been the happiest of Ruben's life. Every moment seemed an adventure, from cross-country skiing the previous winter, to helping Dani and the girls plant and nurture their first garden in the springtime, to the gorgeous September day when they all had merged their lives together in a beautiful ceremony in the little church in town.

Each week seemed better than the one before.

Ruben had always loved the changing seasons along the lake—the new life in the spring, the recreational opportunities of the summer, the quiet and peace of the fall.

He had a feeling this season, Christmastime, would always be his favorite. This was the time of year when he had found the woman beside him, the one who filled his life with more joy than he ever could have imagined.

"You don't think they'll be too cold out there, do you?" she asked, with a worried look at the dogs as the parade started and Ruben guided the boat behind the watercraft in front of *The Wonder*.

"It's at least twenty degrees warmer out there with the radiant heat off all the lights the kids strung around," he assured her.

His poor boat looked like a floating casino at this point, with Christmas lights dangling from every possible spot. A floating casino from the South Pole, he amended. The two giant light-up inflatable penguins from last year had been joined by one more and all three bobbed around maniacally as *The Wonder* churned through the water.

He never would have guessed when he bought the cabin cruiser a little more than a year ago that the boat could end up changing his life. Without it, or more accurately, without a night of mischief by three teenage girls when they spray painted her, he wasn't sure he and Dani would have found their way to each other.

As he thought about how empty his life would be without her and the girls, thick emotion welled up in his chest.

Dani, always in tune to his mood, gave him a concerned look. "Are you okay?"

"Perfect," he said. "I was just thinking about how my world has changed since we did this last Christmas."

Her features softened with a tender look that humbled him. "What a gift this year has been."

He reached a hand out and she rose to join him at the wheel. He kissed her briefly but didn't want to take his attention too far from the boat controls when there was so much traffic on the water. He also didn't want to let her go so he tucked her in front of him, his arms on either side and her back nestled against his front.

Keeping his eyes on the water illuminated by his boat lights, he kissed the back of her neck and was rewarded with a shiver. That was one of her most sensitive spots—and how lucky was he to have discovered most of them over the past year?

"Careful, or you're going to make me wish we weren't in this parade at all," she murmured. "Are you sure we can't sneak off and dock at home for a bit while the girls are gone? Nobody would know."

He grinned. "In case you missed it, Doc, we have three eight-foot-tall light-up inflatable penguins aboard. I think they might draw a little attention, parked at our dock for a few hours."

"Too bad."

Ruben tightened his arms around her and whispered a suggestion for later, something that made her laugh and the dogs look over at them with a resigned sort of curiosity.

They had plenty of time.

They had forever.

★ ★ ★ ★ ★

EAGLE VALLEY LIBRARY DISTRICT
P.O. BOX 240   600 BROADWAY
EAGLE, CO 81631   (970) 328-8800